Also by Amelia Grey

The Earl Next Door

Amelia Grey

St. Martin's Paperbacks

This is a work of fiction. All of the characters, organizations, and events portrayed in this novel are either products of the author's imagination or are used fictitiously.

THE EARL NEXT DOOR

Copyright © 2019 by Amelia Grey.

All rights reserved.

For information address St. Martin's Press, 175 Fifth Avenue, New York, NY 10010.

ISBN: 978-1-250-21430-0

Our books may be purchased in bulk for promotional, educational, or business use. Please contact your local bookseller or the Macmillan Corporate and Premium Sales Department at 1-800-221-7945, ext. 5442, or by e-mail at MacmillanSpecialMarkets@macmillan.com.

Printed in the United States of America

St. Martin's Paperbacks edition / June 2019

St. Martin's Paperbacks are published by St. Martin's Press, 175 Fifth Avenue, New York, NY 10010.

10 9 8 7 6 5 4 3 2 1

Chapter 1

As misunderstandings go, the one that led to the Dowager Countess of Wake being mistaken for a lady of the night would qualify as rather large, unfortunate, and beyond insulting. That it was made by a man who caused the very proper Adeline to imagine just the sort of things that might go on in a house of ill repute only served to make her even more furious than perhaps the misunderstanding warranted.

In her defense, she'd just had a somewhat startling shock after pulling a crimson corset from a stack of neatly folded fabrics when the forceful clank of the door knocker sounded throughout the house. She was working her way through the swatches in the drawing room, trying to make decisions on the gowns she would have made for her first Season since becoming a widow. That the modiste had included the under apparel must have been a mistake. The red was Adeline's favorite color, a flaming decadent shade that no lady would ever wear—even under her clothing.

Especially not a widow.

No doubt it was the "especially not a widow" thought that got to her. When Adeline realized she'd never have another opportunity to put on something so utterly unacceptable, she did, well, the unacceptable. Before she could think better of it, she loosened the front laces and slipped the corset over her head, letting the extraordinary garment settle over her dark widow's dress. The knock at the door was all but forgotten as she inhaled deeply and tightened the crimson ribbons under her breasts before tying the ends together.

It was magnificent. Naughty. But she didn't care. It made her feel, of all things, feminine.

She spied a length of luxurious fabric that surely confirmed this box had been delivered to the wrong address and was intended for someone else. Someone so very unlike her. Not that it stopped Adeline from pulling the gold swath of tulle from the stack and wrapping it twice around her waist. In no time at all she had fluffed the gossamer cloth and fashioned the sash into a big, perfect bow.

It was completely out of character for her to indulge in such unfitting behavior, but why stop now that she'd started? Feeling deliciously wicked to be so brazen, she pulled the sleeves of her dress low on her shoulders and twirled a couple of times. She admired the forbidden elegance enhancing her shape, which was always hidden behind the straight, waist-less fall of her skirt.

What would the ton think if she, a dowager countess, showed up for the first ball wearing such a brilliant shade of red? Or her stays outside her gown? She smiled just thinking about all the horrified expressions she'd see on the faces of Society's elite ladies of the ton. And then Adeline wondered what the handsome gentlemen would think of her. Widow or not, twenty-two was much too young not to ever look at or think about a man again. To want his eager kisses and the soft stroke of his masculine hand against her skin.

So caught up in the freedom of her improper thoughts, the richness of the fabrics, and the childlike innocence of spinning around as if she didn't have a care in the world, she didn't hear the footsteps down the corridor. Somewhat belatedly, she did hear her housekeeper's gasp.

But it wasn't Mrs. Lawton she noticed standing in the doorway when she stopped whirling.

Adeline took in the tall, black-cloaked figure whose gaze was staring straight at her as her skirts settled around her legs and she regained her balance. The housekeeper was trying her best to keep the stranger at bay, but her petite form was no match for the powerful-looking man whose brows suddenly knitted together in a frustrated frown of resolve.

Adeline's first thought was to hurriedly rip off the stays and restore her clothing to suitable order. Knowing that was impossible without making matters worse, she pulled her bare shoulders back and stood fast. After two years of marriage to Wake, she was good at handling embarrassing situations and concealing her true emotions. She would remain seemingly unruffled by the unexpected invasion and deprive the man the entertainment of seeing her flustered or trying to remove the corset.

"I tried to stop him, but he brushed right by me as if I wasn't there," her housekeeper informed her.

"Thank you, Mrs. Lawton," Adeline said. "There's no reason to fret. I'll take care of this."

The woman hesitated before nodding and disappearing into the corridor.

The stranger regarded Adeline so closely she wondered if he could see inside her and know exactly what she'd been thinking and feeling when she'd donned the stays and lowered the sleeves of her dress. She was looking him over, too, and realized there was something familiar about the man's thick, dark, sand-colored hair and how it waved naturally across his forehead and fell to the top of the collar at his nape. Faint curiosity wove through her. They had met, but she couldn't put a name to his face.

This was no surprise considering the fact her husband had never wanted her to look another man in the eyes on the few occasions he'd allowed her to attend parties with him. It wasn't long after their marriage that he'd started insisting she spend her days at his country estate whenever he visited London. There had been no convincing him otherwise, though she'd tried on many occasions. Wake had been gone two years now, and thinking of him and that time of her life had become less and less frequent.

Whether or not she'd ever met the gentleman before her now, this wasn't the way to start a new neighbor visit. Well, no matter now. The deed was done. Adeline expected him to realize his mistake, explain the reason for his action and apologize for barging into her house unannounced, and then hurry penitently away.

"Who are you, sir," she asked, "and what do you want?"

For a moment, she thought perhaps the man might have recognized her as the once-decorous Countess of Wake and make amends, but then, without reference to who she was, who he was, or even a well-mannered greeting, he stated boldly and with definite impatience, "I want to see the madam of the house."

His voice, deep and dark as the mantle he wore, washed through her like a warm sip of spiked apple-and-cinnamon cider. There was no demand in it—there didn't have to be. His determination showed in his countenance. Yet, his demand without benefit of reason or introduction didn't sit well with Adeline, no matter that he might very well be one of the finest-looking men she'd ever seen.

He strode farther into the drawing room, the tail of his cloak flowing majestically out behind him. His wide shoulders moved just enough to add to his roguish, compelling appeal. Adeline sensed a commanding strength within him that most ladies would find attractive.

But not her, she reminded herself.

One husband controlling her life had been more than enough for her.

She was a widow now and decidedly done with men

of all varieties—except the ones in her imagination, of course. Those she could manage.

The man crossed his arms on his wide chest as if he'd done nothing wrong, and looked her over from head to toe. This time, however, his appraisal caused an unaccustomed catch in her breath. He took in every inch of her that was possible to see. An indecent and entirely inappropriate tingle traced a pathway across her breasts and then shivered down to her lower abdomen. That made her feel even more wretched at being caught daydreaming—until indignation struck.

It didn't matter that he looked so dashing he had her senses heightened when he'd stopped a mere step or two in front of her. He was a stranger with no manners and showing no remorse. Anger started to simmer inside her. This ogre was sorely in need of a lesson in manners.

Difficult as it would be, considering her flagrant abuse of respectable attire, she had every intention of handling this ill-mannered scoundrel and making short work of getting rid of him.

Since he appeared to be a determined man on a mission, Adeline asked again, "Who are you, sir?"

His head cocked back in irritation and his expression had a rakish hint of mystery about what he was really thinking. "It's not customary to ask a gentleman his name in a place such as this," he said, seeming to give no weight to answering her simple question.

A twinge of concern pricked her instinct at his comment. She had hoped there would be no problems with opening the small boarding school for unfortunate girls in the building behind the house. Now, he was giving her reason to doubt that. It was perhaps more than a little unusual to put such a charitable establishment in the middle of a valuable street of houses, but she and her two friends and partners, Julia and Brina, had agreed it was simply the perfect place.

They could have never found such an ideal property on their own. Their solicitor had been invaluable in all aspects of starting the school. It was agreed by all that Adeline would live in the main house. She would be completely separated from the school and the girls by the tall yew hedge with an arched trellis for a gate, thereby keeping her at a distance from anything unseemly. Though it had satisfied her wish to be close and available if, for whatever reason, she might be needed after the school commenced. And they'd been purposely quiet while furnishing the school so they wouldn't be disruptive to the neighborhood.

Moreover, this street was in St. James. Not the center of Society's crown jewel, the bustling, prestigious Mayfair—where most of the inhabitants had no inclination to know about, much less be near, the everyday people who made up the larger portion of London's growing population.

Adeline searched the man's broad brow, angular cheekbones, and square chin and jaw, hoping that his comment had nothing to do with the school, and said, "It's the polite question to ask. When a man doesn't offer it no matter where he is," she said tersely. "I'll show you out."

Not waiting for a response, Adeline strode past him without glancing his way. Seconds later she heard his determined footfalls in the corridor behind her, but thankfully not before she'd shimmied her sleeves back up to cover her shoulders, restoring some modicum of respectability to her clothing.

Salvaging her pride might take a little more time.

With his longer stride it took only seconds for him to catch up to her. There was no need to call for Mrs. Lawton to aid her in seeing him out. Adeline would take great pleasure in doing that all by herself. She started to open the front door, but he caught it with his hand and leaned his body forward, stopping her.

Instantly wary, she managed to stifle a flinch and huff, though her heartbeat thumped a little harder. No gentleman should be so blatant toward a lady. Her muscles coiled and tightened in response to his unforeseen action, but for some unfathomable reason she felt no fear for her physical safety.

This, she realized, was a battle of wills between them.

While he was clearly no ordinary gentleman, she no longer was an ordinary woman. Her husband's death had ensured that she would never be under any man's hand again. She had gained a level of freedom she'd never dreamed of before and she wasn't afraid to indulge in it.

"Sir, I bid you good evening."

Powerless to deny herself an attempt to best him, she threw her weight onto one foot and vigorously pulled on the door.

Her efforts didn't even rattle the hinges.

The strength of him wasn't going to be dislodged by her efforts. Nevertheless, she wouldn't relinquish her hold or be cowered by his uncivil display of superior strength. She was through taking orders from men who felt their title, wealth, or heritage permitted them to have—no, to demand—anything or any person they wanted.

Her chest heaving, she looked up at him and calmly asked, "Are you threatening me?"

From beneath thick lashes, his silvery-gray eyes stared into hers and seemed to darken to the color of thunderclouds. He slowly took his hand off the door and stepped away. At his movement, she caught the inviting scent of shaving soap, fine wool, and freshly pressed linen. Much to her consternation her body tingled with errant unladylike sensations once again.

"If you really thought I was threatening, you wouldn't have sent your housekeeper away."

That was perceptive of him, but she wasn't going to let the arrogant man know it. His brashness, innuendo, and vigor should have frightened her—and it did—but not in the way she would have presumed or wanted. It awakened a long-dormant sense of unfulfilled desire. That is what she most needed to fear.

She lifted her brows in doubt as an answer.

"I'm simply asking you to summon the owner of the house," he said in a quiet, but firm voice.

"You weren't *simply* asking," she said. "You were trying to *force* me to do so."

In a low voice, he all but whispered, "I would never force a woman to do anything. I only want to speak to the owner and find out what is going on here."

Adeline's spine remained rigid. So this was indeed about the school. That was a troublesome matter and would have to be dealt with gently. She and her friends had hoped to keep information about The Seafarer's School from the ton until the girls moved in, thinking it would be more difficult for the old guard of Society to object to her charitable project if the children were already settled into the residence. There would be a certain amount of gossip about the reasons she, Julia, and Brina were opening the school, but they were prepared for it. Their hope was that everyone would be accepting as long as the three of them kept their distance from the girls and, as all proper ladies should do, leave the business and management of it solely in their solicitor's hands.

The clock in the drawing room chimed and didn't stop until it had resounded five times. Her gaze remained locked together with his as if neither wanted to be the first to blink. Adeline had to make a choice. She could continue her battle of wills with him, call for Mrs. Lawton to help her toss the man out on his ear, or, less satisfying, relent to his cocksure resolve and find out exactly what he wanted.

The decision was suddenly easy. She only wanted to be rid of him and the desirous feelings of excitement that stole through her when he looked too closely at her. And she looked at him.

Adeline stiffened her back again with all the aplomb her title required and said, "I am one of the owners. You can talk with me."

"You're much younger than I assumed the proprietor of this establishment would be," he confessed. "And as beautiful as you are in your crimson and gold, and in any other circumstances, or any other location, I would be happy to pay whatever fee you charge to fulfill my needs. However, this is a respectable neighborhood and I cannot and will not sit by and allow a madam to move in and set up her business here."

A trio of thumps echoed in Adeline's chest, and then a few more. The pendulum on the clock must have ticked a half-dozen times. Adeline's brain seemed to freeze before the air swooshed out of her lungs. Shock roared through her. Her whole body stiffened before she felt her eyes narrow in outrage.

"Just where do you think you are, sir?"

"A house of pleasure."

Outrage quickly morphed to fury, which flowed hot and fast, consuming her. Oh yes, she knew about such disgraceful, secret places. She'd overheard her husband and his small group of gentlemen friends talk about visiting them.

Adeline was skilled at holding in her emotions, but this man had gone too far. With only one step she stood toe-to-toe with him. Lifting her face, she rose up on the balls of her feet and edged her nose closer to his. "You think this is one of the many private underground brothels hidden from all but Society's most elite gentlemen?"

"Isn't it?" he asked huskily.

There was no time to consider what her next move should be. Hardening her resolve and taking a step back, she proclaimed, "I am the Dowager Countess of Wake and you have trespassed too far. How dare you push your way into my house and speak to me the way you have. You, sir, are an abomination to the term *gentleman*."

She fought to regain every ounce of her normal

calm, her abiding restraint, her guiding sense of deco-
rum in any unpleasant circumstance. But then she acci-
dentally looked at his mouth, felt that long-suppressed
surge of yearning. Adeline didn't want this unusual mix
of longing and angry dizziness to control her. She hated
the truth of how womanly and desirable it made her feel
to see hunger for her in his eyes. Hated the truth of
how she was presented.

And then, in a moment of insanity, she thought of
the very real possibility of those full lips on hers stir-
ring with passion, and reason was gone.

Unable to do anything else before she lost herself
completely, she drew back her hand and struck him
soundly across the face. It was that, or kiss him.

Perhaps she chose the wrong one.

Chapter 2

Lyon's head snapped back.

A jolt of shock whipped through him. He wasn't an easy man to catch off guard, but he hadn't seen that coming.

Hell's horses!

Not a madam, but a countess. And a widow at that. He mentally shook himself and swore quietly again. Flashes of old gossip raced through his mind at hearing her name, but there was no time to plunder his memory for the snippets.

He knew she was telling the truth the instant she'd said her name, though her manner of dress and his aunt's assertions a brothel was being established in the neighborhood belied her words. No wonder he'd thought her too young, too beautiful, and too wholesome-looking to be working in a house of plea-sure when he'd first seen her twirling in the drawing room like a lighthearted miss.

Now he knew why.

In his twenty-eight years he thought he'd seen, heard, and done most everything that was available to a man of his privilege and station in life. But this lady had just proven otherwise.

With unquestionable clarity.

For now, he was cautiously managing, with diffi-culty to be sure, to hold his anger in check. After all, why surrender to the madness of what she'd done and give her the satisfaction.

Lyon Marksworth, the Earl of Lyonwood, had never been slapped. By a madam *or* a lady. That garnered her his admiration *and* his ire. He was accustomed to calm and order in his life, and the countess had just upset both by not being who he thought she was.

"Lady Wake, I am Lyonwood. Your neighbor."

The countess's flushed face suddenly went ashen.

He bowed but offered no apology. At first. She'd had her justice in spades and aces—the whole damn deck. However, she looked appalled by her action upon hear-ing his name so he would take it on the chin and shoulder the responsibility. And he had been wrong, so he added, "For entering your house without an in-vitation and mistaking who you were, my apologies."

So they were both in a deep dilemma. How did an earl and a dowager countess proceed now that their identities were made known after such an unforgettable first meeting?

"Lord Lyonwood," she said, managing a begrudging, rigid, and very slight curtsy.

From his first memory, Lyon had been taught to be a gentleman. He knew all the acceptable rules of proper behavior and manners depending on whatever situation he found himself—a gentleman, a gambler, or a rake. There were certain values a man of honor followed no matter the situation. Above all, he protected his family and others when necessary. He respected life and loyalty, and he paid his debts. Whether or not warranted, he always gave a man he suspected might be cheating at cards the benefit of the doubt—once.

A gentleman lavished gifts, financial support, and satisfaction on his mistresses. Likewise, he bestowed sweet compliments, rides in the park, and when appropriate, flowers on proper young ladies in Society. Lyon had never muddled the two.

Until this afternoon.

Now that he knew who she was, he felt it incumbent that he should say something about her husband.

"It was tragic what happened to your—"

"Please stop." She interrupted him quietly, lowering thick, velvety lashes over her golden-brown eyes and inhaling deeply. "It was a tragic event and a trying time for everyone who was touched by the tragedy. It's been over two years now and no words are necessary."

He could understand her not wanting to talk about that time, so he quietly said, "That long. I hadn't realized."

She lifted her head, as if she'd searched deep inside herself and gained new strength. "There's no reason for you to. And I would appreciate no further mention of it."

He nodded once.

"However," she added, "you should have immediately told me who you were. This matter could have been settled much quicker."

Perhaps he should have stated who he was when he first entered the drawing room, but he'd thought it wasn't necessary. He was only too well aware of how many private pleasure houses were hidden among the cozy streets of respectable London and how easily and quietly they were established. He'd certainly availed himself of more than a few over the years, which was why he'd promised his aunt he'd deal with the one she believed was moving in next door to him and down the street from her.

Lyon could now see that Lady Wake's earlier perplexed expressions and her sense of outrage had flashed warning after warning, which he'd ignored. That the countess didn't immediately engage him with welcoming smiles should have been a swift indication all wasn't as it seemed, but he was already in an irritable state of mind when he arrived at her house and unwavering in his thoughts not to be persuaded from his mission by a tempting woman.

He'd returned home from a laborious meeting with his unprepared solicitor, wanting only to get ready for an evening at White's so he could get caught up on the latest news and indulge in a game or two of billiards, a few hands of cards, and an expensive bottle of brandy. Instead, he'd come home to find his aunt in his drawing room wringing her hands in misery over the possibility of unmentionable women setting up a forbidden business in their quiet neighborhood. And insisting he must do something about it at once.

Given all that was put before him, including the countess's attire, what else could he have possibly done other than assume she was a paid woman preparing to fulfill some lucky man's fantasy for the evening?

"The mistake was mine. I thought this was the kind of house where a man is always free and welcome to come and go as he pleases without hindrance, and not have to reveal his name or wait around to be announced. If I had known you were a lady and not an angel of the evening, I wouldn't have acted so freely."

"An angel of the evening?" She puffed out a breath of exasperation. "What rubbish. Clever words or phrases won't hide what you thought when you entered or how you spoke to me. Now that you know who I am, you are still free to speak to me as before."

That she would suggest he continue to speak so openly with her surprised him and was downright refreshing. Most of the ladies he knew would have fainted when he made the remark about paying her fee for the evening and pray to never hear such a vile comment again.

"Nevertheless, I will give you the respect you deserve and watch my language now that I do know, my lady."

He watched her breathing ease and calmness settle over her as they each assessed the situation. That her recovery was quick and solid was a testament to her strength.

"I heard you were out of Town when I moved into

the neighborhood a few days ago," she continued in a calm and confident voice.

"I returned last evening."

"That doesn't absolve your actions tonight. You should have checked with someone before you came charging over with uncivil actions, assumptions and untrue allegations."

Lyon's jaw clenched tighter. No doubt about that. He should have questioned his aunt more about her suspicions, but he wasn't about to explain that to the countess and implicate his aunt and her friend. "I was reasonably certain I had good cause to act as I did."

"But you didn't."

"No." What else could he say?

"And earl or not, sir," she added valiantly, "you are an ogre as I've found most of your ilk are."

He couldn't argue with that either.

"Before you go, I'd like to know what made you think this was a house of pleasure for men."

Lyon shook his head slowly. She was unbelievable. Asking him to explain what she'd just slapped him for. He wasn't going to get caught in that snare again. "I'd rather not say, my lady."

"Of course you don't want to, but you must. I need to know what caused you to act as you did. Others could make the same mistake."

Something settled in Lyon's chest. A feeling that he'd never had before. Lady Wake was no shy or simpering female. She was courageous, impassioned beyond belief, and probably too strong-willed for her own good.

That intrigued him. It made him want to answer her

with candid freedom, but every fiber of his being as a gentleman warned against such talk with a proper lady.

Yet, after only a brief hesitation, he responded, "If you insist."

"I do."

"It was brought to my attention that there have been some peculiar things going on over here while I've been out of Town."

"Peculiar?" Concern resurfaced in her expression. "What do you mean? There is no reason for us to stand on ceremony, my lord. We are quite familiar with each other now. Speak to me as you would a madam and tell me what made you think my home was a house of ill repute."

"Very well. An abundance of deliveries of bed-chamber furniture going into the building behind this house."

"Why would that be strange, sir?" she asked him crisply. "Beds are necessary for everyone."

"And women coming and going at all hours of the day and night."

"Ah, yes," she said on a breathy sigh as the meaning of his words became clear to her and she relaxed once again. "Now I understand. Beds and women. What else is a man to think of other than pleasure?"

Lyon felt the only thing he could reasonably do at this point was lift his brows, and say, "For that I can offer no apology."

"It's true, there have been many beds delivered. The building behind this house is being furnished as a boarding school for girls, my lord. The women who have been seen coming and going will be their tutors.

Currently, some of the women have different jobs they must return to each day. They are free to leave at whatever time they deem necessary to make their other duties and commitments."

"A boarding school?" he repeated, wondering why the hell his aunt didn't know that. She was usually one of the first to hear the latest gossip.

"Yes. So whatever tawdry vision you'd imagined would be taking place between these walls tonight or any other won't be happening. My home is not what you thought it was, and anyone else who assumed the same will have to look elsewhere for his decadences."

The countess opened the door for him.

Lyon felt his expression softening, his admiration growing. For a number of reasons, including the truth of her words, there was no repairing their inauspicious meeting.

He nodded without further words, turned, and walked out of her house.

Chapter 3

The chill of an early spring wind cooled Lyon's cheek, but nothing else, as his boots crunched the damp ground on the pathway that led to the pavement in front of the countess's house. That the long-shrouded sun was trying to peek from behind gray clouds at the end of the day did nothing to change his mood.

Not that it mattered or that he cared, but he finally remembered why he and the countess hadn't immediately recognized each other. He'd been late attending her debut Season, and she was already betrothed by the time he'd arrived in London that year. Lyon was sure they'd met, but he never pursued another man's fiancé or wife. There were more than enough unattached ladies in the ton to woo without stepping in another man's footprints.

From what Lyon remembered, the countess had never been to London with Lord Wake after they married. The earl must have been at least a decade older than Lyon, and Lyon hadn't known him well. They had a different group of friends, but there had been a few times they sat down at the same table to play a hand of cards or a game of billiards when Wake was in Town. Lyon remembered Lord Wake saying on more than one occasion that his wife was too delicate to make the long and bumpy journey from his country manor to London.

Delicate?

Lyon rubbed his thumb across his cheek. Not the lady he'd just met, Lyon groused to himself. She had not spared her strength when she struck him. He had no idea what disorder may have caused her fragility when she was married, but he could safely say she was over it.

Another flicker of admiration struck him for how she'd handled herself considering what he'd done, and right on the heels of it was a streak of remorse as he opened the tall, creaky gate hanging on the iron fence that surrounded his home. He should have been kinder to her once he found out who she was, he thought as he let the gate clank shut behind him. She was a widow after all, whether or not she had been dressed like one.

Lyon remembered when the ship *Salty Dove* sank in a sudden and fierce storm off the coast of Portugal. No doubt everyone in the ton still remembered, as did the rest of London. It was a stunning blow to all of England, as most everyone either knew or had heard of someone who perished that day. Little more than a handful of the one hundred and fifty people on board had survived to tell what had happened.

Lyon strode into his house, ripping his hat off his head and tossing it and his cloak and gloves onto a side chair without breaking stride. He brusquely waved his tall, portly butler, Brewster, aside as he came hurrying from the back of the house to take Lyon's wrap.

"What did you find out?" his aunt called out to him before he made it halfway down the corridor.

"It's a boarding school for girls, Aunt Delia," Lyon replied, entering his drawing room with determined steps. He walked past his mother's sister, straight to where the brandy decanter was placed on a round table beside his favorite chair. "There's no cause for the state of worry you and Mrs. Feversham allowed and no reason for me to bring down the wrath of Hades on anyone in that house."

"A girls' school?" his aunt questioned from the end of the dark rose-colored velvet settee where she always sat when she came to visit him. "Next door to you?"

"It appears so."

"How can that be?" she asked. "This is a neighborhood. Not a business district where such institutions should be located."

"The school is the building behind the house," he answered, having no reason to doubt the countess' word. "Which, as you know, backs up to the business district. The boarding school is the reason Mrs. Feversham saw so many beds being carried to the back of the house. The women she saw coming and going through the gate during the day and in the middle of the night will be instructing the girls. For now, the tutors have other jobs they must go to."

"That's really quite odd. Mrs. Feversham didn't mention seeing girls living there. Only women."

Lyon lifted the topper off the decanter and covered the bottom of a glass with the amber liquor. "They will be soon. So you can tell your vexed friend across the street that she can stop watching what is going on at the house next door. All is well. And while you are at it, Aunt"—he stopped and gave her a rueful smile— "remind her I don't want to hear that she's been observing my comings and goings either."

"Well, really now, Lyon." Cordelia adjusted the pillow behind her back and smoothed down the folds in her blue sprigged skirt. "What else has the poor lady to do since she can no longer get out into Society?" His aunt paused. "I'll have one of those since you're pouring."

"I was going to open a claret for you. I know you prefer it."

"That not necessary," she said, lifting her chin and giving him a genuine smile. "I won't be here that long, dearest, and you know I won't have more than a sip or two of it, anyway. You'd have to finish off the bottle or let it go to waste. Not much tastes worse than day-old claret."

Maybe for her.

Lyon downed a generous swallow of the strong liquor and breathed in long and heavily, letting it settle in his stomach before adding a splash of the fortified wine to the dainty crystal he kept on the tray just for his aunt's visits. He then added another ounce to his glass. After his meeting with Lady Wake, he needed it to help him put the entire incident out of his thoughts.

For good he hoped.

Having a late afternoon drink with his aunt was nothing new. Mrs. Cordelia Carbonall was his late mother's only living sibling, probably the reason he was so patient with her. That, and the fact she had a bold streak he'd admired and sometimes appreciated. It had always seemed strange to him that his aunt had more the nature, wit, and strength of his father than of her sister, Lyon's mother. As best he could remember her, anyway.

His mother had been gone close to twenty years, and time had started taking its toll on his once-vibrant memories of her. She had been a beautiful lady with a softly sweet voice. He could no longer hear her singing to him in the evenings before his governess took him off to bed, but he knew she had. Time had erased the feeling of the smooth touch of her hand when she cupped his chin in her palm so she could make sure he was listening to her, but he knew she'd done it.

Cordelia wasn't a classic beauty as his mother had been, but she had sparkling, playful blue eyes and a smile that matched her quick drollness and even temperament. Cordelia's husband had passed away only two years after Lyon's mother. Over the years, she'd attracted the attention of several gentlemen. At least two of them had offered for her hand, and more than once. But she'd remained a childless widow, and from all Lyon could tell she was happy with her choices.

Much to his father's liking, Cordelia had never tried

to be a mother to Lyon. That had actually suited all three of them. It didn't mean she hadn't been a part of his life. For as long as Lyon could remember, his aunt hadn't been shy about asking for whatever she wanted from him or his father, be it monetary or a social favor. The only difference was that the Marquis of Marksworth wasn't nearly as accommodating to her as Lyon had always been. Mostly because Marksworth had bestowed a generous allowance on Cordelia after her husband passed. No doubt thinking that would be the end of his duty to her and she would quietly fade away from Society.

He'd been wrong.

Ever since Cordelia had moved to the neighborhood three years ago, she'd made it a point to visit her friend Mrs. Feversham once a week and fill her in on the latest gossip. And of course, Mrs. Feversham, who lived across the street from Lyon, always had plenty to tell his aunt about the neighbors she could see from her first-floor chambers. Cordelia considered it her duty to occasionally stop by for a visit with Lyon, when he was in Town, and share all she'd heard. Lyon listened patiently to every sentence. She was considerate of his privacy and never stayed very long.

Today, her troubled chatter of gossip had led to his barging in on the countess thinking he was going to be keeping the neighborhood safe from being invaded by a bevy of the lesser sort.

"It's curious that a school is going to be next door," his aunt said, taking the drink from him. Not giving him time to answer, she continued by saying, "In my day, a girl was taught in the home with a highly qual-

ified and proper governess. Tutors for French and pianoforte lessons were sometimes brought into the
house, but a good governess could handle it all. Dancing, too." She sighed as she put her nose to the glass
and sniffed its content indulgently. "I've always enjoyed the smell better than the taste."

"As do most ladies, I've heard," Lyon said, swinging the brown velvet wing chair away from the warmth
of the fireplace so that he could face his aunt from the
end of the settee.

"I suppose times are changing—though not too
keenly by some of us, and certainly not for the better.
A boarding school for girls is highly irregular." She
shook her head as if forgetting her train of thought for
a moment and asked, "Why did you say the school is
opening in our neighborhood?"

"I didn't, Aunt," he answered making himself comfortable in his chair. "I have no idea."

He didn't want to mention Lady Wake by name to
his aunt. Cordelia could find out about the countess
living there on her own.

Lyon had known when he left London last November
that his elderly neighbor, Mr. Bottles, was in poor
health and grumbling that his daughter never came to
see him. Perhaps the man had passed and the new Earl
of Wake had bought the house for the countess as part
of her allowance. Not that it mattered to Lyon what the
spirited lady did or who occupied the building at the
back of her house, he reminded himself again. Right
now, he wasn't interested in getting better acquainted
with her.

He sipped his brandy again. All he wanted to do

was forget about her and their meeting, but he was finding that difficult to do.

"Why didn't you ask more questions about the school? I would think you'd have great interest since it's so close to you."

"I arrived at an inconvenient time and, quite frankly, I'm not as inquisitive as you and Mrs. Feversham. I had no reason to ask many questions after it was made clear to me the neighborhood was not in jeopardy."

"I can't fault you for that. Men have never been as prying—" She stopped and smiled knowingly at him. "I mean as curious as ladies. I suppose there's nothing wrong with teaching deserving, decorous young ladies how to be proper, as well as enhancing their skills with a needle and quill. It sounds quite admirable. Perhaps they'll have a French tutor as well. Do you know?"

"I'll leave it to you to find that out, Aunt," he said patiently. At least Cordelia was now curious instead of upset. "I only returned from Lyonwood late in the evening yesterday. I spent the entire day meeting with my solicitor, who didn't have all the account books in his possession that I'd requested to see. Most of the ones he put before me had pages that had somehow gotten damp and were unreadable. The man had all winter to get them in order and hadn't. I arrived back home to find you here and in a fit of concern thinking something dastardly was happening next door. I erased that fear. It's all I can do."

"And you did it quite well. I do thank you for asking Brewster to let me know you were back in Town. I'm sure you didn't expect me to come over on your first day back, but I couldn't ignore Mrs. Feversham's pleas this afternoon."

"I'm always happy to see you, Aunt," Lyon said, and meant it. "I never mind you stopping for a visit." He couldn't take out his frustration on his aunt for an unsuccessful visit with his solicitor or his disastrous meeting with Lady Wake.

"Still, I shouldn't have burdened you with our concerns. Mrs. Feversham was really quite unsettled and I'm afraid I let that influence me. I mean what else were we to think after what she saw?"

Lyon smiled. "Perhaps that she shouldn't spend all her days and nights looking out the window in hopes of seeing something her neighbors are doing."

"Now, don't be harsh. It's really a shame she couldn't walk after her fall last spring."

"I'm not trying to be insensitive. Why don't I walk you next door so you can explain to her there is nothing unsavory going on and ease her mind."

Cordelia gave him a wry smile. "Are you not going to let me finish my drink?"

That would take three days at the rate she sipped a thimbleful of brandy. Lyon smiled indulgently. "Of course, finish it and tell me what's kept you busy over the winter."

"When the weather wasn't too cold and dreary to leave my house, I did the usual—cards, parties, teas, and gossip. Goose feathers! What a boring life I lead. Now, do you want to tell me what kept *you* busy while at Lyonwood?"

"No." He then took a sip of his brandy.

Cordelia laughed with vigor. "I thought not. Nor do I really want to know what a handsome young gentleman does."

"Have you seen the marquis over the winter?" Lyon asked, though it was the irritating countess who kept sweeping through his thoughts, invading his peace.

"Yes, of course. Your father wouldn't miss a social gathering of any kind, and you know I seldom do either. The dreadful man is his usual self. Handsome and arrogant as ever. My hair grows thinner and grayer by the hour and he never seems to age a day. It's most unfair how life favors that man. But, of course it's fine that you take after him with your dashing appeal."

"You have always been too coldhearted with my father and not severe enough with me."

"That is the way it suits me." An innocent smirk quivered the corners of her mouth. "Marksworth was never good enough for my sister, but he was good enough to give us you. I do appreciate him for that, though I'd never say it to him. And I don't expect you to say it to him either. It would be lovely if he were to begin to stoop a little. Maybe hobble when he takes a step or two. Perhaps lose one of his front teeth, or at least forget what he was going to say once in a while. The man is still so robust it's simply maddening to watch him grow old but not get any older."

Lyon shook his head over his aunt's comments and watched her put the glass to her lips as if she was going to take a sip. He knew she never tasted the brandy. It amused him that she always wanted to have a glass with him but never took a drink.

"Did you see him today?" she asked.

"There was no time."

"I heard he planned to return to Marksworth for a few days. Perhaps he has already left."

"You know, life would be much more pleasant if you two would settle your differences and, if not become friends, at least speak when you see each other."

"Oh, we speak if we must," she said with a smile. "But why would we want to change anything between us after all these years? Everyone so enjoys gossiping about how we're sometimes seated beside each other at the same dinner party and never say a word of greeting."

Lyon often wandered if their dislike of each other was really just a game they played because they realized how much alike they really were.

"He has taken very good care of you, Aunt."

"Yes, of course he has, but only because he knows my sister would rise from the dust of her grave to haunt him if he didn't." She inhaled the brandy again and smiled over the edge of the glass. "You do know he's going to marry again, don't you?"

Lyon leaned forward in his chair and cupped both hands around his glass. "No. I haven't seen or heard from him since I left his estate shortly after Boxing Day." Not that hearing about pending nuptials surprised Lyon. His father was as active today as the day Lyon was born. By a cruel twist of fate, the marquis had outlived Lyon's mother and two other wives. Whenever Marksworth was a widower, matrimony was always on his mind even though he had mistresses all over London.

"Who is she?"

"Miss Helen Ballingbrand."

That was a bit of a surprise considering his father was now nearing the age of fifty. "Another miss?"

"An older one this time, it seems. Still quite a few years younger than your father. Apparently her uncle, Viscount Chrisville, who is very wealthy as you know, decided to gift the spinster with a sizeable dowry of fertile land, and suddenly Marksworth couldn't seem to resist her beauty or her charm."

"Ah, yes," Lyon murmured before sipping his drink and leaning back in his chair again.

What the bride brought into the marriage was always important to the marquis. From his own lips, since Lyon's mother passed, his father hadn't married for love. As mercenary as it sounded, Lyon knew that increasing Marksworth's estate holdings was always at the forefront of his father's marriages. And if it had been up to his father, Lyon would have married years ago and for the same reasons. But that's not what Lyon wanted.

"I'm sure I must have met her when she made her debut a few years ago," Cordelia said. "I don't remember her and apparently you don't either. I'm told she was extremely shy and hated the crush of people at the balls and dinner parties. She never returned after the second week of her first Season. I'm assuming she'll attend the parties this year and we'll all be reacquainted with her. I know your father will attend every event he's invited to." She sighed. "I don't know where he gets the energy to do so night after night, month after month, and year after year. It seems to invigorate him."

Aunt Delia kept talking, but at the mention of the

Season Lyon's thoughts turned from his father to Lady Wake as easily as waves washed upon the shore in the warm days of summer. If only the emotions she caused inside him were as peaceful. They were turbulent and seemingly as relentless as swells upon the deep blue sea during a storm.

That he could remember, he'd never experienced being truly angry at a woman. And certainly not one he desired. How could the two emotions even go together? It wasn't the normal order of things, but it was both desire and anger he'd felt when she struck him.

Thoughts of her suddenly reminded him just how long it had been since he'd been with a woman. He'd returned to London with the aspirations of changing that drought, but right now it didn't seem likely.

No matter what had transpired between him and Lady Wake, or with his unsettling feelings about it, the countess was the only woman on his mind.

Chapter 4

He was a beast. Except he wasn't.

For three days Adeline had stewed about her neighbor. Well, some of that time she'd simmered and a time or two she'd sizzled. But no matter when or how she'd thought about the man, heat was always involved.

Which was ridiculous. What kind of gentleman simply assumed the worst about a neighbor he'd never met and barged into their home? And, it had taken him far too long to tell her who he was and express his regret for thinking her the madam of a secret brothel. Even then she had her doubts whether it was a sincere apology.

She would never forget how he boldly took in every detail of her face as if taking a thorough inventory of something valuable before letting his gaze skim down her neck, across her breasts, and over her bare shoulders. Remembering it now, her breaths deepened. She'd never seen any man peruse her so openly and show such real, unadulterated appreciation of her beauty in his expression. A thrill of something akin to desire had raced through her.

It was unexpected and heady.

She was horrified that she'd slapped the earl. Not that he didn't deserve it. He did. Invading the privacy of her drawing room. No matter that he thought he had good reason. Assuming she was . . . well. Suggesting he would like to . . . But neither of those things had disturbed her nearly as much as the fact that she'd thought about kissing him. That was where her true anger lay.

With herself.

How could she have even considered the possibility of his lips on hers? And why wouldn't thoughts of him go away and leave her in peace as had every other man she'd seen and had discussions with since becoming a widow?

At night Lyonwood plundered her dreams. Every morning she'd sworn she wasn't going to think about the dastardly earl anymore, and every day she'd failed.

Today would be different, she promised herself. She had reason to celebrate and be joyous with much more important and wonderful matters to occupy her mind than a brazen rogue. Except for a few minor details yet to be settled by their solicitor, Mr. Clements, everything about the school had been properly negotiated and signed. Even though she and her friends were now freer to carry out their own choices concerning every aspect of their lives than when they were married, it was still almost impossible for a lady to make her own business decisions without the aid of a male to negotiate for her. Thankfully, Mr. Clements was a young, forward-thinking man who'd allowed them to lead the way in how they wanted the school organized and managed.

The girls had arrived yesterday, and Julia and Brina would be joining her soon. The three of them were going over to the school together to welcome everyone.

Adeline stood in the small portion of her back garden that separated her house from the plain, white, three-story building that used to be a servants' quarters. It had been quietly transformed into The Seafarer's School for Girls. The name hadn't been her choice, but now that she saw it written in small simple lettering posted over the entrance, she knew it was the right one. At first, Adeline thought it carried too many sad memories of the people lost in the sinking of the *Salty Dove*. Now, looking at the name, she saw it more as an honor to all the sailors and workers who went down with the ship. It showed how something good was coming from an event that had been so devastatingly horrific for so many.

She could have waited inside for her friends to arrive, but she was anxious to be out in the morning sunshine and underneath a rare flawless blue sky so early in the spring. There was something comforting and satisfying about it warming her shoulders and the back of her neck while the chilly air cooled her cheeks. It always gave her an inspiring feeling of renewal to see the trees and bushes budding with tiny bits of green after the last vestige of winter days had passed.

An errant wind fluttered across Adeline's face, causing a few strands of hair to find freedom from the side of her wool-covered bonnet and tickle the side of her face. She continued to stare at the school sign and slowly, unbidden and unwelcomed, Adeline's thoughts started clouding with memories of how the idea for the school took shape. It was as if her mind had been a void waiting to be filled with recollections that suddenly wouldn't be shut out.

She wasn't in London when news arrived that the *Salty Dove* had broken apart and gone down off the coast of Portugal in a ferocious storm that took the lives of almost everyone on board.

When Adeline heard her husband wasn't among the few survivors, she was where she'd spent most of her married life, at Wake's country estate in Sussex. She left for London immediately and took up residence in their Town house, which she realized had, in the blink of an eye, become her brother-in-law's—the new Earl of Wake's—house.

Over the next few weeks, he had gone about doing the things that were necessary for him to officially assume her husband's title and possession of all its entailed properties. Adeline had begun to heal her body and spirit. The new earl and his wife were kind, insisting she stay with them during her mourning—the mourning that only she knew never took on the deep sorrow a wife should feel. She couldn't find a place in her heart for that, but she understood and respected his family, friends, and others grieving over his loss. That was all she could do.

It was months after the ship sank that Adeline's new, freer life truly began. She'd renewed her acquaintance with Lady Kitson Fairbright and met Mrs. Brina Feld. Their husbands had also lost their lives on the *Salty Dove*. Neither the place nor the reason for the widows meeting was a pleasant one, but she'd never forget that fateful afternoon. It was where the root of her idea for the girls' school was planted.

Before that day, Adeline had never been anywhere near London's docks. It wasn't an area for ladies.

Unsettled swirls of fog had drifted in off the water. Nestled between the occasional distant squawk from a seabird were irreverent shouts and sometimes-raucous laughter from men working on lines, hulls, or decks of the boats and ships. She was close enough to hear the continuous clank of riggings tapping against wooden masts and water lapping at seawalls. The smells would be forever etched in her mind as well. Dank water, dead fish, and putrid waste were mixed with faint, vagrant traces of salted, muggy air.

A large square near the waterfront and down from the shipping channel had been chosen to display what few belongings had been recovered from the passengers aboard the *Salty Dove*. The items were lined up in rows, available for family members who wanted to wander through the collection and retrieve their loved one's final possessions.

Adeline's brother-in-law had asked her to join him for the heartrending but necessary task since she would know better than anyone what personal items her husband had with him on the voyage. Nothing could have been further from the truth.

She had learned early in her marriage that she didn't know her husband at all. And the awkward truth was that he wasn't a man she wanted to know or to mourn. She was grateful for the generous allowance he'd left for her, but she would never return to the estate where he'd forced her to live, and demanded to know day after day after day why she wasn't in the family way. He didn't seem to care that Adeline wanted a babe, too. A child would have given her someone to love.

Near the waterfront that sorrowful afternoon, the three widows were drawn together because none of them had the need to sift through the articles that had washed ashore. They couldn't watch the few who did.

Off to the side and down the boardwalk, Adeline noticed another group of people huddled together. Mostly women and children. She heard gentle crying, sniffling, and softly spoken words from some of them. All were poorly dressed, but there seemed to be a special bond among them as they hugged, talked, and comforted one another.

Adeline found herself drawn to them because they seemed to be experiencing the true mourning she'd never felt for her husband. She overheard a red-haired, freckle-faced little girl asking, "Mum, what are we going to do now that Papa is gone?"

"I don't know, my little one," the mother had whispered desperately, brushing through the girl's tangle of long, red curls with a shaking hand. "Ye know I don't have a delicate hand when it comes to a stitch and that yer Papa was only being kind when he said I made the best bread he ever ate. I can find someone who'll pay me a wage to clean their shop for 'em. Don't worry yeself, lassie. I'll find work somewhere."

"I won't worry, Mum. I'm big now. I'll help take care of you now that Papa's gone."

Adeline watched the mother smile and then kiss the top of her young daughter's head with dry, trembling lips. She hugged the little girl with such tightness, Adeline felt as if her own chest were being squeezed. The woman looked up and saw Adeline watching her. Tremendous anguish and deep confusion showed in the woman's face, causing Adeline to wobble on her feet. That's when she realized that death, grief, and fear respected no one. That's when the first tears of loss rushed to her eyes and trickled down her cheeks. The woman gave her a comforting smile and a curtsy. Adeline was profoundly touched by the woman's show of respect even while bearing the weight of her own immense tragedy.

Wanting to help ease her pain in some way, Adeline stopped a worker and asked about the small group. He told her they were the family members of the ship's workers. They would be allowed to go through the belongings only after the members of Society had finished.

She spoke to her brother-in-law regarding the insensitivity of the rule, but he brushed aside her concerns about how unfair it was to make them watch and wait their turn to search for their loved ones' possessions until after they had been picked over and disturbed by others. The new earl considered her anxiety a part of her grieving and suggested she wait in the carriage for him. That's when Adeline knew she wanted to do something to help the wives, the daughters, and the sisters of the men who'd worked on the *Salty Dove*. At the time, she didn't know what it would be, but with some thought she realized the best way to help the families was to educate and teach their girls a skill so they could one day earn a wage. There were boarding schools where boys were educated and learned skills. Why couldn't there be one for girls, too? Learning to sew would be a respectable way for them to earn a living.

After coming to that conclusion, she hesitantly mentioned it to Julia and Brina. To her delight they were eager to be included. Like Adeline, neither was interested in marrying again, and they were intrigued by the idea of doing something more useful and worthy than simply reentering Society after their time of mourning ended.

It hadn't been easy. None of it had. Not finding the place for the school or the families of the workers. Her solicitor, Mr. Clements, had been a tireless advocate from the moment she mentioned her plan to him. With more diligence than she ever expected, he secured the large property from an elderly gentleman named Mr. Bottles. The house had a separate building that had housed the servants. It was situated in the middle of a privately secluded cul-de-sac near the business section and not far from the park. Everything about it suited their needs perfectly for the school.

Mr. Bottles finally agreed to sell after they agreed to let him name the school. That was the easiest thing about starting the school. It took time to find the families, explain to them what the widows wanted to do, and talk them into allowing the girls to come live at the boarding school, a way of life that was usually made available only for boys. The girls would be taught to read and write as well as learn the seamstress trade. With Mr. Clements' invaluable assistance, it had been accomplished. Adeline, Julia, and Brina realized they couldn't help the families of all the workers on the *Salty Dove* who had perished that day. That task would have been impossible. But they could help some of their young daughters and sisters who would be nearing the age to learn a trade.

The nine girls who would be attending the school wouldn't have to worry about not being prepared to find employment one day as had their mothers near the docks that foggy afternoon. They would be taught the differences between fine threads for sewing and embroidery and thicker threads for darning and knitting. They would learn the distinctive textures and costs of fabrics. The way to pleat, gather, and rush them. How to cut and sew them into clothing and draperies. Some would learn how to cover hats in a decorative fashion with feathers, beads, and ribbons while others would learn to make the delicate silk roses, fancy knitted lace, and perfect satin bows that decorate the gowns ladies of Polite Society wore. At the school, they would each be free to go in the direction their talents took them. Once they accomplished their skills and came of age, Adeline would see to it they gained employment at a reputable shop so they could earn a wage and help take care of themselves and their families.

"Lady Wake?"

Startled from her pensive thoughts, Adeline immediately knew that masculine voice coming from behind her. The earl. Despite her intentions to remain unaffected when she next encountered him, her heartbeat faltered. Her throat thickened. Her breaths became shallow and fast. Didn't he know he was the last person she wanted to see again? Ever. He'd insulted her. Angered her. Caught her in a weak moment indulging in a young lady's fantasy. Worst of all, he'd made her want to think about the actual possibility of warm embraces, sweet kisses, and soft touches.

Slowly, she turned. Her gaze fell on a wide chest and strong-looking shoulders covered by a crisp white shirt and neckcloth, dark green waistcoat, and chocolate brown coat. Lifting her lashes, her gaze rose up to the clean-shaven, handsome face of Lord Lyonwood, standing on his property just beyond the waist-high garden wall, staring intently at her. Oh, he was a splendid-looking man. Whoever invented the word *dashing* must have been looking at a painting of the earl. Yet, there was something more than just the build of his body or the handsomeness of his face that conveyed his strength. Something she sensed inside him that she couldn't yet decipher.

It was maddening that just the sight of him made her think about being cuddled against his chest. And the intensity in his expression made her wonder if he might be sensing some of the same feelings that affected her.

Not that either of them wanted it. Adeline was dismayed he'd seen her so openly displaying her womanly longings, and though he'd hid it well that afternoon, she knew he must be angry that she'd slapped him even though she had just cause. It certainly wasn't the sort of action anyone would welcome. But it was as if none of those things seemed to matter when they looked into each other's eyes. The yearning for something more was there between them. She couldn't deny it and had no idea what to do about it.

"What are you doing here?" she asked a little more abruptly than she'd intended, but he unsettled her in a way that made her wary.

"I came outside to see if you were all right."

"Yes, of course," she answered, her tone returning to normal. "You can see I am. That is, I was before you startled me. Why wouldn't I be?"

"I don't know," he said, walking closer to the withered vine-covered border between them. "That's why I came out. I noticed you standing here and wanted to make sure nothing was wrong."

It seemed strange hearing genuine concern in his voice and seeing it in his expression after their last meeting. There was a long moment of silence as each took in what the other had said. His eyes were as gray as she remembered. She tried to stop the fluttering in her chest with a deep breath, but it wouldn't cease. When her gaze met his it was as if she couldn't control her senses or feelings. Feathery wisps of sensual awareness curled through her and made her even more curious about him. It made her want to forget the disaster of their first meeting, especially his ungentlemanly behavior, and indulge in all the experiences her sensations offered.

"You can see, I'm perfectly fine," she insisted softly. "What made you think there is anything wrong with someone standing alone in their garden on a beautiful spring day?"

"You hadn't moved."

She thought about that. "Really? I mean, surely not."

"You've been in the same place, looking at the same spot for a very long time."

He was watching her. For a fraction of a moment it seemed a heavenly thought that he was interested enough to do so, but her rational mind quickly returned. With it came the memories of when her husband had her monitored each day so she wouldn't do anything strenuous. She hastily brushed aside those unpleasant feelings and asked, "How would you know that? Were you deliberately observing me, my lord?"

"Do you really think that?" he asked skeptically.

"Shouldn't I? First you invade my home and now it appears you have been watching me in my garden."

He grimaced for a moment or two and then his features relaxed into more of an amused expression. "You think I've been spying on you from afar?"

Did she?

"That's what it sounds like to me," she suggested, trying to sound outraged or at least serious, but wasn't sure she had because her body and mind betrayed her again by thinking she wasn't so sure she would have minded if it had been true. Confused by her own scandalous thoughts and irritated by his amusement over the idea of her assumption, she quipped, "I discovered the other afternoon the sort of things you are capable of doing, my lord, and they aren't gentlemanly."

"Let me put your mind at ease. No," he said emphatically, placing the palm of his hands on the top of the wall and leaning toward her.

The strength of his grip on the stone communicated his message more than the words he spoke. Though he was still some distance from her, it was almost as if she felt his heat, caught his scent, and sensed his power as surely as she had when he held her front door shut and was so close his breath fluttered against her cheeks.

"What happened in your home was a regrettable error, Lady Wake, and I wasn't watching you earlier. There was nothing intentional about noticing you standing so still for so long. Every morning I tie my neckcloth where I can see out the window to this section of your garden. It's natural for me to look out."

Adeline glanced over his shoulder in the direction of his house. The first and second floors could be seen clearly from where she was standing. *Oh.* She swallowed hard, believing his explanation.

After all, he was her neighbor. That wasn't something that was going to change in the foreseeable future. It would be best if they forgot the past and were civil if not trusting of each other. He'd obviously made the first move toward that end by coming over to inquire about her well-being, and she would do the right thing and meet him halfway.

"Thank you for letting me know. I'll remember that whenever I walk outside, my lord. And again, I'm perfectly fine and need no one checking on me when I'm in the garden enjoying the day."

She'd had enough of being watched almost every moment of the day the two years she was married.

"Good. I'm glad to know it wasn't a snake or a spider in a web that stopped you for so long," he said with a twitch of a grin.

After a shiver at the thought of such creatures being in her path, and much to her consternation, Adeline gave a hint of a smile, too. That seemed to satisfy him.

"I'll leave you to enjoy your morning in the fresh air." He nodded and turned away. Adeline looked down at the pathway and then scoured the air space in front of her for any telltale signs of a web.

Maybe the earl was a beast after all, and he was certainly one who knew her fears.

Chapter 5

With a deep sigh of vexation Adeline looked up at the trellis she stood beneath. She had to admit that she hadn't had the opportunity to be alone with very many men, but the earl had to be the most intriguing of that lot. He was a menace to her peace of mind. She must keep her intimate thoughts and feelings for Lyon under control. And she would. Just as soon as she figured out how.

The last of the brown leaves of winter had fallen away, and buds of greenery were showing in patches all over the archway. Several vines were woven in between the ivy, but not enough of the plants had grown out for her to know what type of flower would adorn the structure in the next few weeks. Glancing down at her heavy dark blue widow's skirt and matching velvet pelisse, she found herself hoping the blooms would be bright, cheerful colors. Light shades of pinks, vivid blues, deep purples, sunny yellows, and brilliant reds.

Any color that wouldn't remind her of the drab gloominess Society expected her to wear.

Shaking her head, and blaming even her complaints about her clothing on the disturbing Lord Lyonwood, Adeline stared back at the school building determined to focus on the girls. The boarding school deserved her complete attention. She was eager to meet the girls, eager for their time at the school to begin.

The back door of her house opened. Adeline turned to see Brina coming out.

"I'm sorry we're late," she called and waved.

A smile stretched across Adeline's face. She suddenly felt uplifted. "It's about time you two got here."

"It's my fault we're tardy, as usual," Julia called, gliding up beside Brina and waving, too. "I hope you didn't give up on us and meet the girls without us?"

"Of course not," Adeline answered, squinting against the glare of sun that hung above the roofline of her house, and motioned for them to join her. "I've been waiting for you out here because it's such a beautiful day. Come on."

Brina, the youngest of the three friends and benefactors of the school, was tall, willowy, and a natural beauty. Even in her widow weeds and with her gorgeous silvery blonde hair covered by a wide-brimmed straw hat, as it was today, everyone took notice when Brina walked by. To most of Society she was the epitome of all a widowed lady should be. Devoted to the memory of her husband, and kind to a fault. There was

an enticing grace about her that most ladies envied but
never attained. Everything about Mrs. Brina Feld spoke
of loveliness and goodness.

Adeline knew Brina's countenance was held together
by an enormous, fearless inner strength. Though not
much past the age of nineteen when asked, she'd had no
reservations about helping fund and plan the boarding
school from the moment Adeline suggested it. Brina's
round face and almond-shaped blue eyes always held
a smile for everyone be they friend or stranger. Her
words were always carefully chosen and gentle. Only
Adeline and Julia knew how deeply Brina still mourned
her husband. She'd been married less than three months
when the ship went down. Her husband had been heralded as a hero, saving the lives of a few but losing his
own. Brina's sorrow for the loss of her beloved ran deep
as the sea.

Julia came hurrying down the steps behind Brina.
Known in Society as Lady Kitson Fairbright, Julia was
the opposite of their dear friend Brina in appearance
and deportment. Julia's shiny chestnut-colored hair always seemed to be falling out of her chignon whether
or not she'd donned a bonnet that day. She had rare
dark violet eyes and the fairest complexion Adeline
had ever seen.

While Brina always said and did the right thing in
every situation, Julia couldn't seem to, at all times,
manage the strict rules of propriety. Her carefree spirit
was difficult to harness. Never intentionally, but she
had been known to walk to Town without a proper
bonnet or hat covering her head and, according to gos-

sip, unthinkingly lift her skirts a little too high when stepping over a puddle crossing the street. Sometimes her venturesome, impulsive nature led to unexpected incidents that were difficult for a lady to explain. But Lady Kitson Fairbright had been irreplaceable when it came to helping start the school even though she'd struggled with her own troubles since her husband's death.

"I've missed you two," Adeline said after hugging first Julia and then Brina. "I hope both of you are never out of Town at the same time again. I had no one to talk to while you were gone."

"We were not together, remember," Brina reminded her teasingly. "We had no one to confide in either."

"I'm not trying to scold you," Adeline smiled impishly. "Only let you know how wonderful it is to see you. What made you so late? Did you have to stop for Julia to rescue a cat from a tree or to make sure a stray dog had clean water to drink today?"

"No," Brina answered with a slight roll of her eyes. "Not this time, but Julia told the driver not to go fast. She didn't want to tire the horses so early because she knew they'd have a long day."

Julia smiled sweetly. "You two cannot shame me for making us late. I only wish everyone had the affection for animals that I do."

"We do," Adeline insisted lightly. "We simply don't always show it in the many ways you do. You are a good example for us all. Tell me how Chatwyn is doing. Did he love the coast?"

"Oh yes, very much so, and I did too, of course,"

Julia answered. "He didn't want to leave. What's not to love about running barefoot along the water's edge when you're two years old? He was delighted."

"Wasn't the water freezing cold?" Brina asked.

"And rocky?" Adeline added with surprise.

"Yes, but he didn't care. He ran right over every pebble, shard, and broken shell as if skipping through a soft bed of grass. Every morning he would beg to go to the shore and play. The duke was very attentive. He would have let him go every day had I not insisted that if it continued, Chatwyn could catch a chill and become a weak, sickly child in the future."

"I think you did the right thing in standing up to the duke," Adeline said. "And how about you? Was the duke any kinder than when you were in London?"

Julia gave them a breathy sigh. "A trifle I suppose. I do hope it continues now that we've returned to get ready for the Season. I think he would keep me and Chatwyn at Sprogsfield forever if he could because it's so isolated and difficult for me to break any of Society's rules there. What about you, Brina?" Julia asked, turning to her. "We know what Adeline has been doing all winter, making sure Mr. Clements had everything accomplished. How was your visit with your family?"

"Lovely but wearisome," Brina said respectfully. "They won't leave me be. There was a steady stream of eligible gentlemen visiting. Some just for dinner, some for overnight, and others for several days, but all for me to consider as my next husband."

"And you rejected every one," Adeline offered as fact.

"Of course." Brina smiled contentedly. "You two

seem to be the only people who understand I have no interest in ever remarrying. But enough about us for now. I want to know if all the girls are here."

Adeline looked back at the school and laughed. "Yes, every one of them. Mrs. Tallon came over earlier and told me all nine are accounted for and waiting to meet us, so let's go."

Julia and Brina walked under the trellis and into the small schoolyard with Adeline. They stopped to stare at the name above the door.

"It sounds very quiet in there."

"I'm thinking the same thing, Brina," Julia agreed. "I would have thought with almost a dozen girls gathered in one place there would be a little noise."

"I'm sure it's because they are getting settled into their new home," Adeline said, feeling a rare moment of trepidation herself. "Leaving their families must have been traumatic for them."

"I didn't want it to be," Brina said compassionately.

"None of us did," Julia answered softly.

"They need time to adjust to what is now going to be their normal lives," Adeline offered. "We knew that. And they will. It's best they are quiet for now and get to know each other."

"I think part of my queasy feeling inside is that it isn't just a dream any longer. It's real now and the weight of knowing the girls are here because of us. Even though we won't actually be taking care of them or teaching them, they are our responsibility. Before it was just an idea, planning and talking about them. Now we are going to put faces to their names."

"But we all agreed this would be best for their

futures," Adeline added cheerfully, hoping to mitigate the concerns all of them were having now that the girls were on the property. "Many children go to boarding schools—mostly boys—and they do exceptionally well and so will these girls. Learning to read, write, and sew will be invaluable to them when they are old enough to earn a wage, which they will need to do one day, unless they are fortunate enough to marry a shop-keeper, silversmith, or some other tradesman who can take care of them."

Both friends nodded.

"Besides, we aren't forcing them to live here," Adeline reminded her friends. "Their families made this choice for them. If any of them want to return to home they can. Mr. Clements assured me every family he contacted was grateful for this opportunity."

"It's just that I know how the mothers must feel about their daughters leaving home and living elsewhere," Julia said wistfully. "They'll miss them terribly."

Adeline knew Julia had feelings and thoughts she and Brina couldn't yet comprehend with any depth. Julia was a mother. She'd been awaiting the birth of her first child when the *Salty Dove* sank and took her husband's life. Her son's grandfather, the Duke of Sprogsfield, was constantly threatening to take responsibility for little Chatwyn away from her if she dared to stir up gossip about herself. They all knew the duke was powerful enough to do it, so Julia had to rein in her free spirit and acquiesce to the duke's demands that she behave prudently at all times.

"Well," Brina said in a softly dismissive tone. "We

won't think about any of the sad reasons for this school. Only the good ones. And whenever these girls leave, they will have more knowledge than they can possibly have reasons to use it. And the skills to be a superb seamstress."

"Speaking of which," Julia said, looking a little oddly at Adeline. "I wanted to tell you I went to see Mrs. Le Roe yesterday, and she was in a dither. She asked me twice if I had received a box of fabrics from her. She was quite fretful, saying that a disgruntled employee might have intentionally had some intimate samples delivered to the wrong clients in hopes of ruining her reputation."

The earl came as easily to Adeline's mind as slipping a linen chemise over her head and down her body. She had forgotten him for a few minutes while she talked with her friends, but the infamous box that had contained the crimson stays soared him and all that he made her feel back to the forefront of her thoughts.

"What's wrong, Adeline?" Julia asked.

"Nothing," she answered softly.

"I'm not believing you," her discerning friend stated. "There's something you're not telling us. I can sense it."

"No," Adeline said absently, thinking she should have returned the fabrics to Mrs. Le Roe. But really, how could she after she'd—after he'd—

"Adeline, what are you trying to hide from us," Brina said. "Something's bothering you and there's no reason to keep it a secret from us."

"I think it has to do with a box from Mrs. Le Roe," Julia declared. "Your demeanor completely changed when I mentioned her name. Has she done something to you or someone else?"

"What? No. That's preposterous."

Brina quickly removed one of her gloves and placed her palm against Adeline's forehead. "How long have you been standing here in the sun waiting for us?"

"Not long," she answered defensively, leaning away from her friend's touch and willing the evocative images of Lord Lyonwood to fade completely away. "There's nothing wrong with me. Really." She paused. "It's just that—" And then suddenly the words came tumbling out like a waterfall before she could stop them. "Oh, all right, I might as well tell you. I was mistaken for the madam of a brothel, but other than that, I'm fine."

Adeline watched shock flare in her friends' expressions.

Oh, dear.

Brina jerked her hands to her hips. "You can't be serious."

"She is," Julia said.

"Yes, it's true." Adeline inhaled a deep sighing breath. "In your wildest dreams, would you have ever imagined anyone thinking I was a madam and opening an underground house of pleasure rather than a boarding school?"

"Who are you talking about?" Brina whispered on a broken gasp.

"What are you talking about?" Julia demanded. "Who would dare be so vulgar as to assume such an outrageous thing about you?"

"A tall handsome man with the most intriguing gray

eyes I've ever seen. My neighbor. The Earl of Lyonwood."

Brina shook her head in disbelief. "How could he?
I remember him. We chatted a few times. He's always
seemed a gentleman."

"What I want to know is why he would think such
a scandalous thing?" Julia asked.

"Apparently it had something to do with the amount
of beds being delivered to the school."

"What did you say to him?" Julia asked.

"I really didn't know what to say," Adeline admitted.

"Of course you didn't," Brina consoled. "I wouldn't
either. But what *did* you say? I know you. You wouldn't
have had a fit of the vapors or rushed above stairs to
hide from him."

"You couldn't have stayed silent either."

"No, of course I didn't. I had my say about his actions and words."

Adeline supposed she'd have to tell them about the
incident. Most of it anyway. Not even to Julia and Brina
could she admit that the earl had openly looked her
over so thoroughly she'd shivered. She couldn't tell them
how he'd made her long for kisses and caresses, or that
in a desperate attempt to absolve her guilt over her wayward feelings she'd slapped him. No, she couldn't tell
them any of that. But donning the stays—they would
understand.

She began the story by saying, "They were crimson."

Several gasps, ahs, and sighs later, Adeline concluded
her story. "Lyon believed me without question, but not
without a bit of rancor because of his mistake I'm

sure. You both know earls and dukes well. They think they have the right to do and say what they please to whomever they want."

"What an absolutely fascinating story," Julia whispered, still clinging to every word.

"I always thought him a gentleman, but I've changed my mind. He's a beast!" Brina exclaimed.

Just what Adeline had thought.

Julia crossed her arms over her chest as if she wasn't so sure of that and said, "I know Lyon. He is a handsome devil, but what I want to know is did you keep the stays?"

"What?" Adeline shook her head. "No. I threw them into the fire as soon as I could rip them off. The gold bow, too."

Brina and Julia looked at each other, and then back to Adeline.

"What gold bow?" Julia asked.

"Oh," Adeline whispered. "Didn't I mention the tulle?"

"No." The edges of Julia's lips lifted with a smile. "Exactly where were you wearing it?"

Suddenly the three friends started laughing. It felt wonderful to feel something other than anguish over the incident. Adeline filled them in on the strip of fabric she'd tied around her waist before saying, "As you can imagine it was an awkward meeting for both of us once our identities were made known."

"Have you seen him since the night it happened?" Julia asked.

"Once," she admitted honestly but decided not to

tell them it was only a few minutes ago. "Over the garden wall, and we were tolerant of each other."

Adeline didn't want to go into further details about that conversation where there was somewhat of a peace made between them, so she added, "I fear he will not be an easy neighbor to live beside. When I returned home yesterday from seeing Mr. Clements there were so many carriages waiting in front of his house they had clustered in front of mine as well. My driver had to let me off down the street and I walked home. Which I didn't mind the stroll, of course." Adeline smiled. "But I did wonder why he had so many people visiting."

"Perhaps it was his tailor, his boot maker, and his milliner getting him ready for the Season," Julia offered.

"Maybe even a button maker, too," Brina added. "A beast like him needs to be buttoned up tight."

The friends laughed again.

"Enough about Lord Lyonwood," Adeline said, feeling better now that she'd shared the story with her friends. Most of it anyway. "We have spent enough time discussing him."

"Very well," Julia said. "But it does sound as if Lyon is an exciting man to be around."

"Yes, he is," Adeline said without thinking and then quickly added, "Let's go meet the girls."

At first Julia and Brina were reluctant to give up the stimulating conversation about the earl so quickly, but Adeline remained adamant that she was through with her story and they had no choice but to follow her into the school. She had told them all she was going to about her neighbor.

Adeline had personally selected Mrs. Tallon out of all the applicants for the headmistress of the school. She was a robust, stern-looking woman who was, at least, twenty-five years older than Adeline. There was a motherly appeal to her, too. She opened the door, curtsied, and then waved her hand toward the girls.

"My ladies, come inside. The girls are waiting. Girls, show the proper respect to your benefactors."

Adeline saw the nine girls ranging in age from eight to twelve standing in a line as straight as toy soldiers until they each made their curtsy and mumbled their greeting. All were different in size, shape, and color of hair and eyes. They all wore the freshly pressed dresses Mrs. Tallon and her helpers, Miss Peat and Miss Hinson, had made for them. Two of the girls stood out from the rest. They were holding hands. She might have thought they were sisters had they looked anything alike.

One was almost as tall as Adeline and had the gangly rawboned look of a male youth. Her blue eyes were large. Slightly protruding front teeth enhanced her sharp nose and chin. A timid smile stretched across her thin lips. Her light brown hair was unusually short for a girl, barely touching her shoulders. She was introduced as Mathilda, but the girl whose hand she was holding was the one Adeline had most wanted to see.

Fanny Watson. The little girl she'd seen that day on the docks had been found. A lump grew in Adeline's throat. Fanny was a head shorter than Mathilda with vibrant long and curly red hair. Her bright blue eyes, her nose and mouth, were small, lovely. She was stout and her rounded cheeks had more freckles than Adeline had ever seen on anyone.

That day near the docks wafted across Adeline's thoughts once again as she looked at the girls with a feeling of awe. When her brother-in-law had seen her in tears that afternoon, he thought she was crying for the loss of her husband. But the tears had not been for him. Would never be for him. She'd lost all feeling for her husband when, after a few months of marriage, he'd yelled at her in anger that his mistress had given him child, but his wife hadn't, and it was damn time she did.

That admission from him had been a blow she didn't think she would ever recover from, but now she had.

There was a fleeting rush of sadness for what the girls had been through. It faded quickly and was replaced with a hopefulness. Their futures were filled with possibilities.

It would always hurt Adeline that she was barren, but now she had nine girls she was responsible for. They wouldn't ever take the place of having a child of her own, but they would give her a purpose in life that she hadn't had before.

She inhaled a deep breath, smiled, and said, "Good morning. Welcome to The Seafarer's School."

Chapter 6

$\mathcal{L}$yon's eyes popped open.

His blurry mind couldn't make out what had roused him. A high-pitched noise? A scream?

No, nothing, he told himself, lowering his fluttering lids, shutting out a gray slice of light that threatened to further disturb his slumber. Shaking off the intrusion, he snuggled deeper into the welcoming warmth of the comforting bed.

A squeal pierced the silence, and Lyon came instantly, fully awake. He bolted up in bed and listened. What in Hades was going on? He glanced about and listened. He was home. Not in a bawdy tavern east of Bond Street playing cards with friends and foe alike.

Nothing seemed out of place except for the host of young feminine shouts, shrieks, and laughter that splintered and crackled all around him. By all that was sacred, what had happened in St. James to cause such a ruckus?

"Damnation," he whispered, realizing his head felt like an anvil being pounded with a hammer. A low hum reverberated in his ears. It had been a long time since he'd overindulged in the bottle. Those years were behind him. Or so he thought. He would be mindful not to let it happen again. His temples were throbbing.

Lyon shook the warm coverings off his legs and rose, feeling as if he'd just fallen asleep. The chilly bedchamber and icy cold floor against the bottom of his bare feet helped clear his groggy mind as he walked over to the window. He yanked the top of the draperies apart to look outside. His neighbor's extended back grounds was swarming with girls.

"Lady Wake's garden," he whispered to himself. It was obviously now a play area for the boarding school she'd told him about. And these were the consequences. Toe-curling shrieks. He shouldn't be surprised. The girls were apparently as undisciplined as the lovely, merry widow.

Some of the lasses were running together, others were all by themselves, either hopping, skipping, or jumping. He wasn't sure which. Dressed alike, they wore gray bonnets, black gloves, and dark brown coats. And each one was making some kind of shrill noise that shuddered all the way through him. They chased, laughed, and yelled at each other. Their coattails flapped and long tresses bounced on their shoulders. Why would girls run and squeal if no one was chasing them?

The hoydens were so loud, he would have sworn to

anyone they were standing in the room right beside him. Irritably, he checked to see if the window had been properly closed. It was secure. Glass panes and wood were no match for the girls' gleeful merriment.

It wasn't natural to be that boisterous so early in the morn. The sounds they made would have sent winces through him whether or not he'd dipped once too often in the brandy last night—and Lady Wake was probably the reason he had. He had a devil of a time keeping his mind off her and on his card games.

With an annoyed jerk, he pulled the draperies together, dragged himself back to the bed, and tumbled down. He wrapped the blanket high on his neck and around his shoulders. Closing his eyes, he planned to ignore the sounds outside and sleep for several more hours. Then get up at a reasonable, more normal time.

But the noise didn't stop. Gaiety from next door continued. Grew louder. Girlish giggles and frolicking. Sleep continued to elude him as frustration built. It was the jubilant, youthful sounds of free spirits enjoying life. He hadn't actually heard such happiness since he was a boy at Eton and given an occasional day to play without instructions of any kind. Perhaps he wouldn't have minded the girls' loud cheerfulness so much if it had been at a different time of the day.

When he wasn't home.

Sleeping.

Lyon inched the blanket up and over his ears. He turned from one side to the other seeking relief. In desperation he rolled onto his stomach, pulled the pillow from beneath his head, and tightened it over his ears with his hands.

Nothing was going to block the sounds. Their voices could penetrate anything. Each squeal seemed to drill through his skull like a hot lance. He couldn't drink enough brandy to make him sleep through the clamor. For the sake of his sanity and the other neighbors as well, he had to put a stop to this nonsense and not let it go on any longer. There was nothing else to be done to restore order to the neighborhood.

Shucking off the blanket and pillow, he tossed them away, hopped off the bed, and went to his shaving chest. Shaking off the chill of the morning, he splashed a double handful of frigid water onto his face. He then quickly stepped into his cold trousers and buttoned the front flap with one hand while hastily pulling his shirt over his head with the other. There was no time for collar, neckcloth, or waistcoat. Not even stockings.

Frustrated, he shoved his bare feet into his boots as he tucked the tail of his shirt beneath his waistband. In his haste, he forgot about his usual method of dressing. He grabbed his stag-colored coat on the way out the door. At the last moment he thought about his uncombed hair but decided all he needed to do was rake through it with his fingers while hurrying down the stairs. Presentable enough for a flock of young females who were disturbing the peace, he argued with himself.

Lyon stomped out the back door and across his lawn, and jumped over the low garden wall. He skimmed down the tall yew hedge that separated Lady Wake's garden from the schoolhouse. He walked along the side of her house to her back garden, his head and ears pounding with every step. A natural-stone pathway led him to the archway the countess had stared at for so long a few days ago. Passing underneath it, he saw the little girls romping and playing to their hearts' content.

Smiles and happiness that he hadn't been able to see from the window brightened their faces. The sight gave him a moment's pause and more than a little doubt concerning his intentions. Perhaps he was being a bit hasty.

But then, a shrill shriek shuddered through him, underscoring his headache once more.

Why, he didn't know, but he'd always assumed girls were quieter, calmer, and more genteel than rambunctious schoolboys. He could understand little fellows exhibiting such uncontrolled behavior. But, whether boys or girls, this was an ungodly hour to be outside running about and disturbing the neighborhood. He would ask them to be quieter and suggest they find a different time of day for their playfulness. Perhaps in the afternoon, when he was usually gone from home.

That should do it and put an end to such nonsense today and every day.

"Girls," he called in a normal voice.

Not a one of them paid him any mind. Perhaps they couldn't see him. Or hear him. Small wonder with the commotion going on.

His quest continued. Impatiently, he stepped closer and called louder, "Girls! Girls!"

In an instant they all stopped. Not just the laughter, but their arms, legs, heads, and bodies became motionless, too. In fact, everything surrounding them went quiet. Distant horse and carriage traffic seemed to suspend sounds, as well. But only for a second or two. The smallest miss, who looked to be no older than eight or nine, started screaming, and hell broke its chains. All the girls started screaming at the top of their lungs. Not with the earlier joyfulness, but with terrified sounds.

Good lord, what did he do wrong? They were acting as if he were a wild boar charging toward them and they feared for their lives.

Lyon didn't know what to do. His ears drummed, his head hammered, and his heart slammed against his chest. The girls huddled together, locking their arms around one another, looking at him as if he were a monster that had been unleashed and was getting ready to devour them. He'd never seen or heard anything like it. When it came to women and ladies, Lyon knew what to say and do. How to charm or coax them into understanding whatever situation they might be in at the time.

He didn't know anything about girls.

A tall buxom woman about the age of his aunt Cordelia came running out of the building and down the three steps, two younger women following behind her. Good, he thought. Someone strong to calm and settle the girls. But no. She started yelling at him to go away, as she gathered the girls around her.

"Wait," he said, in a reassuring voice. "No, no, don't worry, girls. It's all right. There's no need to be afraid of me."

But then he must have done the inconceivable and walked closer to them. Though he didn't think it possible, the screams became louder. They couldn't have been more frightened if he'd been a ghost that had risen from a grave in the dead of night.

Lyon stopped moving and held out his arms and hands as if he were showing a thief he had no purse to steal.

From the other side of the yew hedge he heard, "What in the name of heaven is going on out here?"

Bloody hell.

Lyon knew that lovely voice. Lady Wake sounded out of breath, as if she'd run down three flights of stairs. He turned and saw her rushing under the vine-covered trellis with her dark brown skirts swirling about her legs. His stomach tightened at the sight of her. She hurried over to where the girls were huddled near the front of the school door.

"Mrs. Tallon, is someone hurt?" she asked with evident dismay. "Stung by a bee? Bitten by a spider? What?"

"No, nothing like that," the woman said in a strong voice and pointed. "It's him."

That's when Lady Wake's gaze aimed straight as an arrow at Lyon. He had no choice but to incline his head in a polite greeting.

Surprise lit in her eyes before she gave him an expression that could have easily froze boiling water.

She ignored him, turned back to the woman, and asked, "What about him? Why was everyone screaming?"

That's what Lyon wanted to know.

"I heard this man yelling at the girls," the woman said in a sputtering of words. "I don't know why, but he shouldn't be here saying anything to the girls. He frightened all of us."

The countess whirled back toward him and snared him with another penetrating gaze. "Did you do that?" she asked unbelievably. "Yell and panic everyone?"

"Certainly not," he answered testily, not used to having to defend his actions to anyone and certainly not to a saucy widow who made him want to pull her into his arms and kiss her every time he saw her. However, feeling a little guilty, he added, "I might have spoken a little loudly."

"A little loudly? Don't be ridiculous." She glowered at him. "That is the same thing as yelling."

He frowned and took a step closer. One of the girls screeched again, so he stopped once more. By Hades, didn't the girls know by now he wasn't going to harm them?

The countess turned immediately back to the girls and said, "This gentleman doesn't intend to hurt you." She glanced back toward him with cool irritation seething in her expression. "Right?"

"Rest assured," he said stiffly, trying to hold on to what little patience he had left.

"This is our neighbor, the Earl of Lyonwood. I want all of you to stop whimpering and give him a proper curtsy."

They obeyed without question, though some of the girls continued to sniffle. Others looked as if they'd quite literally seen a ghost—the kind that ate little children. Only one was smiling, Lyon noticed. A blue-eyed redhead whose chubby cheeks were covered in freckles. She seemed to be the only one who saw humor in the madness of the situation that had taken place, and she was enjoying it.

"Mrs. Tallon," Lady Wake said, "please take the girls inside. Make them some tea to calm them. Give them a few minutes to collect themselves before you resume their lessons. I'll take care of things out here. The earl was obviously looking for my house, became confused, and ended up at the wrong door."

Confused? Not bloody likely, Lyon thought but remained silently fuming so he wouldn't upset the girls any more than he already had. He'd have his say to the strong-willed widow once the girls were out of sight.

Lady Wake crossed her arms over her chest and gently tapped one foot as she watched the teacher scurry the girls into the schoolhouse. The woman then closed the door behind them so quickly and firmly it rattled the windowpanes.

"Follow me," she said, and started marching back under the trellis and into her garden.

"Gladly," he muttered, his mouth tightening and his resolve strengthening.

Lyon had a feeling this wasn't going to be an argument he could win. But he wasn't going to back down from the fight. Especially not with this spitfire. He'd give it all he had despite the fact he thought they'd soothed over their initial meeting a few mornings ago when he'd seen her standing in her garden. Apparently, he'd been wrong. Lady Wake had already proven she wasn't a frail weakling. Usually he didn't mind a lady with a bold temperament, especially such an intrigu-

ing one, but it appeared the countess was itching for
another quarrel with him.

And he was in a good state of mind to give her one.

The petite housekeeper he'd met a few days ago was
standing on the back step of the house holding onto the
tail of her apron. "Is everything all right, my lady?"
she asked in a timid voice. "Can I do anything to help
you or Mrs. Tallon?"

"No, thank you, Mrs. Lawton. Everything is fine
and under control. You don't need to go for help.
Thankfully, no one is hurt. You can go back inside
now."

After throwing a not-so-well-hidden disdainful expression in Lyon's direction, the housekeeper pivoted
on her heel and went back inside. Apparently she
wasn't ready to forgive him for upsetting the girls or
brushing past her and into the countess's drawing room
without permission.

Lady Wake confronted him with glinting, golden-
brown eyes that he somehow managed to find more
attractive than fierce. Her cheeks were flushed with
exertion and single-minded dismay. She wore no bonnet, so a breeze nipped at her dark honey-colored hair,
sending wispy strands blowing against her cheeks. The
sides and crown of her long tresses were pinned up, but
the rest hung down the back of her shoulders in beautiful tumbling waves.

Lyon knew, just as he had the previous two times
he'd seen her, that he was attracted to her in the most
primal sense, but her strength of determination and
bold personality made her just as desirable.

"What happened just now?" she demanded as he

halted in front of her. "What in the name of all the saints were you doing at the school making the girls scream?"

The short hair at the back of Lyon's neck rose. He'd never met a lady who could rile him so quickly. "They were already running around screaming when I arrived."

Her lovely winged brows flew up in skepticism, and that bothered him all the more.

"They were *playing*," she assured him.

"At this time of the morning? Barely past sunrise."

"What are you talking about?" she asked, keeping her gaze solidly on his. "In another hour it will be afternoon."

Really?

He managed a light shrug. He hadn't realized it was that late. His thumping temples made it feel as if he'd just gone to bed when the racket had first startled him awake. "No matter the time of day, just seeing a man and hearing him call to them loud enough they could hear over their own voices shouldn't have frightened them."

"Perhaps it wouldn't have if you didn't look like a ruffian or as if you'd just—"

She looked at his tousled hair, and then let her gaze flutter down his face to the open neckline of his shirt. Lyon sucked in an unexpected breath of arousal that not even his pounding head and lack of sleep could hold at bay. She was too tempting.

"As if I just got out of bed?" His voice sounded huskier than he'd intended.

"Yes," she admitted softly, lowering her lashes, obviously uncomfortable and as if feeling suddenly shy to admit to such an intimate thought to him.

"It's true it could have upset the girls because I'm not properly attired. I was sleeping when the noise started."

"Noise?" she scoffed, staring up at him again with renewed resistance to his claim and seeming to overcome her moment of gentleness along with the truce he thought they'd reached a few days ago.

He nodded. "I walked over thinking only to ask them to be a little quieter."

Her eyes rounded instantly and her hands clenched tightly at her sides. Clearly she had no fear of doing battle with him and felt prepared to do so. Not that after their first meeting that should amaze him.

"You admit that?" she demanded.

"With no hesitation."

She listened to him in stunned disbelief and then said, "What do you have against children?"

That took him aback, and he resented her implication he didn't have a fondness for children. He would welcome the sound of children playing one day—in the future. He looked forward to his sons and daughters laughing and romping about the grounds of Lyonwood. "Nothing. I like children."

She folded her arms across her chest and harrumphed defiantly.

"I don't have a problem with them," he insisted. "Just the noise they were making earlier."

"You are unbelievable, my lord! You complain about delightful squeals from girls having an enjoyable time when I am sure you will enthusiastically sit in the midst of more than a hundred men shouting and yelling insults, swears, and jeers in your ears at a pugilist match, a horse race, or a cock fight. Yet, you let the sounds of little girls having a playful time disturb you. What kind of man are you?"

The fiery countess wasn't going to budge an inch, but neither was he. "The usual kind, my lady. I expect to hear caterwauling at those events. And they don't take place in the morn when respectable people are sleeping."

"Are you saying the girls aren't respectable for playing?"

He would not let the intriguing lady get away with a statement like that no matter how fetching she was with her sparkling eyes, rosy cheeks, and indignant manner. Controlling his anger, he said, "You are deliberately mistaking my words, Lady Wake."

"How can you say that? There is no other meaning that makes sense to what you said."

"It's not that I don't like children. I've never been around them." Not for many years anyway. "I didn't realize they could be so loud. Girls were running around everywhere and no one was even chasing them."

"That's no excuse. Children need time to enjoy a few minutes of normalcy. You are an impossible man to deal with. What is wrong with you?"

You, he almost said aloud but caught himself and only replied, "Nothing."

"I think not, Lord Lyonwood. You charge into my house and accuse me of amoral behavior before gathering the first fact about who had moved in next door to you. You watched me from your window, and now you storm into my garden to reprimand the students without coming to me first with your complaint. Not only all that, *you* have managed to scare the girls and their teachers half out of their wits for no good reason other than you spent your night swimming around in the bottom of a grog barrel."

Grog?

"Your nerve is so out of bounds, Lady Wake, it would take weeks to find should anyone go looking for it."

"I'll take that as a compliment."

"Then let me give you another," he said softly, his gaze sweeping down to her lips. "I appreciate and commend how you've come to the girls' defense."

For a moment her face softened and she looked as if she might take his praise as he intended. But then, as he suspected she might, considering her propensity to boldness, she spoiled it by saying, "Perhaps you should try drinking a little more while you are spending all night with your cohorts at the gaming halls. That way it won't be so easy for you to awaken in the morning at the lovely sound of girlish laughter."

Lyon wasn't sure if he grimaced or grinned at her comment. Today she was clearly not interested in the modicum of a truce that had been struck between them.

Fine.

"That idea has merit, Countess. I'll only have to decide which gives me the greater headache. Too much drink or shrill merriment exploding into my bedchamber." He stepped closer and looked right into her eyes.

"I will allow that I'm not a patient man and that I like order and calm, but I'm not a wild ogre out to harm children."

"You are just heartless."

"No," he insisted, not that it seemed to matter to her. "I want them to play. Just quietly. This is a neighborhood. If the little chicks can't play quietly, then you should move your boarding school to the country and give them all the ground they want to run around."

The countess looked aghast at what he said. Fearing she might tempt him to say more and disprove his staunch oath that he wasn't an ogre, Lyon turned and stomped off. He'd never met a lady with such a fearless spirit. One who stood her ground no matter the odds or the situation in which she found herself.

The devil take it. A brothel would have been easier to deal with and far more quiet.

His temples were throbbing like a thumb that had been caught in a slammed door, and worse, his stomach was cresting up and down like a huge wave. Nevertheless, he thought he'd been quite good controlling his temper toward the willfully strong widow, considering his splitting head. He needed a splash of brandy and breakfast. In that order.

And coffee.

Lots of coffee.

After that, he needed to talk to his solicitor. He wanted to see what could be done to move Lady Wake and her school out of the neighborhood to somewhere more appropriate.

Like the northern coast of Scotland. That should be far enough away to suit him nicely.

Chapter 7

Adeline paced in her garden until she wore herself out. All because of the tempestuous earl. He had the gall of the Prince himself. And then some. Lyon simply wasn't worth all the effort she was putting into thinking about him time after time. It was exhausting.

Yet, she couldn't seem to stop.

They'd had what she thought was a respectable, neighborly conversation just two or three days ago. Except for the carriage traffic his visitors caused in front of her house, she was beginning to believe they might dwell in peace as good neighbors. Now he was back to his old tricks of storming over without just cause and distressing her.

Still too agitated and not ready to go inside, Adeline wandered over to an old wooden bench that stood against the back wall of her house and plopped down. That he'd upset the girls so terribly, after all they had been through, angered her beyond words. Their tragic losses, and getting used to living with strangers in a boarding school under the strict environment of learning skills, were frightful enough for them without him adding to their fears.

Rushing over half-dressed to chastise them for being too noisy was unforgivable. Calling them *chicks*! In fairness, she knew it had been a rash comment he made in the heat of the moment. It's not that a baby bird was such an appalling name to call the girls. Chicks were actually extremely soft with their downy newborn fluff before their feathers appeared. They were warm, cuddly, and quite precious to hold in the palm of one's hand. Perhaps they made a little squeak from time to time, but it wasn't a repulsive noise. It was high-pitched, but sweet and innocent sounding.

Besides, as far as she was concerned the earl's erratic actions showed he was more undisciplined than girls at play.

Suddenly Adeline blew out a soft laugh. Maybe in retaliation she would have the girls come outside at eleven o'clock every morning and scream to the high heavens. That would be fitting for the late-sleeping earl. To bother him as much as he had her would bring sweet satisfaction.

It felt good to think of the possibility of such an action, but she would never do it. That wouldn't be advantageous. Adeline was rational enough to know that if Lyon was disturbed by the girls playing, others might be, too. It was important that the school become a part of the neighborhood and blend in. Not disrupt it and cause problems that would be difficult to settle. It was best she take care of this now. She would speak to Mrs. Tallon and tell her to take the girls to St. James Park three times a week to play and run to their hearts' content. And she should come up with another respite they could do each day. Singing would probably be a good pastime. That shouldn't annoy anyone, including the earl.

She laid her head against the siding of the house and closed her eyes. Maybe if she shut out the light of day, she could also resist the temptation to foster more thoughts about her infuriating neighbor. How many times would she have to tell herself there were more important things to dwell on than a man who not only jumped to conclusions before he had the facts but also disliked children?

Peace wouldn't welcome her.

She kept seeing his intense gray eyes searching hers and the way his uncombed hair fell attractively around his forehead and face. The light stubble of beard on his cheeks and chin had enhanced his roguish good looks. He really should have had on a collar so she couldn't see his strong neck and the intimate hollow of his throat.

Dash the man. Did he follow any of the acceptable rules of proper behavior?

Adeline knew her knowledge of men in general was limited, but she was fairly certain disagreeable, insufferable aristocrats weren't supposed to be as attractive as the earl. Lord Lyonwood made her feel anger and outrage, but he also made her want to explore the warm and delicious feelings he caused inside her. Whenever she looked at him she felt as if her insides were melting into a hot swirling pool of anticipation and she didn't understand why.

It was obvious he didn't like her. She didn't like him. He didn't like children, and he probably didn't like dogs or cats, either.

She smiled to herself. It might be going a little too far to think Lyon didn't like animals, but he clearly had no patience when it came to children. And no respect for a lady's privacy.

That last thought brought other memories to mind. The concentrated pressure from her husband to produce, the criticism from him because she didn't, and the hurts and feelings of inadequacy for not measuring up to what her husband had expected of her when they married.

A wife to give him children.

Wake never believed she was as devastated as he was by her inability to conceive, but she was. That was the reason she agreed to all the things he made her go through. Things that were supposed to ensure she would have a babe.

Only after they married did she learn that Wake had picked her out of all the young ladies making their debut that Season because he thought she appeared to be the most favorable to give him a strong, healthy son. He didn't charm and woo her so diligently because he thought her the most beautiful or wittiest, or even for her generous dowry. No. It was because she appeared to him to be the best young lady to withstand the rigors of childbearing.

All that was behind her now. In the past. Where it would stay.

Determined to keep the invading thoughts from lingering, Adeline tried to settle more comfortably into the bench, wanting only to breathe deeply and relax. It would have been much easier to accomplish if the seat had cushions. She made a mental note to ask Mrs. Lawton to put some out every morning. The days were getting warmer and there was no reason she shouldn't come outside and enjoy the spring air—while reading a book, or stitching a flower on a handkerchief, or having her morning tea.

A shadow fell across Adeline's face. She thought perhaps a thundercloud had eased across the sky. Or maybe Mrs. Lawton had come outside to check on her. What if the earl had returned? Her eyes popped open. Startled, she saw a little girl standing over her.

Adeline jumped to her feet.

"Good heavens. What's wrong?" Adeline asked. "Did the earl return?"

The red-haired child with freckles sprinkled across her nose and crest of her rounded cheeks innocently glanced from one side of the house to the other. "I don't see him anywhere."

The girl didn't look distressed, but Adeline bent down to her level and said, "You don't have to be frightened. I'm going to make sure he doesn't bother any of you again."

"He didn't frighten me," she said confidently. "I'm not given to fits like some of the other girls who are living here. I only screamed because they were. He seemed like a nice man to me."

That wasn't an answer Adeline expected. All the girls were shrieking in terror as loud as humanly possible when she came out. "Then what are you doing here?"

"Looking at you."

Squelching her first instinct to show her displeasure at the simple answer, Adeline reminded herself she was talking to a child not more than ten years old and then cleared her throat and smiled. "That was quite obvious. I meant to ask why you aren't in the schoolroom having tea with everyone else?"

"I don't care for tea," she said in a matter-of-fact tone.

"I see," Adeline said, though she really didn't. She didn't know of anyone who disliked tea. There had to be another reason she was out of the school building. The thought that she might have been thinking about running away concerned Adeline. She didn't have on her coat, bonnet, or gloves, though. "Your name is Fanny, right?"

She nodded and clasped her hands to the back of her skirt and gently swung her body back and forth.

"Did Mrs. Tallon or either of her helpers give you permission to come out here?"

"No," she admitted calmly. "But I didn't ask them."

At least she was honest about it. "Don't you think you should have sought someone's consent before you left the school?"

She shrugged.

Fanny certainly wasn't giving the appearance of a child who was trying to run away, but she wasn't say-

ing much either. Adeline asked, "Did you have plans
to go anywhere in particular when you came outside?"

"No. I'm curious and just wanted to look around.
Mum said it's good to be curious. That's how you learn
things."

"Fair enough. I can understand that. All your sur-
roundings are new to you. It's natural to want to see
everything. We won't worry about that this time, but
I'm curious about something. How did you get out of
the schoolroom without Mrs. Tallon knowing?"

"I was real quiet."

Adeline made a mental note of that.

"And her back was turned to me. Irene was crying
and Reba started crying, too. And another girl." Fanny
rolled her eyes. "I don't remember her name. Mrs. Tallon was busy with them."

Adeline's heart constricted for all the girls and what
they were going through. This change in their lives
wouldn't be easy, but the difference it could make in
their futures would be immeasurable. That is what she
had to focus on. The girls and their families had to
make the sacrifices today so they would have a chance
at better lives tomorrow. Boys went to boarding schools
and managed it and ended up well educated, and so
would these girls. They would realize they were just
as strong and capable, and do beautiful seamstress
work one day, too.

"I know this may not be the easiest of paths, but it
will be the most rewarding for all of you," Adeline
said, feeling quite somber at the depth of her undertaking. "I wish I could hurry it along, but it can't be

done that fast. Learning to read and write and be good at a trade takes time."

"I'm in no hurry," the little girl offered as she looked around the garden. "I like it here. I think it's the most beautiful place I've ever seen."

That appeared to be the case for Fanny. She didn't seem at all disturbed. Maybe it was only mere curiosity that caused her to leave the school building.

"When I met all of you a few minutes ago, I noticed you were holding hands with one of the other girls. Was it Irene?"

As she shook her head, her long red curls bounced. "No. That was Mathilda. She doesn't cry. She's brave like I am and doesn't mind being here either."

"That's good to hear." If some of them were coping already, there was hope in time all of them would and without too much trauma in the meantime.

"We haven't done much sewing or learning, yet, but I liked seeing the workroom. It has a lot of thread in it. I wanted to touch the spools but Mrs. Tallon told me I couldn't. I didn't know there were so many different colors. I could look at them all day."

Her comment pleased Adeline. The room was also full of most anything they could want or would need to add frippery to all types of clothing, hats, and bonnets. Mrs. Tallon had stocked the room with various colors of embroidery and tatting threads, yarns, lace and ribbons, and many different kinds of trim. There were feathers, dried flowers, and jars of beads lining several shelves.

Though the headmistress had argued against it because of the cost, Adeline insisted a few lustrous fabrics must be included with the many bolts of inexpensive muslin that had been purchased for teaching. The girls needed to appreciate the texture differences among a coarse, worsted wool, heavy cotton, and a fine silk tulle or lightweight brocade when pushing a needle through it or cutting it from a pattern.

"You're young enough that you'll probably have the opportunity to use every shade that's in there before you are ready to be employed by a dressmaker."

"I hope Mrs. Tallon lets me pick the colors I get to use first." Fanny scrunched her nose and then twitched it a time or two. "But she probably won't."

"That will be up to her."

Adeline wasn't getting any closer to finding out what Fanny was really doing outside the schoolhouse. If it wasn't fear of the earl, or that she wanted to run away, perhaps it was . . .

"Tell me about Mrs. Tallon and her helpers? Have they been kind to everyone?"

Fanny hesitated as if she wanted to study on what she wanted to say. "Mrs. Tallon says I need to answer her when she speaks to me, but sometimes I don't have anything to say. Mum says I don't talk enough either." She breathed in deeply and shrugged.

Adeline couldn't help but think of herself and Lyon. They probably said too much to each other and could take a lesson from Fanny and just be quiet. "I'm sure you miss your mother and that she misses you, too."

Fanny nodded. Her blue eyes continued to gleam confidently. "But I need to be here. She said I'm going to learn how to read and write my name. I already know how to sew."

"Really? Well enough to cut up an entire piece of fabric and make a dress out of it?"

She shook her head. "Not that much. I can't make a fancy dress like you have on, but I can sew on a button, hem a skirt, and darn a hole in the elbow of a sleeve."

"That's quite impressive for someone your age."

"Mum says I'm good help to her but she wants me to learn how to read." Fanny's lashes suddenly lowered. "Papa knew how. He used to read to us when he was home, but he's been in Heaven a long time now."

Adeline swallowed down a lump of sorrow that sprung up in her throat. She supposed two years was a long time for a child. "I'm sorry he can no longer do that."

"That's all right. I'm going to learn so I can read to Mum the way Papa did, and then she won't be so sad. Papa will be happy when he knows I can read, too."

"And it will bring a smile to your mother's face when she hears you reading to her."

"Papa will be watching from Heaven."

"I believe he will," Adeline said with a smile. "I'm glad to know you want to be here and you weren't trying to run away from the school when you came outside."

Fanny unclasped her hands and held them up as she shrugged again. "I don't have anywhere to go."

"All right. Let's start heading you back to the school. If Mrs. Tallon realizes you're gone, it would worry her." Fanny fell in step with Adeline. "You do know you can't be walking out of the schoolhouse again without Mrs. Tallon's permission, don't you?"

"Why, if I'm not going to do anything but walk around and look at everything?"

"You might accidently walk too far away and get lost. That would concern all of us. And, you might miss out on an important lesson she's teaching. You wouldn't want to do that, would you?"

Fanny shook her head again, causing her curls to bob across her shoulders. "Mum told me it was very important that I mind all the rules and eat all my food when it's put before me whether or not I like it and don't say a word."

"She sounds very wise."

"I'm not to give anyone any trouble so that I have to come back home before I'm properly schooled."

Feeling quite pleased, and hopeful about the future success of the school, Adeline smiled. "I agree with your mother and that's not going to happen, is it?"

"No, I'm going to be a good girl. She made me promise to do everything I'm told to do and not to be hitting anyone or pulling any girl's hair."

Adeline considered what Fanny said for a moment and then she stopped, bent down once again to be on Fanny's level, and said, "You haven't done anything like that before, have you?"

The little girl looked at Adeline with sparkling, mischievously calm eyes. Her lips pursed together and she shook her head, swinging her shoulders as she did so.

Finally she said, "No, my lady. Not since I've been here."

Chapter 8

Lyon walked through the door at White's, swinging his cloak off his shoulders. He handed it and his hat off to the attendant and headed straight for the reading room. A quiet place to peruse the day's newsprint was just what he needed. After his unusual start to the morning was disrupted, he wasn't sure he'd get that at his house. His club was the next best place. It was early enough in the day that he had no reason to believe many of the members would be gathered for their afternoon card games or billiards.

White's had a grand history as far as gentlemen's clubs went. Only the elite of male Society had ever made it past the front door—according to tradition. But, there was legend that contradicted that long-held belief. He'd heard rumors that in the past there'd been a few occasions where ladies had managed to slip inside the hallowed rooms by donning gentlemen's clothing and either putting on a wig or cutting their hair in a short, manly fashion. One lady was said to have posed as a server rather than as a member or guest.

He wasn't sure he believed any of the rumors had truth to them. To Lyon, it didn't matter the size, height, or age of a woman. And certainly not how she was dressed or the style of her hair. Women and ladies alike had a softer look about them, a different way of walking and talking. They had an undeniable demeanor that spoke of feminine qualities that couldn't be hidden beneath the trappings of a man no matter how clever a disguise.

After a hearty breakfast of ham, eggs, and several pieces of toasted bread smothered in a tasty mixture of preserved figs and butter, his headache went away, though in its place came the remorse that he'd scared a dozen girls so badly they'd probably not want to go to sleep tonight and would have horrific nightmares when they did. He'd considered going over to apologize for interrupting their playtime but decided that could frighten them all over again.

He'd paid a call to his solicitor only to find the man was out of his office for the day taking care of another client. Perhaps he should look into the possibility of hiring a different solicitor. Lyon had been annoyed Mr. Burns had all winter to have the account books and ledgers in order and ready for him to review last week. Four months and the man hadn't managed to accomplish it.

For now, Lyon would see the man tomorrow. He

wanted to find out all he could about how the lovely but contrary Lady Wake ended up next door to him with a boarding school in the back half of her garden. As well as whether or not there might be the possibility she could be convinced to move the school elsewhere. Knowing the fearless Lady Wake, she would probably insist he should be the one to sell and move away.

Hell would freeze over first. His house had been in his family more than fifty years.

A low laugh rumbled in Lyon's throat as he entered the doorway of the reading room. He paused and tapped the side of his leg with the newsprint he'd picked up from the front room.

This was not his day.

The Marquis of Marksworth had already seen him, so there would be no chance of ducking out quickly and heading to another club to avoid him. Lyon nodded to his father and he returned the greeting. Lyon might as well pick out a spot that had two empty chairs. Marksworth would be joining him as soon as he finished his conversation.

Aunt Delia was right about his father, Lyon observed, deliberately walking in the opposite direction of the group of men engrossed in a quiet discussion that seemed to be of some importance, considering the apprehensive expressions on their faces. The tall, strapping marquis, with a physique most young men would envy, looked half his true age of near fifty. It was never more prevalent than when he stood beside gentlemen his own age. Unlike the rest, there were no wrinkles making deep trails around his eyes, not a hint of pudginess around his middle, and seemingly not a hair lost from his head. Lyon had long grown used to hearing that he and his father looked more like brothers than father and son.

But in the way they lived their lives they couldn't be more different.

The Marquis of Marksworth wore his title, privilege, and wealth with a gusto few gentlemen could match. Sharing the Prince's love of art and other cultures, as well as having the Regent's ear for local and foreign political matters, made the marquis sought after by friends and foes alike for any piece of advice or warning he might dole out. Marksworth relished the power and attention the friendship with Prinny gave him and took pride in the advantage of being so noted. That he had conspicuously taken care of three mistresses for years also elevated his standing in the difficult-to-impress gentlemanly community of the ton and made him the cause of much envy and awe. The marquis embraced and enjoyed his status as London's most lusty swordsman.

Marksworth lived by the long held conviction that most gentlemen didn't consider it a terrible offense to cheat on their wives, but if they caught a man deceitful at cards, they'd be ready to meet him at dawn or see to it he was never accepted in the houses of Polite Society again.

His son's lack of interest in the politics of London, much less the whole of England or elsewhere, was a great disappointment to the marquis, but he'd never pouted about it. Marksworth considered Lyon's refusal to set up a mistress in a home of her own and gift her with money, jewels, and nightly visits an even bigger tarnish to his name and an affront to all mankind who could afford to do so and didn't.

Lyon wasn't a saint. When he was younger, he'd tried his father's lifestyle but didn't feel the need to boast about it. He freely took pleasure and gave it. A mistress was an easy way for a man to enjoy and satisfy his primal need for a woman in his bed and was the best way to stay away from innocent young ladies. It didn't take Lyon long to realize he didn't want a mistress at his beck and call year-round. And he didn't plan to live a life separate from his wife after he married, as did most titled men once they produced the mandatory heir or two.

Lyon wanted only one lady to cherish—a wife whom he loved and adored with all his being.

Wanting no more drink, he waved the server aside as he settled into an upholstered chair near the back of the room. He smiled as he opened *The Times*, remembering Lady Wake had the nerve to call fine brandy grog. No doubt about it, she was a lady to be reckoned with. Before he could finish reading the headlines, he heard his father making himself comfortable in the chair beside him.

"I've already read it and there's nothing to take notice of in there today," Marksworth said. "Most of it is rehashing yesterday's stories. But, if you have nothing else to do with your time, you might as well glance through it and see for yourself. Welcome back to London."

Lyon looked over at his father and smiled. "Thank you." He refolded the newsprint and laid it on the table beside him before giving his attention back to his father. "Why didn't you write and let me know that you planned to marry again?"

"You mean aside from the fact it appears I'm the only one in the family who's interested in wedlock?" Marksworth grunted. "I would have written if I'd thought you cared a dram one way or the other about my matrimonial status."

His father had always been skilled at making his point.

"I don't," Lyon admitted. "But I do care about you."

At that comment, his father returned his smile. "That's heartening. There's no need for you to worry about me or my upcoming nuptials. You'll like Miss Ballingbrand. It's true, as no doubt you'll recall, she had a miserable time of her first Season, but she's older now and has put that behind her."

Lyon couldn't say he remembered her at all, so he stayed silent.

"She didn't know how to deal with the crush of people at all the parties and idle conversation, but she is fairly intelligent. Not a young belle but she's no weed on the shelf either. She's not too fashionable as you'll notice: quiet, pleasingly demure, and manageable."

"Ah—manageable. Your favorite kind of wife."

The marquis nodded. "The marriage will be an attractive convenience for both of us. Her uncle is old and wants to see her settled. She needs a husband to take care of her."

"So she's grateful, too," Lyon commented, deciding not to be brash and mention that Cordelia had told him

Miss Ballingbrand's dowry had been generously padded with rich lands.

"For sure," he remarked, giving Lyon a satisfied grunt. "I don't know how I left out that admirable attribute when I was describing her. She's all the things *most* gentlemen would desire in a wife."

Marksworth's hint of a nudge didn't go unnoticed by Lyon. Those weren't the qualities he was looking for in who he married. They both knew Lyon couldn't give a damn whether or not a lady was demure. He'd actually prefer she wasn't. He wanted a wife who was passionate. About him, about their life together. Why would he want a quiet spouse who seldom spoke to him or didn't seem to care whether or not she was married to him? He wanted a lady who was vigorous, brave, and forthright in all things, especially her attitude toward him.

Lady Wake came to mind. Wearing the provocative red stays. No, she wasn't demure. She wasn't afraid to speak her mind, either. Her passionate nature had been blatantly on display every time he'd seen her. She was headstrong to a fault. And he surely couldn't say she was lacking in courage or a will of her own. She'd taken him to task with a vengeance when she thought he'd threatened the girls.

Marksworth laughed softly and said, "I've missed our visits, son. I'm glad you're back."

Brushing thoughts of the countess from his mind, Lyon gave his attention back to his father and said, "Me too."

Lyon had little appreciation for London in winter. He'd rather be at Lyonwood riding across his lands, checking the barren fields and frozen ponds, and visiting his tenants to see how they were faring through the coldest days. Occasionally he'd have friends come for a visit to enjoy hunting, target shooting, and all-night card games. Winter life in the countryside had suited him nicely for the past few years.

Yet, he had to admit to himself—but not his father—that he had been thinking more about sons to tramp around the estate with him and a beautiful, loving wife to come home to after a day of plundering the land or hunting its game. Someone to dine with, play chess, converse, and laugh with in the evenings. A wife who wanted to be in his bed and actively share in the intimacies it provided. Fiery and zealous in his arms. He wanted her soft and warm snuggled next to his side when he went to sleep and awakened in the mornings.

And unlike his father, who left the tedious affairs of land holdings and business ventures to his accountants and solicitors, Lyon took great interest in checking all of the books and records of the various assets himself. It wasn't that he looked for discrepancies because he didn't trust his managers, overseers, or accountants. He did it because he enjoyed the challenge of going through each entry, cross-checking the debits and credits, and making sure all the numbers were correct.

"You may think otherwise, Marksworth," Lyon said, "but I'm not against you having the companionship of a wife."

"Yes, I know. You just don't understand me keeping a mistress as well."

"You have three."

"I've known two of them for many years," he argued as if that explained it, and then sighed ruefully. "I don't have the heart to turn them off, and I do still enjoy going to see them from time to time."

"It's not for me to approve or condemn the way you choose to live your life. Nor is it any of my concern how a woman chooses to earn a wage for herself."

"Thank you," his father said sarcastically and then grunted another laugh. "You are just like your mother. Always trying to understand me—and it can't be done."

Lyon bristled at that statement. It wasn't that he was trying to understand his father. He simply didn't agree with him about love, ladies, and women. That said, Lyon would still rather have a conversation with Marksworth than anyone else. It was always a challenge.

"But, I loved her anyway," Marksworth continued. "She never understood why I was never satisfied with what I had for long. She knew and accepted the time would come when I'd want more. Horses, land, businesses . . . women. I can't explain it now any more than I could explain it to her twenty years ago. There's nothing to say other than I gain a tremendous amount of satisfaction from obtaining and keeping whatever it is I want."

There was no doubt about that. And, Marksworth was well-respected and envied for his business acumen. He improved his holdings in some way every year. Lyon wasn't against acquiring more wealth. He appreciated it. Took great care of it and enjoyed it. But he had no desire to live his life trying to add to it.

Lyon noticed a server walking toward them, and his father said, "I'll order us a glass of port."

"I'll have one later," Lyon said, shaking his head.

"Too much of it last night?"

"Much to my head's distress this morning," he answered with a dismissive wave of his hand. He'd not paid attention to how many times his glass had been filled while playing cards.

Marksworth shook his head at the server. "I thought you were past those days."

"So did I."

"Tell me, is there any chance you plan to select a wife this Season?" his father asked when their conversation grew quiet.

"This is old, rocky terrain, Marksworth, and no use going over it again. My views haven't changed since last you asked."

"Nor have mine."

"You swear you loved my mother, so would you allow me to fall in love before I marry, too?"

"Of course," Marksworth said with a slight frown. "I want you to. But as they say, the day grows late for the harvest while your heart searches for love. Keep in mind you were going off to Eton when I was your age. A man with a title to pass down shouldn't wait so long to have a son. You could do me a favor and at least tell me there is reason to hope you might find *love* this Season."

Unbelievably, Lady Wake crossed Lyon's mind again. He shrugged off thoughts of her, but he couldn't shake the sudden feeling that he was ready to find love.

Someone other than his friends to share Lyonwood with him.

Irritated by his lack of possibilities, he said, "I don't want to look for a bride as if I were looking for a mare to furnish my paddocks with colts."

Marksworth quirked his head and lifted his brow, and gave Lyon an exaggerated smile. "I'll be happy to do the honors for you. Mr. William Palmont's daughter is making her debut this Season. I met her a few nights ago in their home. Quite by chance. She's lovely, delightful and full of vigor. I think you could *love* her." His father looked pointedly at him. "She has serious brown eyes, which should appeal to you. She's most definitely extremely intelligent, which you would insist upon and appreciate. And she seemed quite discerning, which should suit you perfectly since you're so picky."

"Picky?" Lyon shifted in his chair. It was unusual for Marksworth to deliberately rile him. Though he couldn't say his father didn't know what he was looking for in a wife. "I'm selective."

"If you prefer that word, fine. Use it." He paused, then inhaled loudly. "I suppose the meaning of both fit though I suppose you aren't old enough to be jaded."

"And I don't need your help finding a wife."

Marksworth cleared his throat and looked about the room before settling his gaze on Lyon again. "You haven't done a very good job of it so far. At the rate you're progressing, I'll be an addled, decrepit man before you give me a grandson."

Lyon shook his head and smiled warmly as he looked at his father. There was no getting the best of him. And Lyon suddenly noticed Cordelia was wrong about his father not aging at all. His aunt must not have looked closely at the Marquis recently. He had a smattering of gray in his hair, though it hardly showed in the light-brown color. Not much of the aging color, but enough to be sure. In any case, it was nice to know his father didn't think that nearing fifty was old.

"Perhaps a change of subject is needed," Marksworth offered as a sign of peace. "Have you had the opportunity to speak to your new neighbor over the hedgerow?"

The mention of the countess caused a slow roll in the bottom of Lyon's stomach. He sat up straighter in the chair. "Lady Wake?"

"Or Lady Kitson Fairbright or Mrs. Brina Feld. Though I'm told those two don't live on the property. I have no idea how often they might visit. They helped Lady Wake finance the school."

Interested in what else his father knew about Lady Wake, Lyon shifted in his chair again. "How do you know about this?"

"The same way I knew Miss Ballingbrand had changed her mind and decided she didn't mind if she married after all. You should know by now not many things happen in London I don't know about."

Yes, Lyon did know that, but it hadn't occurred to him to ask his father about his incensed neighbor.

"How did it come about? The school. Does Lady Wake own the property? Is she leasing it from Mr. Bottles?"

His father's brows rose and he looked keenly at Lyon. "You are inquisitive about this, aren't you?"

"There's a half dozen or more girls living next door to me. I'm curious," he offered, hoping his father wouldn't start asking him questions he didn't want to answer and wasn't sure he could.

"Yes, but there's more to it than that. When you said Lady Wake's name, you suddenly looked as if someone had just sat down on your favorite hat."

Lyon smiled. His father didn't miss much. Lyon was irritated with the countess, but that didn't mean he wasn't also interested in her and what she was doing. She intrigued him with her bold, hot-blooded spirit.

"Just the simple facts will do, Marksworth."

"Very well. I'm fine with you hoarding your thoughts and keeping me in the dark. Mr. Clements, Lady Wake's solicitor, was Mr. Bottles' representative as well. Lady Wake wanted to buy a property large enough for a small school, and Mr. Bottles wanted to move to York to be with his daughter. Clements put the two of them together and they settled on a price. Are those facts simple enough for you?"

His father grinned. So did Lyon.

So Lady Wake owned the house. That was good to know. The thought that he could purchase it from her immediately entered his mind. At a hefty profit to her, of course. He'd even help her find a more satisfactory place to move the school. Where there was plenty of land for the girls to roam and play.

"Do you know why three ladies of considerable means would want to open a boarding school to teach the finer arts of manners and whatever else girls are taught?" Lyon asked. "I would think they'd be more into teas, card parties, and reading societies."

"I don't know what you've heard, but it's not an ordinary boarding school. It's not for the girls of Society. Not even those whose families find themselves financially embarrassed for one reason or another. It's unique in that it's only for girls who lost a father or brother when the *Salty Dove* sank. The men who worked on the ship. The stewards, attendants, and so forth. I really don't know the finer details, but the girls are from those unfortunate families. They would probably never have the opportunity to be taken in by anyone to learn a trade unless someone took them in to train as a scullery maid. I'm told the widows' school will teach the girls to sew. Quite admirable of the widows to take on such a charitable project."

By the time his father finished, Lyon felt as if he'd swallowed a lead ball. He couldn't believe he'd wanted to stop the girls from playing! What a blasted thing to do.

"I hadn't heard that about the school," Lyon said, his admiration for Lady Wake growing. She was not only daring and zealous, she was kindhearted, too.

Most of the ladies he knew wouldn't even toss a coin of their pin money to a street urchin, much less take a portion of their inheritance and open a charitable school to teach girls how to sew. To even think about the hardships of the workers' families was compassionate. To financially help them meant she had a generous, giving nature. That impressed Lyon. He'd bet his stable of stallions no one other than the three widows had done so much for others after the tragedy that took so many lives. Now, he was wishing like hell he hadn't marched over to quiet the girls. He'd no idea about their past and certainly not the connection they had to Lady Wake and her friends.

No, he couldn't consider trying to buy the property from her after all. The girls' lives had already been upset enough with the tragedy. He wouldn't add to it or their fears again. He would endure the school. How, he didn't know.

"Identifying the families and then finding them was quite an undertaking as I understand," his father continued. "Apparently Clements hired excellent people and handled everything for the widows in this endeavor so they didn't and shouldn't have to get involved in the intricacies of the school."

Lyon wasn't so sure about that statement. The countess seemed very involved and protective of the girls. He had a feeling Mr. Clements didn't do anything without the capable Lady Wake's suggestion or permission.

"You'll remember all three of the ladies lost their husbands when the ship sank."

"I do remember that." Lyon was also thinking he might well be the ogre he swore to Lady Wake he wasn't.

"There's been spots of gossip about it for the past two or three days," his father pointed out. "But if you haven't been to a dinner party, you probably wouldn't have heard. It's not the kind of talk you'd hear at a card game. Some ladies, mostly the older ones, think they've gone too far from what's acceptable with this endeavor, but others think it's fitting they are doing something so benevolent. I assume in a way to memorialize their husbands. They're being hailed as the wonderful widows by a few."

"I agree," he said, wondering why Lady Wake hadn't told him more about the school. Perhaps because he hadn't bothered to ask. "They should be recognized. This was very charitable of them."

The conversation fell quiet again for a few moments before his father revived their earlier discussion by saying, "You know I gave serious consideration to not marrying again."

"I would have assumed the idea crossed your mind from time to time," Lyon said dryly.

"Many times. I decided it was worth another try. Perhaps fate will smile upon me this time and give me another son."

Lyon considered his father's statement. He couldn't say that the thought of a child had crossed his mind when he heard his father was going to marry again. But it was always a possibility.

"The truth is, I want to make sure my legacy is the one that carries on the title and not that of my brother. I'm not sure I can depend on you to do that for me."

"Bloody hell, Marksworth."

"Be as scornful as you like."

"Thank you."

"But it's the truth. Have you stopped to think lately that if you don't have a son, our titles will go to Irvin who by the way already has a son, even though he is two years younger than you? I would twist and turn in my grave through all eternity should the title ever go to him. I dare say he'd gamble away everything but the entailed property inside a year, and he'd go through that as well if he could."

Lyon chuckled. "I'm not going to let you goad me

into proposing to the first lady I see. Besides, I don't hear rumblings of discontent at any of the clubs concerning my cousin's behavior. Irvin always manages to find a way to pay his debts."

"Yes, by laying off the cards and dice until his pockets are plump again from his allowance. He'd like nothing better than the opportunity to pay them with my earnings. Whether or not his inheriting the title disturbs you, it does me. I intend to protect my legacy and see that doesn't happen. I'd like a little help from you in that area. It's past time for you to do your duty and find a wife." Marksworth suddenly chuckled good-naturedly and slapped his hand on his knee.

"Do you intend to let me in on what humors you?" Lyon asked grudgingly.

"Certainly," his father said. "Just this morning a wager was entered in the books here at White's that I'll have another son before you have your first one."

Before making a comment, Lyon swore under his breath and shifted in his seat. "Our private lives shouldn't be the subject of a wager," Lyon said scornfully.

"I know, but what can we do?" Marksworth shrugged without the least amount of compunction. "A man has a right to wager on anything he wants to, and right now I'm the only one of us set to marry, so take a guess on where the bets are being placed. If you'd get busy, you could end all the speculation within a year."

Lyon would happily have a son—if he found a lady he wanted to be his bride and give him one. At that thought, Lady Wake entered his mind for the third time. It was damnable how he couldn't stop thinking about her.

Marksworth watched Lyon with a stare that seemed to be far more searching and deeper than necessary and asked, "Why the wrinkle in your brow?"

Lyon groused inwardly but said nothing. There was no need. His father had made his point clear. There would be an heir to carry on the title from his bloodline. And it didn't matter to his father which of them accomplished that.

"Ah, well, we'll have to save your answer for another day anyway. There's Mr. Leeds. I must be off to my appointment with him." Marksworth rose and looked down at Lyon with a hearty smile. "Do you want to come for dinner on Thursday?"

"The usual time?" Lyon asked.

"Of course."

Shortly after his father left, Lyon realized there would be no peace for reading the day's news at White's. He shouldn't have expected it. Everyone who passed by stopped and wanted a *moment* of his time— which turned into minutes, which turned into half hours, which turned into most of the afternoon. The members of the prestigious club looked upon it as their duty to let him know they had laid their money down on the newest wager in the infamous books, and most of them made sure he knew their money was on his father.

Fine.

When Lyon had had enough of the interruptions, he went home to find Brewster waiting in the vestibule for him with his usual professional expression, holding a note.

"I'll read it later," he told his butler, laying his outer clothing aside.

"It's from your neighbor, Mrs. Feversham, my lord. You may want to read it now." Brewster turned toward what appeared to be a very large flower basket filled to overflowing with something that was covered and tucked in a white cloth. Elaborate bows of what seemed to be every color imaginable had been tied on the handle, and ribbons of varying lengths were streaming from them. A note had been tied to it as well.

"What is it?" Lyon asked.

"A basket of scones and tarts, my lord."

"Take it to the kitchen."

His butler cleared his throat. "It's not for you, my lord. It's for the girls' school next door."

"What the devil?"

"I was told Mrs. Feversham's note will explain it to you." He held the folded paper out to Lyon. "However, her footman said she heard the girls wailing this morning, felt compassion for them, and thought a few fruit tarts and fried dumplings might assist them in feeling better and improve their emotional disposition."

"Damnation," Lyon muttered. "A few? Looks as if there's enough to feed an army for three days. Why didn't her footman take them? Does she consider me her servant to do her bidding?"

Brewster blinked slowly and remained still, seeming unperturbed by Lyon's bluster. "I don't know, my lord. Would you like for me to send someone over to ask?"

Lyon laughed gruffly, took the note and opened it. It was two pages long. The woman had written a book instead of a simple message. He didn't have the patience to read it at the moment. He handed it back to Brewster and stared at the basket.

For some reason, Lyon had the feeling Mrs. Feversham suspected he was the one who'd made the girls shriek and cry. She must have seen him stomping over there. She was either getting back at him for doing it or trying to help him appear apologetic by asking him to deliver the sweets to them. In either case, he couldn't take the basket over to the school. The sight of him might start the girls screaming again. He could send Brewster, but that had possibilities he didn't want to think about. They might consider the tall, portly butler another strange man showing up at the school, and that could distress them, too.

What he wanted to do was have Brewster march the basket right back over to Mrs. Feversham's house and put the responsibility on her doorstep where it belonged. But Lyon was feeling a tinge guilty for unnerving the girls so greatly, and a bit remorseful, too. He'd like to think that if he'd known of their past sorrows and what they'd been through, he wouldn't have gone over complaining about their girlish squeals and giggles.

They deserved the sweets. And he supposed he wasn't above helping an incapacitated neighbor.

There was only one solution that he could think of to do. Take the frilly, pastries-laden basket over to the saucy Lady Wake's house and let her take care of it. Besides, the idea of seeing her sensuous mouth, honey gold hair, and thick dark lashes framing her sparkling eyes appealed to him right now. He took in a deep breath and let it out slowly. But he couldn't fool himself. He doubted she wanted to see him after their heated conversation.

That would be *her* problem.

Not his.

"Give it to me," he said, reaching to take the basket off the chair where it was sitting.

Not bothering with his hat, cloak, or gloves, Lyon strode to the door and opened it. His aunt Delia stood in front of him, a small covered basket swinging from her wrist.

"Lyon, I was just about to knock."

He blew out an exasperated breath and shook his head in frustration. The trials of some days seemed to never end.

"Aunt," he said, with a nod of greeting.

"I stopped by to see if you would go with me to see Lady Wake. I've been wanting to meet her, so I had my cook pack marmalade and biscuits to welcome her to the neighborhood. Since I don't know her, and she is a countess, I was afraid she wouldn't see me without an appointment—unless I had a handsome earl by my side." Cordelia looked at the basket he held and then up to his eyes and smiled. "However, I see my gift can't compete with yours."

Chapter 9

A scone had been placed on each saucer and the cups were full.

Adeline sat on the settee in her drawing room opposite Julia and Brina listening to the two of them talk. The afternoon was windy but not cold, so they'd discussed the possibility of a walk in St. James Park later in the afternoon. She had missed her visits with them. Listening to them now made her realize how lonely the winter had been. Their chatter was a refreshing change for her usually quiet house.

If only her mind could enjoy such tranquility. But no. Lyon was a constant disruption to peace. She kept thinking about how he looked standing in front of the school. Half-dressed. Hair tousled from sleep. Passionate with anger. Filled with vitality. If she hadn't been so angry with him, she would have wanted him to kiss her. Maybe she had wanted him to, anyway.

"Do you agree with that?" Julia asked.

"Yes," Adeline answered, hoping she was agreeing to something she wanted to do. "Tomorrow I'll be at Mrs. Le Roe's for a fitting. Will either of you be there?"

"Not me," Brina said. "I don't even want to talk about the Season. I've been in London less than a full week and already three gentlemen have sent notes asking to call on me."

"Only three?" Julia said with a wry smile.

Brina wrinkled her forehead and placed her napkin on her lap. "I know it sounds callous of me not to be flattered, but I'm simply not interested in a gentleman who is trying to win my hand or even asking me to save him a dance at the first ball. It's the truth and I don't want to pretend otherwise with you."

"We don't want you to," Julia defended. "But I'm afraid I'm not feeling the freedom a widow is supposed to have. I think I would rather have a family who was pushing me to marry again than a duke who is watching my every move in hopes I'll cause a big enough scandal he can justifiably cut my allowance and take my son from me."

"Oh, Julia, I'm sorry. You know we don't want that," Brina said. "I sympathize with you because the duke is so old and strict with what he feels is appropriate behavior." Brina touched the back of Julia's hand briefly, then gave her a teasing smile. "You know I do, but can we switch places? I think I'd much rather have your problem than mine. It seems as if every man I see is being pushed upon me."

"That's because you are young, beautiful, childless, and wealthy."

"You are all those things, too," Brina argued. "Well, not childless, of course."

Adeline stayed quiet once again and let her friends have their battle. It wasn't a conversation she wanted to get involved in. Brina and Julia knew Adeline wasn't interested in matrimony, but for different reasons from Brina. She had loved and adored her husband and wasn't ready to give up her mourning. Adeline struggled with guilt for not mourning her husband enough. It simply wasn't in her to do more than feel deep sorrow for his family's loss.

She knew a wife's primary duty was to give her husband a child. A son, if he had a title to carry on. Adeline had failed. She'd drunk every potion put before her, stayed flat on her back in bed for days as Wake had ordered after he'd lain with her. She'd endured every examination he'd insisted upon. To no avail. Perhaps all he had asked of her would have been easier to bear if he'd just once identified with her rather than constantly remind her of the shame she brought on him because his mistress had given him a healthy child.

Adeline hadn't.

So, matrimony? No. Adeline would never put herself through that again, but it didn't mean she didn't desire a man's touch.

"Speaking of gentlemen, Adeline," Brina said, "have you seen the beast, Lord Lyonwood, since we were here last week?"

Images of the handsome earl flashed through Adeline's mind. She cleared her throat, relaxed her shoulders. "Yes, we had words this morning," she said cautiously, not wanting to get into what had happened with the girls. She knew Brina and Julia wouldn't like his storming over to quiet the girls any more than she had.

"Was the meeting any more civil than the first time you met?"

"Probably not."

"Why?" Brina asked. "Did he not apologize again for thinking this a pleasure house?"

"No, thank goodness. I'd really rather he never bring up that conversation again. It was extremely uncomfortable for both of us."

"Yes. Of course." Brina sipped from her cup and gave Julia an expression that let both of them know she hadn't meant to tiptoe onto what was so obviously the thorny side of the garden path concerning Lord Lyonwood. "I don't know what I was thinking. It should be forgotten by all of us."

"But really, how can we?" Julia stated, insuring she wasn't going to be as accommodating as Brina and reminding Adeline she was more perceptive than their younger friend. "Apparently, the earl is not putting forth his best efforts to win favors from you. What kind of words did the two of you exchange this morning?"

"It was only a slight tiff about the school." Had she really said it was slight? "We each had our say, and that was the end of it."

Julia would not be put off. "What was it about?"

"Noise," Adeline admitted. "And perhaps the girls were a little loud for such a quiet neighborhood, but he and I settled it."

"For now perhaps," Julia said. "But the school isn't going anywhere and neither are you. Is the earl?"

"I have no idea about him," Adeline said.

"I would think not," Brina offered, "but he could cause us trouble concerning the school."

Adeline was determined not to start thinking again about how attracted she was to Lyon. She wished she could tell Brina and Julia with all truth that she hoped she never saw the man again. But she couldn't. The unescapable fact was that she was drawn to him. It didn't matter that he'd thought her a madam and had yelled at the girls. There was a strong charm about him and his reasons for doing so. She sensed a code of honor inside him that what he was doing was right. Defending the community from an unsavory element or a calamity of noise.

Adeline placed her untouched tea on the tray in front of her. Wanting to change the subject from Lord Lyonwood, she said, "But I have a favor to ask of you, Julia."

"What?" she asked expectantly and then took a bite of her scone.

"I want you to bring Chatwyn with you the next time you come for tea."

"Yes, please do," Brina added quickly. "We haven't seen him since you left for the coast last fall. I'm sure he's grown taller."

"Oh, no." Julia dabbed at the corners of her mouth with her napkin and then said again, "No, I couldn't do that. You don't know what a two-and-a-half-year-old is like. He's never still. Except when he's sleeping, of course. When he's awake he is always running or talking—though no one knows what he's saying yet. He grabs everything he sees and usually puts it in his mouth."

Adeline laughed. "Perfect. It would be wonderful to see him again and hug his little body up close."

"Yes," Brina agreed. "I do want to give him a hug. He makes us laugh and smile. Something I know I don't do often enough."

"Neither do I, so it's settled," Adeline stated. "You'll bring him with you the next time we have tea and scones, and he can enjoy them with us."

"Scones!" Julia exclaimed, her cup rattling in the saucer as she put it on the tray. "Never. You haven't seen him eat and you don't want to. He's such a happy little fellow that he laughs and chatters when food is in his mouth and it goes everywhere. Half of it ends up on his face and the other half is either on his shirt or in his hair. Believe me you don't want to see him after he's gobbled down a scone covered in plum preserves."

"It sounds delightful, Julia," Adeline said. "I do want to see him. Don't deny us his company."

"No, of course I won't, if you're sure. I'd love to share him with you. But, I warn you, his manners are—"

"That of a child," Adeline exclaimed, cutting off the rest of Julia's sentence. "We want to watch him grow up, hold his little hands, hear his babble of words."

"Kiss his chubby cheeks," Brina added. "Do this for us, please. And if it causes you anguish, suffer through it."

"All right, all right, I will. But mark my words, we won't have any peace. We will be constantly watching him."

"Excuse me, my lady."

Adeline looked up and saw her housekeeper in the doorway. "Yes, Mrs. Lawton."

"The Earl of Lyonwood and Mrs. Cordelia Carbonall are here to see you."

A tight curl of expectancy knotted Adeline's stomach. Had the girls agitated him again? And who was this lady with him? Had he brought someone from the ton to take her to task about the school? What could he possibly want after their quarrel earlier in the morning? Perhaps he merely wanted to share with her some other thing he felt she'd done wrong?

Adeline glanced at Julia and Brina, who were giving her questioning looks. "I have no idea why he's here." She turned back to Mrs. Lawton. "Please tell him I have guests."

"No," Julia said quickly. "Don't dare. I would like to know why he's come to see you."

Of course she would, Adeline thought.

"I want to know, too." Brina placed her cup on the tray beside the other two. "Perhaps he simply came to apologize and make peace for whatever he said to you during your tiff this morning."

"I feel quite confident that isn't the case, Brina. Not every gentleman is a gentleman."

"What did he do other than complain the girls were too loud?" Julia asked, being her typical self and not missing anything Adeline said.

"Nothing." Other than arouse feelings inside her she wanted to stay buried.

"Then do invite him to join us, Adeline," Brina encouraged. "I thought him a handsome man the last time I saw him. Now that I know how rude he's been to you, I want to see if he now looks like a monster since he's been acting like one."

Adeline could say without equivocating that the earl did not look like a monster.

There was nothing to do but acquiesce to her friends. Besides, if he wanted to discuss the school, it was best Julia and Brina be available to have their say. "All right." Doing her best to calm the knot of trepidation in her stomach, Adeline turned to Mrs. Lawton. "Ask them to come in."

All three ladies rose and looked toward the entrance.

A short, small-boned, older lady with an inquisitive smile came through the doorway first. The earl entered and stopped beside her. Lyon's gaze immediately met Adeline's. Suddenly it was as if every one of her senses spoke to her at once. *Let me touch him. Let me taste him. Let me smell him. Let me hear him. Let me see him.*

He bowed. "Lady Wake, you should have told me you had guests."

Julia moved to stand just ahead of Adeline and to her right. Brina did the same on Adeline's left, leaving the earl no doubt that no matter the reason he came over, they stood protective of Adeline. Which also meant that he would know she told them about their first meeting. So be it. She appreciated her friends' support more than they would ever know. But with this man—she had to stand alone.

"My lord," Adeline answered with a curtsy and then

left the safety of her friends and walked around the settee toward him. "It wasn't necessary. They asked that you join us. I believe you know Lady Kitson Fairbright and Mrs. Brina Feld, but I'm afraid I haven't had the pleasure of meeting the lady with you."

"Lady Wake, may I present my aunt, Mrs. Cordelia Carbonall."

Julia and Brina joined them, and proper greetings and brief pleasantries were exchanged by everyone. Adeline found it difficult not to keep glancing at the large, beribboned basket gripped in Lyon's masculine hand. He must have noticed her inquisitive expression for he placed it on a chair.

"I brought fruit tarts for the girls," he said.

Adeline felt as if she had a hundred butterflies in her chest and all their wings started fluttering at one time. She was wrong. He had come to apologize for his outrageous behavior that morning. And in the nicest of ways. Bringing the girls something sweet to enjoy. She would have never thought it possible of him. "Thank you, my lord. That's very kind of you. The girls will be very appreciative of the treats."

"They are from Mrs. Feversham across the street. I'm not sure if you're aware of her condition, but she's unable to walk. She asked if I'd deliver them to you."

Oh, what a beast!

Just as her heart was melting over his compassion, he showed his true self once again. Adeline should have known something as enjoyable as tarts for the girls couldn't have come from the earl. What had made her even consider the thoughtfulness was *his* idea. He was a brute of the first order and that wasn't likely to change. It was a shame such a handsome face and powerfully fit body had been wasted on him.

"I wasn't aware of that," she said tightly, and forcing herself not to stiffen so he wouldn't know the frustration he caused her. "I'll be sure to send her a note."

"On the other hand," Mrs. Carbonall said, stepping forward and placing a much smaller basket on the chair, "the biscuits and marmalade in here are from my kitchen to you. Welcome to the neighborhood, my lady."

"I thank you as well," Adeline managed with a genuine smile. "Please sit down and join us for tea."

"We wouldn't think of intruding, my lady," Mrs. Carbonall said. "But before we go, I want you to know I think what you three have done in establishing a boarding school for those poor girls in light of what happened to their families is most admirable."

The lady's sincerity touched Adeline warmly. "Thank you for letting us know."

"Before you go, Mrs. Carbonall," Julia asked, walking over to her, "do you mind if I ask if you have knowledge of the condition of Mrs. Joan Hawtry's son? I only returned to Town a few days ago and I haven't heard. I know he was ill when I left late last autumn."

"I remember that as well," Brina said, joining them. "And I haven't heard any news about him either."

"Yes, of course, I'll be happy to tell you what I know about his ailment. He's been quite sick for some time, but now I can say he's better, though still unable to get out of the house."

The three ladies started talking, which left Adeline

to stand in the entrance way to the drawing room with Lyon. She had no doubt that Julia had a sincere interest in Mrs. Hawtry's son, but her perceptive friend had also obviously felt the undercurrents of tension between Adeline and Lyon and wanted to give them some time alone—whether or not Adeline wanted it.

"Why didn't you tell me this school was for daughters and sisters of workers who perished on the ship with your husband?" Lyon asked.

A shiver stole over Adeline. It was an inexplicable feeling, but she didn't want to think about her husband when Lyon was near. "I don't want to talk about that time, about what happened. It's past and what I am doing now is for the future. That's where my focus is now."

He was silent for a few moments, and she thought he was going to change the subject, but instead, he said, "That I understand and I'm accepting of it, but I'm talking about the girls and the school. Not your personal sufferings. I understand your need for privacy on that."

There was tenderness and concern in his voice. She wanted to respond to it but was afraid it would reveal too much of what she felt when he was near so she kept silent.

"You never mentioned that it was a charitable endeavor this morning or the tragic loss they'd endured."

"Was that my fault or yours, my lord?" she asked with a hint of humor in her voice.

"Mine," he replied without hesitation.

"Yes." She took in a deep breath, feeling a little shot of victory at hearing his admission. "It was. Would it have kept you from storming over to complain if you'd known the girls' situation?"

He seemed to study on that for a moment. "I'd like to think so, but the truth is I don't know. I have no patience for things that aren't orderly."

"I've discovered that. Thank you for being honest."

"Here's more truth for you," he said, moving so that his wide shoulders were blocking the other women from Adeline's view. "I believe your courage in doing this is extraordinary. I wish I'd known their circumstances. I might have acted differently. A difficult neighbor wasn't something they needed."

"No, they didn't," she agreed, feeling surprisingly moved by his tone. "They are fine now. And, tempted though I am, I'm not going to stand here and list all the things you have said to me in the last few days that you shouldn't have said."

"Good," he replied easily. "I don't need a reminder."

"I don't think you have ever taken the time to ask me anything. You are usually just barging over and demanding whatever it is you want."

His gaze swept effortlessly over her face. It was intimate, and a warmth of pleasure washed over her. A quiver of desire to touch him seemed to shudder so deeply inside her she felt it in her bones. She had no doubt that he felt the same currents of fascination for her flowing naturally between them.

He gave her a mischievous smile. "I knocked this time."

As much as she hated to, Adeline smiled, as well. He wasn't a beast, but he was a danger to her.

Chapter 10

Hammering rain beat upon the roof of the landau and slashed against the small glass panes in the door. It was as if the heavens had opened up to empty buckets of water upon London. Strong gusts rocked and shuddered the lightweight carriage.

Adeline had made it out of her solicitor's office and inside the compartment before the worst of the early spring storm hit, but not until after a fierce whip of wind had turned her umbrella inside out and rendered it completely useless. Her cape was wet but not completely drenched; her thin silk dress and satin shoes were damp and cold. She could warm herself quickly enough when she made it home, but she didn't know how long that might be.

The heavy downpour had traffic moving at a crawl.

No matter. She would weather the storm in stride. All the minor details of the school that had been left unresolved for one reason or another had now been settled and money to ensure the financial soundness of the school for the next five years was set aside in the proper accounts. She, Julia, and Brina had left Mr. Clements' office, where they'd signed the last of the documents concerning the organizational structure and security of The Seafarer's School for Girls.

Adeline leaned her head against the soft velvet cushions and smiled as the carriage rumbled along. Sounds of the pelting storm should be disturbing, but as she listened to the rage outside, she realized she was peaceful inside and had been for quite some time now. Occasionally a memory from the past would haunt her, but she was learning to busy herself with other things when they wanted to invade her thoughts.

Now there were children in her future. Not any she would be a mother to, but ones who would grow up to have a better life because of her. It was fitting that she was helping children with the money Wake had left at her disposal. She had to appreciate him for that. Some widows weren't taken care of as well as she had been.

She was at peace.

Yet, something was missing in her life. The Earl of Lyonwood had made her aware of what it was. What she had dreamed of having from her marriage but never received. Someone to hold her possessively. To touch her with passion. To love and desire her.

Lyon had awakened those dormant, now-unwelcomed longings to be romanced the way she'd dreamed she would be when she'd married. The fascinating earl next door was the culprit. It wasn't that she hadn't seen, met, or chatted with strong, handsome men since her husband's death. She had. None of them had come close to making her feel the powerful, sensuous sensations that Lyon had. It seemed unfair that the irascible man should be the one to catch her attention.

A sudden jolt of the carriage threw Adeline forward. She steadied herself with her feet and glanced out the window. Visibility was so poor she couldn't see anything but gray. Over the squalling wind and pounding deluge on the roof, she heard her driver shouting and then distant, muffled replies.

After a few more annoying bellows, the carriage started moving but only for a few seconds before the conveyance halted once more. Further words were exchanged between her driver and someone else.

Adeline looked out the window for a second time. She rubbed the pane with her gloved hand. They'd stopped on her street but not in front of her house.

"Not again," she whispered to herself, impatience gathering quickly in her chest.

More shouts were heard and moments later, her driver, covered in an oilcloth and a dripping, wide-brimmed hat, yanked open the door. "I'm afraid we can't go any farther, my lady," he said disgustedly. "I've tried. Appears your neighbor has the street completely blocked with the coaches of his visitors again. We'll have to wait."

Adeline drummed her fingers on her damp lap in irritation. Sitting in a cold carriage wearing damp clothing in the midst of a storm when her house was right down the street was quite disconcerting. She probably wouldn't be as uncomfortable had she donned a woolen dress and her walking boots, but she thought the lightweight fabric and dainty shoes more fitting for the occasion. But truthfully, it wasn't really the wait in the icy compartment that bothered her.

It was the earl.

His habits were becoming a routine and a nuisance she would rather avoid. It was the third time the entrance to her house had been obstructed since Lord Lyonwood had returned to the neighborhood. The two previous times there had been no problem. Adeline had simply gotten out of the carriage and strolled the short distance home. That was fine. It wasn't that she'd minded either time. Today was different. It was pouring buckets. Her umbrella was broken, she was already wet, and her feet were going numb.

How dare this man ruin her happiness about how well the day had gone at her solicitor's office with inconsiderate behavior. She'd been feeling absolutely serene and now she was quite annoyed. Why would the earl be so thoughtless as to allow the stack-up of carriages to happen at the end of the cul-de-sac in front of her home on a regular basis?

That had to be stopped.

What was he doing anyway? Holding court like the Prince for his friends and acquaintances every other day? Surely he knew he was inconveniencing his neighbors.

"Do you know what the reason is for the waiting carriages this time?" she asked the driver, resisting the urge to tap her foot in unguarded frustration.

The man nodded, seeming not to mind the drops pelting his face. "It's a card game today, my lady. I was told the earl has one every week when he's in Town."

"A card game?" Adeline almost choked on the words as she slipped the corded handle of her meticulously knitted reticule over her wrist. The devil himself couldn't bother her more than Lyon.

"I asked one of the drivers to move his coach forward and let me pass. He said there were too many carriages in front of him and he had nowhere to go. The other bloke told me he didn't budge the Duke of Middlecastle's carriage for anyone."

"How rude!" she exclaimed.

"I'd consider it an honor if you'd allow me to call out the duke's man for his disrespect of you, my lady," her driver offered.

"No, of course not," she said emphatically. "Heavens, please don't even think about doing such an uncalled-for action. I don't want you in a squabble about this with anyone, but it does make me wonder what kind of friends the earl has."

"Sounds like they're important ones, my lady."

Adeline smiled at the driver. She wasn't really expecting an answer from her statement.

So, it appeared she now had two choices. She either had to walk in the slashing rain to her house where she could change into dry clothing and sit before a hot fire with a warm cup of chocolate, or stay in the cold carriage wearing damp shoes that weren't going to dry out anytime soon while twiddling her thumbs for only heaven knew how long.

No one had to tell her that rain and card games could go on all night long.

What nerve the earl and his friends had to place anyone in this situation, she thought as she searched around the cushions and floor for an extra umbrella. Lord Lyonwood had barged into her house and the schoolyard thinking to tell her how she could use her home and then assumed he could do whatever he pleased around his own—with no concern whatsoever as to how it upset the lives of his neighbors.

Her search for an umbrella came up empty. Not even a fancy parasol had been left inside. Exasperated, she looked over at her driver and asked, "Do you have an extra umbrella?"

"Don't have one at all, my lady. But the rain should let up soon."

"Not soon enough for me," she mumbled to herself; and then louder, she said, "I'm sure the rain won't harm me and it might possibly cool my temper. I'll walk. Help me down and then you can get the horses and yourself out of this weather."

"It's not for me to tell you what to do, but I suggest you wait out the downpour right where you are. It's not fit for you out in this. The wind is fierce and the rain is cold."

That would be the civil thing for her to do, but she wasn't feeling civil. She was feeling quite fierce herself. Adeline reached to pull her hood over her head and realized the cape she was wearing didn't have one. Oh, what rotten luck. And it was all Lyon's fault. She'd have to rely on her short-brimmed bonnet to keep the rain out of her face, but a freezing walk was preferable to spending another minute trapped in the carriage.

"I appreciate your concern and it's kind of you to offer advice, but it's not that far to my house from here, and I'll probably run most of the way. Help me step down, please, and I'll be on my way and you can be, too."

Adeline's foot hit the ground in an ankle-deep puddle. Inhaling deeply from the unexpected water, for an instant she rethought her assertion that she could hurry home. Wet feet had always chilled her to the bone, and for a moment she couldn't have felt more vulnerable if she'd been wandering the dark moors alone at midnight. Wincing from the weakness of the feeling, she fought it down and shook if off. Lifting her shoulders, she thanked the driver.

A gust threatened to take off her bonnet. She held it on her head, dashed across the street, and started toward her house at a fast pace.

Without benefit of a hood, a trickling stream quickly seeped around her neckline and down the back of her dress. Wind blew open her cape and within seconds the front of her dress was soaked. She took her hand off the bonnet to close the flapping wrap. Her bonnet flew off and whipped madly at the back of her shoulders.

She ducked her head lower, worrying with bonnet and cape at the same time, when from the corner of her eye she saw a glimmer of light and lifted her head for a glance. It was the earl's house she was passing. Her steps slowed. His stately home looked like a beacon of warmth, rest, and hope in the blinding torrent.

It was brightly lit with what appeared to be a welcoming lamp glowing in every window.

Anger churned inside her.

Adeline took a few more steps past his residence and then abruptly stopped. What was she doing letting Lyon get by with such abominable behavior? She hadn't been afraid to start a charity school for unfortunate girls even when her late husband's brother refused to help her in any way. And by heavens, she wasn't afraid to speak her mind now to this earl.

She turned around and marched back toward Lyon's house. Wanting to be neighborly after the incident with the girls playing outside last week, she'd allowed the inconvenience of not being dropped off at her door the two previous times without saying a word. Perhaps she could understand the earl congesting the cul-de-sac with carriages for an important political meeting with members of parliament. He was a powerful man after all. But a card game! That was unacceptable.

That sort of pastime could be held at a club or the drivers of the coaches could take turns exercising the horses around the block. That was the polite, neighborly thing to do.

Flinging wide the tall iron gate that led up to his home, Adeline splattered through the puddles, not caring that the gate slammed shut behind her. After stepping onto the entranceway, she clanked the door knocker three times. Moments later a tall stout-looking butler opened the door.

Before she could think better of it, she swished past him without a word and headed down the corridor dripping water as she went. She heard the man calling behind her to wait. To stop.

Adeline did neither.

She followed the sound of male talking and laughter. Her feet squished in her shoes with every purposeful step she took. Entering the lion's den and facing his pride of debauched peers was easier than she thought it would be—until she rounded the corner of the doorway and stepped into the drawing room.

Pausing, she took it all in.

There were two white linen-draped tables with four men at each, holding cards in their hands, drinks sitting by their lace-covered wrists. A fire blazed soothing warmth into the room. From somewhere in the distance, she caught the inviting scent of bread baking in an oven. The entitled gentlemen fell silent. All of them were staring at her. Some with astonished expressions and others clearly annoyed that anyone, especially a woman, would be so bold as to charge in the earl's home and disrupt their gaming.

And then she spotted Lyon. Their gazes met across the room. Adeline felt as if her stomach rolled over and her chest swelled. His silvery gray eyes were curious and questioning her.

Questioning?

She had no doubt she looked like a kitten that had been fished out of the Thames, but that was of no consequence. Society dictated one rule she wouldn't ignore. Delicately grabbing the sides of her wet, clinging dress, she curtsied. "My lord, and gentlemen."

The earl tossed his cards on top of the table, rose,

and bowed. "Countess Wake," he said, taking time to assess her from head to toe.

At the sound of her title every chair scraped across the fine wood floor. The men laid their cards on the tables, too, rose, and bowed.

The earl stood tall, handsome and powerful-looking among all the men. Without a doubt, without wanting it to happen, she was reminded how immensely attracted she was to him. That angered her even more. Suddenly she felt every frigid bead of drizzle running down her body, every strand of rain-soaked hair curling around her face. She shivered all the way down to her toes.

"Has something happened?" he asked, his expression suddenly changing to concern.

Stubbornly ignoring the worry that appeared in his features, Adeline gathered her courage and ire around her as if they were her soggy cape. Taking further steps into the room, she gripped her wringing wet reticule tightly and plopped it down on the gaming table beside the earl's cards and then quickly wrenched off her ruined gloves and threw them beside it.

"How dare you gentlemen sit here snug, warm, and may I say *dry*, sipping your fine cognac, without a care in the world while your coaches clog the street causing others to slog through a slashing storm to reach the same amenities awaiting them in their homes." Adeline's gaze swept around the room meeting every face as she spoke. When she settled her attention on Lyon again, she added, "The street in front of my house is not your private parking area."

Some of the gentlemen continued to be astonished,

staring at her with eyes wide and mouths open. One gentleman abruptly cleared his throat and looked away. A couple of them coughed inconspicuously, while still another peered at her over his spectacles with great interest.

She felt no intimidation from any of them.

"I will thank you gentlemen to be more considerate in the future of blocking access to *my* home with *your* carriages and horses while you visit with the earl."

From seemingly out of nowhere the butler appeared beside her with an umbrella in his hands and said, "Perhaps, my lord, since you have guests, I could see that the lady reaches her home."

Before anyone could speak, and with hot eyes, Adeline shot another blistering look toward Lyon and then took the umbrella from the butler's hand. "Thank you," she said, "but that's not necessary. Since I managed to find my way this far in a slashing rainstorm, I think I can get along home just fine."

Confident in her inner strength, Adeline snatched her knitted purse off the table and without further ado whirled and strode out of the room like a queen, reaching the vestibule the same time as the butler. She paused and opened the umbrella while he opened the door.

As determined as she entered, she walked back into the driving rain.

Chapter 11

F or the first time in his life Lyon was aroused in mind as well as body.

Every man in the room had remained silent and in awe of the audacious, hot-blooded lady who'd just stood before them, verbally dressing them down to their toes. Not a one of them moved. All continued to stare at the doorway Lady Wake had disappeared through. Only the crackle of the fire was heard.

Lyon was as mesmerized as the rest. Where the devil did she get the courage to be so bold as to take on a roomful of gentlemen?

The countess was mightily impressive. Her eyes had blazed with the right amount of justifiable anger and indignation. Her softly rounded shoulders had been thrown back defiantly. Her breasts heaved as if she'd been running for miles, and the skirt of her drenched silky dress had clung to her shapely legs with indecent splendor. Without question, Lyon knew every man in the room would be dreaming about her all night. The image of her admonishing not only him, but a duke, a viscount, and several other well-respected gentlemen in London Society would be burned into Lyon's memory forever.

And theirs, too, he had no doubt.

He was also reminded this wasn't the first time he'd been so stunned by her provoking boldness that he wanted to make her his. From their first encounter he'd known she was a lady with strength and spirit who wouldn't fold up at the first sign of adversity. He'd sensed her deep feelings, innate passion, and honorable intentions. Opening the boarding school had proved she had a kind, generous heart. A woman most men would want.

Now, his gaming club knew it, too.

Everyone heard the front door shut. Still no one moved until, at last, the Duke of Middlecastle said, "My God, what a lady! A fiery one to be sure," before plunking back down at the table with a flabbergasted expression still on his face.

"That she is," Broward agreed, pulling on the layers of lace at his cuffs. "The Dowager Countess Wake. Hmm. I never knew she was so comely or so vigorous. I'd always heard she was of the delicate sort and never left her house."

"Me too," Charleston added. "But, she's no bird with a broken wing, that's for sure."

Mumblings of agreement sounded around the room as heads began to nod in agreement.

"If I weren't already married," Pritchard said, grunting as he lowered into his chair, "I'd have to have her myself."

"When did you ever let being married stop you?" Charleston grumbled. "Don't act as if we don't know of your numerous dalliances."

"Now, see here," Pritchard argued defensively. "You'd be after her yourself if you weren't too old to catch her attention."

"Who are you to call one old, my dear man?"

Broward chuckled. "Neither one of you would have a chance if I decide I want her."

Lyon's breath was heavy with anger. Each man was issuing his threat to possess Lady Wake as if she'd have no say in the matter at all. Too often widows were easy marks for men and their baser needs. Hostile vibrations thrummed in his chest. Lyon's natural, primal need to defend her and claim her for his own took over and left little room for civility for the three men verbally going at one another over who could best win the attention if not the affection of such a prize as the countess.

"Shut your mouths," Lyon snarled, realizing the words could very well start a predatory confrontation in his own home.

The verbal conflict between the men ceased immediately and they all stared at him.

But Lyon wasn't through. It was a rash, harsh but necessary statement of warning to the men fighting over her. There would be no backing down from this. He would defend her honor and not permit such gutter talk whether or not she'd want it or approve. He waited a few moments to see if anyone was going to test his order and challenge him. No one said a word.

"You are talking about a lady—a countess. You're all married and should respect your wives and stay silent about your lusts for other women."

The tension and glowering between the men lingered until Pritchard said, "Very well."

"Is anyone courting her presently?" Lord Thurston asked to no one specifically after several seconds of silence. He looked around the room. No one answered so he scooted his chair back up to the table, seeming to take no offense at Lyon's reprimand to the three men challenging one another's masculinity.

Lyon looked over at the viscount and thought, *"She's taken."*

If any of the men present had a chance of catching Lady Wake's eye it would be Thurston, and he was eligible if it was marriage he had on his mind. Lyon doubted that. Right now none of them had the right to tell any of the others hands off—including Lyon. Though he was on the verge of doing it anyway.

It wouldn't be the first time he'd upset the countess.

By the look on the viscount's face, and his low derisive laugh as he picked up his cards and shuffled them in his hands, Lyon knew the man didn't give a damn what any of them said.

Lord Thurston intended to call on Lady Wake.

Fine. Lyon enjoyed a good fight.

If any of them thought the reason he'd been so aggressive was that he wanted her for himself, none had the courage to call him on it.

Which was best.

He sat down and picked up his drink with one hand and his cards with the other. "There'll be no further talk of Lady Wake," he said to everyone in the group, maintaining his ruthless tone. He might not have claimed her for his own, but he'd left them no doubt he would not hear another suggestive word about her. "Next week find another place to have your carriage wait. Let's get back to the game."

A muttering of grumblings, grunts, and scrapes of wood against wood rumbled around the tables as the rest of the men seated themselves and prepared to resume their games where they left off. No doubt there would be much talk of this incident in the homes and clubs tomorrow. Lyon didn't care. If they didn't like the measure he took to halt their challenges or if they thought he was kowtowing to the countess about their coaches or anything else, they were free to confront him—and no one did. Lyon would have defended any lady against such talk.

He looked down at his cards and caught sight of a pair of soggy kid gloves lying beside his drink. Her reticule was gone. Had she left them there for a reason?

As a challenge?

An invitation?

He didn't know but he had a feeling she hadn't simply forgotten them when she picked up her purse. His mind and his heart teased him for a moment, making him think that she was the lady he'd been waiting for and there was no way in hell he was going to let anyone take her from him.

Lyon had an edge. Unlike the other gents in the

room, he already had her attention—for the good or bad was questionable.

Returning the gloves to her might prove to be a good start to finding out what she had on her mind when she left them behind and put him on the path of garnering more than just her attention.

Chapter 12

The storm had left with the descending darkness, taking the greater portion of Adeline's outrage with it. She was now cozy, dry, and sitting snugly in front of her own fireplace dressed in her black velvet robe, smelling the pleasing aroma of cooked fruits that still wafted from the kitchen, though dinner had long past.

Crashing a gentleman's card game wasn't the way Adeline expected to make her debut back into Society, but it was too late to regret her hasty decision to charge in on the earl without being announced as he'd done to her not so long ago. Taking peers to task wasn't the proper or advisable thing to do, yet she was unwavering that it was deserved. There could be some possible consequences in Society. If the older ladies in the ton decided to shun her for the scandalous behavior, every-one else would, too. That was simply the way of it. There was also her brother-in-law, the Earl of Wake, to consider. He was still in control of a good portion of the wealth from her marriage, but he'd never denied her use of it in any way she wished. She hoped he wouldn't decide to now for her breach in proper manners.

Adeline sighed. Lyon had been nothing but trouble for her since he'd returned to his house. They'd man-aged to have a civil, if not friendly, exchange the day he'd brought over the tarts from Mrs. Feversham. Her exploit this afternoon had probably put an end to any friendly relationship they could have had going for-ward. That bothered her more than she expected. That Lyon had stood quietly and let her take him to task sur-prised her, too. She had to admire him for that. Gentle-men did not like to be taken to task by a lady—especially in front of other gentlemen.

Adeline rubbed the back of her neck, trying to ease the tension that had settled between her shoulders. She might as well close the book she held in her lap. There was no use in pretending to read. She couldn't concen-trate on the ghost story, and they were her favorites to read. A young maiden walking past gravestones in the middle of the night to get help for her ailing father just couldn't hold Adeline's attention tonight.

Thinking about the earl was the only thing on her mind. Whether she was looking at him or thinking about him, he haunted her with deep longing feelings she would like to explore but had little knowledge of how to go about letting him know.

It was maddening.

"Sorry to interrupt you, my lady."

Adeline turned toward the doorway. "You know it's not a problem, Mrs. Lawton. I am doing nothing other than wondering why I had that second slice of sweet cake after I ate the delicious pheasant soup you made for me tonight. It was very comforting and just what I needed after such a wet afternoon."

The petite woman smiled appreciatively. "Thank you, my lady. It was my pleasure. I didn't know if you wanted to receive anyone this late, but Mrs. Tallon is here and asking to speak with you."

"Yes, of course." Adeline laid the book aside and rose. "I'll always speak to her no matter the hour. Ask her to come in and then you can retire for the evening. I'll turn out the lamps when I'm ready to go up."

Mrs. Lawton nodded and said, "Yes, my lady."

Adeline made sure the lapels of her robe were secured and then bushed her hair away from her shoulders to her back. There was no time to make it more presentable. She'd left it down so it would dry before weaving it into her nighttime braid.

Mrs. Tallon walked in a moment or two later and stopped just inside the entrance. "I'm sorry to disturb you, Lady Wake. I didn't realize you were ready to retire for the evening. I can come back tomorrow."

"Nonsense. You're here now. You know I've encouraged you to come to me if you thought I might be of assistance. What can I do for you?"

"I wanted to make you aware of something disturbing that's been happening." She hesitated.

A prickle of alarm came over Adeline as she walked around the chair she'd been sitting in and stood before

Mrs. Tallon. "Has the earl been back over again to complain about the girls' giggles?"

"Oh, no, no, my lady." Mrs. Tallon dismissed the idea with a wave of her hand. "We've not seen or heard from him since that morn."

"Good," she said, her feelings of disquiet easing a little. "I'm glad. Please, feel free to speak your concerns."

"I wanted to make you aware that one of the girls, Miss Fanny Watson, continues to disobey me and wanders away from the class and into other rooms. She's gone outside the school building twice without permission."

Adeline was more than a little surprised to hear that. She'd told Fanny that leaving the building without someone knowing was unacceptable and she must not do it again. "Did she wander away from the school grounds?"

"No. Both times I found her sitting on the front steps. But after the first time I found her doing so, I told her not to do it again. She disobeyed me and did it anyway. She's very bright and articulate. She's not disruptive in any way, but she's—sly."

Adeline blinked. That seemed a callous word for a ten-year-old, but she decided not to voice her opinion on that.

"Has she been mean toward any of the other girls? Has she pinched anyone or pulled their hair?"

"No. Most of the time her hands are behind her back."

"That's good to hear."

"She's not disrespectful at all. She finishes her work

quickly and accurately. Most of the other girls need more help and attention than Fanny does. Some aren't adjusting as well as others, which we talked about and expected. It's natural, but when we get busy calming them, we'll suddenly realize Fanny is gone."

"Gone?"

"From the classroom. Sometimes she's simply looking at the threads and fabrics in the workroom. She needs to stay where all the other girls are, no matter that she's finished and they are not. I appreciate that you wanted me to be kind to them because of the unfortunate circumstances of their past, but I feel there must be a harsher punishment for Fanny because she continues to disobey me after verbal reprimands she clearly understands."

After listening quietly to the woman, Adeline said, "Has she said why she doesn't do as you asked?"

"Most of the time she only shrugs. She's quiet. Even in the classroom she hardly speaks to anyone except Mathilda. Quite frankly, it's much easier to deal with a child who talks too much because then, at least, you know what they're thinking."

Adeline remembered that Fanny had shrugged a few times the day she'd wandered into the garden, and she wasn't very verbal at first. Still, once she'd started, she seemed to want to talk about her mother and father.

"Sitting on the front steps or looking around the workroom doesn't seem an especially serious disobedience to me, but I do agree she should do as you instruct at all times."

Mrs. Tallon pursed her lips and twisted her face into a stern frown. Her back stiffened.

Obviously, the headmistress didn't think Adeline's words were strong enough.

"To ensure everyone's safety," Mrs. Tallon said, "I must know where all the students are at all times. If every one of them wandered off any time they so pleased the school would be chaos and I'd have no control. As they become used to living here, I can give them more privileges, but it's too soon for that. What kind of school would we have if they all did what they wanted when they wanted?"

Adeline understood perfectly what Mrs. Tallon was saying and probably should have told her about Fanny slipping out of the schoolhouse the day she wandered into the garden. But Adeline really didn't want to get the little girl into more trouble.

"I know how disconcerting it must be to suddenly realize one of the girls is not with you and you don't know where she is. I agree Fanny and everyone must abide by your rules and always stay with the others."

"She might be a willful child. They are clever and can quickly learn how to control others and lead them astray, too. She needs to be dealt with in a strict manner now so as not to influence anyone else later. If I'm to be in charge I must . . . be in charge."

The word *strict* wasn't to Adeline's liking, but she couldn't disagree with Mrs. Tallon's assessment of the situation so she asked, "What is your recommendation for a suitable punishment?"

"That she write her numbers and all her letters an extra fifty times each day. It should keep her busy so she won't have time to go wandering off while I'm helping the girls who are struggling to cope with being away from home and learning their lessons, too."

Thankful she wasn't suggesting anything more severe, Adeline smiled and said, "Yes. It seems a fitting and fair punishment to me. And if you find she does the extra work too quickly, perhaps one of your helpers can spend more time with her and move her forward at a faster pace since she learns so easily."

"I'll keep that in mind," the schoolmistress said stiffly. "Thank you, my lady. I won't take up any more of your time."

After showing the woman out, Adeline walked back into the drawing room. She found solace in its quietness. She always felt more comfortable when her housekeeper had gone to her own room for the night. Not having servants constantly around her was essential to Adeline's peace of mind. And probably always would be because of her husband's dictates.

Memories Adeline didn't want to relive darted along the edges of her mind. Wake never wanted Adeline to be left alone after he'd seen her descending the stairs much too quickly. How could she ever be in the family way and bear him a son if she walked too fast, if she carried a small basket of flowers, or if she bent over to tie the ribbons on her slippers? Wake would have preferred for her not to walk at all, but Adeline had finally made him see the ridiculousness of issuing an order for her to stay in bed until she delivered a child to him.

Not wanting to dwell on those thoughts, Adeline decided that since she'd dismissed Mrs. Lawton for the night, she would rekindle the fire that had been banked and find interest in the book she'd been trying to read. Surely something or someone would jump out at the heroine soon and cause her to scream and run for her life. Adeline's heart beat a little faster at the thought. Before Adeline reached for the poker, a soft knock sounded and then the door opened and shut quickly.

It was presumptuous of Mrs. Tallon to reenter the house, even if it had been less than a minute since Adeline had seen her out. Adeline waited and heard faint, masculine footfalls coming down the corridor. The trespasser wasn't the headmistress returning.

Lyon stopped at the entrance when he saw her. A gale of anticipation washed over her at the sight of him. Fluttering warmth swirled in her chest.

Her breath trembled in her throat as it did every time she saw him. It didn't matter if he was upset with her, smiling at her, or trying to look into her soul. Her feelings were always the same. She wanted him to take her into his arms and kiss her.

His expression wasn't angry or even annoyed as she would have expected because of what she'd done. Mysteriously, he looked pleased. That, she realized, unsettled her far more than the fact he'd entered her house *again* without permission. Or maybe he assumed he had her consent. He was clutching the gloves she'd deliberately left on the table in front of him. At the time she didn't even know why she had been so brazen. She had known he'd return them at some time. Maybe some part of her was hoping he'd do it tonight.

Inhaling a deep breath, she steadied herself and met his gaze without worry, confusion, or invitation. She prepared herself for whatever temperament he might be in and listen to what he had to say about her afternoon rant.

"My lady."

"Lyon," she said, and then without forethought and before she could stop herself, she launched into somewhat of an explanation. "I shouldn't have rushed inside your house as I did this afternoon, trailing water with every step I took. That be as it may, I shouldn't have lost my temper over the situation I was confronted with and caused a scene in front of your friends and colleagues. It was an extremely improper thing to do but at the time I felt I had no choice."

Not saying a word and while she was still talking, the earl strode toward her, throwing her gloves onto a chair he passed. He didn't stop until, to her surprise and pleasure, he slid his strong arms around her waist and quickly caught her up firmly and tightly against his wide, hard chest with commanding strength. He must have known that this is what she'd been waiting for.

"You were magnificent," he whispered.

An excitement like she'd never known spiraled through her body, mind, and soul. He was letting her know he wanted to kiss her and he wasn't going to let her or anything stop him.

Her lips parted just before his touched hers with a searing hunger that took her breath and stole her heart. His tongue swept into her mouth, deep and probing. She shoved her arms around his neck and cupped the back of his head with her hands, letting her fingers slip into his thick, rich hair. It was exhilarating to be held so close, kissed so relentlessly, and to feel desperately desired.

Adeline had longed for such feelings to become reality.

Their kisses were searching, persuasive, and savoring. They continued second after second. Ravenous. Desirous. Welcoming. Thrilling tingles raced across her breasts, speared down past the depths of her abdomen, and settled as an unfulfilled ache between her legs. She shared his ardor with an overwhelming, long-denied fervency of her own. Pressing her body against him, she encouraged his touch with an abundance of coveted passion waiting to be released.

"My guests thought you were magnificent also," Lyon whispered as he kissed his way down to the crook of her neck, tasting her skin as he went.

"Truly?" she asked breathlessly, and quickly added, "No, I don't believe you. They couldn't."

"I have many faults, my lady, but lying isn't one of them."

Adeline smiled beneath the onslaught of his kisses, satisfied he was telling the truth.

"I see my admission pleases you," he rasped.

"Very much," she answered, enjoying the way his lips felt against her cheeks, her neck, her chest. Loving the way his slight beard-roughened skin felt against hers.

"The blackguards deserved every ounce of your dressing down for their insolence and for being so inconsiderate with where they leave their coaches."

"You deserved it, too."

He paused and looked into her eyes. "That's why I came to apologize for causing you such duress."

A soft breath of laughter echoed past her lips. "Consider it accepted and keep kissing me."

Lyon chuckled softly, huskily, kissing her cheek, over her chin and down her neck again, past the hollow of her throat to where the lapels of her robe folded together between her breasts.

Their conversation didn't hinder or wane the urgency in their kisses. His caresses were impatient and fervent yet gentle and confident as he parted her robe to taste and cool the heated skin between her breasts. She allowed him to walk her backward a few steps until her weight leaned against the wall. His lower body pressed against hers as one of his hands came up to caress her breast beneath the velvet. Adeline savored his touch and willingly accepted the hardness of the rigid bulge hidden beneath his trousers and trembled.

She pulled at the shoulders of his coat, wanting to feel the strength of his arms, shoulders, and chest. As if annoyed with the tight confines of the garment, he swiftly shrugged out of it and slung it away. Adeline explored the firm muscles of his back beneath the fine linen of his shirt and waistcoat. Their kisses and caresses were tempestuous, powerful, and deliciously uncontrolled. Movements were soft but eager, passionate but not harsh.

Complying in earnest with her demands, Lyon pushed her robe off one shoulder. It fell open at the bodice and skirt, leaving only the long sleeves and knotted sash to hold it onto her body. His hand covered her breast with teasing, beautiful strokes meant to arouse and satisfy her before taking her nipple into his mouth.

Gasps, sighs, and moans blended, dissolved, and were swallowed into their heated passion.

Adeline unashamedly craved and enjoyed the pleasure she received from his touch, taste, and the ragged sounds of his breathing.

Her body trembled again and she whispered, "Yes, yes."

The intensity and eagerness of his kisses, his wanting, thrilled her as she matched his hunger. A deep, torturous yearning for more settled inside her. With their hands working together, his trousers were unbuttoned and lowered.

Without words, without warning, without waiting, he filled her. Moved inside her, bringing her to the brink of desire with each thrust. Adeline gasped with exquisite bliss each time. She slid her hands down to grab his buttocks firmly in her hands, intending to see he didn't stop until he finished what he'd started.

Seconds later an intensifying bundle of complex and twisted sensations exploded inside her. She felt as if her body had turned into liquid fire. And it was oh so good, forceful and satisfying. She wasn't sure her legs would hold her as the tremors of gratification continued. Moments later, after a long, desperate-sounding sigh Lyon trembled and gently settled against her.

It was over, but Adeline's senses were still reeling from the depth of their passion and the reward of its ending. She was out of breath, but the faltering eruptions of passion lingered, teasingly active, and she laid her forehead against his linen-covered chest.

Being in Lyon's arms, in his possession was more than she could ever have expected. It was what she'd hoped for and desired when she'd married, but had never received. With the earl, she'd felt wanted and equal. Not groped and used. She smiled and had the wild urge to laugh victoriously from the sheer thrill of what she'd experienced from all they'd shared.

But she contained her happiness, and with her face nestled in the crisp folds of his neckcloth, she whispered softly, "I've been waiting for that."

"From me, or just anyone?" he asked, his lips resting just above her ear.

His question surprised her and she lifted her head. Their gazes met. He was serious. Could he tell she'd been starving for just the kind of passion she had felt in his arms? That she'd never had the ending joy of coming together with a man before.

Adeline moistened her lips and swallowed. "I don't know," she answered; but as soon as the words left her mouth, she knew they weren't true. She was sure it was Lyon she wanted. No other. There had been opportunities to be with other men, but she'd never been tempted. Why she had answered differently, she really couldn't fathom. Perhaps it was because she was reeling from the aftermath of having been completely satisfied for the first time.

His tight hold on her loosened a little and his eyes gazed into hers. "Is this the only time you've been with a man since becoming a widow?" he asked.

"Yes," she admitted and lowered her lashes. It was easier to admit than she'd thought it would be, so she lifted her lids and added, "I didn't expect it to go so fast."

"It's been a long time. For both of us." He smiled, bent his head, and kissed the hollow of her throat softly. "Just as the poets say absence makes the heart grow fonder, abstinence makes desire flame bright but burn quickly."

She wanted to stay wrapped in the embrace of the strong, solid man holding her. It would be so easy to take hold of his hand and lead him to her bedchamber, but instead, she gently pushed against his chest. Seeming reluctant, he stepped back and turned away to adjust his clothing. With steady fingers she closed her robe and retied her sash.

Lyon looked around the room and then walked over to a tray that held a pitcher of water and glasses. Obviously not wanting water, he opened the top doors of her secretary and from the depths of the cabinet pulled out a bottle of brandy. He poured a small amount into one of the glasses and walked back over to her.

"Drink this." He held it toward her. "It will help settle you about what just happened between us."

Adeline's breathing grew shallow as she looked at the amber liquid. She had to force herself not to back away from it and the sudden memories it stirred in her mind.

"I thought you poured it for yourself," she said quietly.

"I will need nothing to help me sleep tonight," he answered and extended the drink closer to her.

How many times had she taken a glass of brandy

her husband held out to her? Too many to count. Not because she wanted to drink it but because Wake insisted it was the only liquid strong enough to hide the vile taste of whatever concoction his latest apothecary had created for her to drink. A brew of herbs and things she didn't want to think about. All of them were guaranteed to make her conceive.

Nothing had ever worked.

"Maybe you don't like the taste of it," Lyon said softly. "It's strong and stings a little, but I think you'll sleep better tonight if you drink it."

"No," she said, continuing to look at the glass as she swallowed down the memories. "I don't want it. I actually used to like the taste of brandy, my lord. But not anymore." She lifted her gaze to his. "I'm quite settled without it."

As if sensing there was more to her rejecting his offer than she was telling, he placed the drink on the chest behind her. "It's here in case you want it later."

"I'm fine." Neither of them spoke for what seemed a long time, and then she said, "I shouldn't have slapped you that night. I've never done anything like that before and believe me, I've had good reason to in the past."

He gave her a quick smile. "I deserved it."

She smiled, too. "Yes, maybe you did."

"When you rose up on your toes to confront me that afternoon I really thought you were going to kiss me."

"Did you really?"

His gaze stayed steadily on hers. "I swear it's true."

So he was as perceptive as she'd thought. "Then what I did must have been a shock for you."

"As was this afternoon. And tonight. You are constantly surprising me and I find I like that very much. When I first saw you walk into my drawing room, gorgeously wet and steaming with hot emotion, I thought to myself what could I have possibly done this time to make her angry? Make her angry enough to come over to my house in the middle of a rainstorm and confront me. But, an instant or two later, I thought perhaps something had happened at the school. To one of the girls and you needed my help."

Adeline inhaled sharply. Yes, she remembered seeing a moment of uneasiness in his features but assumed her action was the cause. "It was kind of you to think about their welfare."

He remained silent, but his expression told her he spoke the truth about his thoughts. Concern for the girls wasn't what she'd expected from him. Nothing could have pleased her more than to know he was worried about them. And it reminded her that his own sense of honor was one of the things that drew her to him.

"Did you truly have no idea why I was drenched and so upset I invaded your privacy?"

He shook his head. "Not until you told me."

"Today is the third time my carriage hasn't been able to let me off at my front door since you've been here."

His eyes softened even more and he took a step toward her. "Why haven't you said something?"

"I was trying to be neighborly," she answered truthfully. "Usually I don't mind a walk in the cool, fresh air. It was the downpour today and a dozen carriages blocking the entrance to my house that made it more than I could accept."

The earl chuckled softly, invitingly. "There couldn't have been that many as I only had two tables of four and I was one of the players. It's never been a problem for any driver to stay in the front before. Mrs. Feversham across the street never leaves her house because she can't walk, and Mr. Bottles, from whom you bought the house, seldom left either. When he did, he walked. You won't be bothered or inconvenienced again. From now on my friends will find another place for their drivers and carriages to wait."

Considering how vocal and unbending he'd been about the girls when they were playing outside, Adeline hadn't expected him to be so accommodating—so quickly.

"Thank you," she said, and then asked, "How did you know I was alone?"

"I didn't. I came over to return your gloves and saw you saying goodbye to the headmistress. I assumed if you were seeing her out, your housekeeper had retired for the night. You really should lock your doors at night."

"Yes. You're right. I usually do when I retire for the evening."

"You're avoiding talking about what just happened between us," he said cautiously.

Because of all she'd been through and endured in the past, she concealed the mountains of emotions that were swirling inside her. He didn't need to know that he'd just brought to reality so many of her dreams; he didn't need to know her secrets.

"There's nothing to say about it."

"There's a lot to say," he argued in a soft, determined tone.

"I expect you to be a gentleman about it and slip out the door as easily as you came in and we'll say no more about this."

Lyon didn't move, but his eyes continued to search hers. She didn't waver and neither did he. He looked as if he was trying to decide whether he wanted to take her to task in disagreement or do as she asked.

Adeline hoped he wouldn't fight her on this. Her reserve of strength wasn't feeling very strong right now. If he tried to pull her into the warmth of his arms once again she would go, rest her cheek against his chest, enjoy his embrace, and ask him to make love to her all over again. She didn't have one smidgen of regret for taking him into her arms and quite possibly into her heart, too.

Finally, showing the mark of a good man, Lyon nodded. He reached down, picked up his coat, and granting her wish, he left.

Chapter 13

A cold wash might work wonders for the body, but it did little to enhance peace of mind or comfort a turbulent soul, Lyon thought as he threw the daily newsprint aside and stood up in the tub. He stepped out and wrapped the towel around his waist before heading toward the window, which was now a daily ritual. He parted the top half of the drapery panels with the backs of his fingers and searched the garden.

The countess was nowhere in sight. Not that he expected her to be. Still, he looked every morning since the day he'd seen her standing under the trellis. He should have never told her he could see that section of her grounds from the window in his dressing chamber. She would probably never stop in that part of the garden again.

Letting the panel go, he walked over to where his clothing had been laid out and picked up his shirt. He'd tried to shake it off, but it still rankled that Adeline had told him she didn't know if she'd been waiting for him last night or if any man would have fulfilled her desires. That was a damn good way to make a man feel like a convenience. He didn't know what had made him ask the question. Maybe he'd had doubts because she'd been so willing. She'd felt so fresh and innocent in his arms it was almost as if she'd never been touched by a man. *Damnation*, he hadn't had any misgivings about who had been in his arms. He didn't think she had, either.

Until it was over.

He was now sure Lady Wake left her gloves in plain sight on purpose—as an invitation for Lyon to go to her. Knowing the other men at his table noticed them too, Lyon had made a show of picking them up, saying convincingly he'd have Brewster see to it they were returned immediately to Lady Wake.

But, of course, that's not what he'd told his butler.

When he'd seen her standing in the lamplight dressed in the deliciously provocative black velvet robe with her long honey gold hair curling about her shoulders, he saw a beauty, tempting him beyond his control. And he'd wanted her madly.

Not just any woman. *Her*. And he thought she'd been waiting for him. Not just any man. *Him*.

She was a daunting, alluring vixen and had been since he'd first seen her. It troubled him that even after they'd come together, he didn't know what she was feeling or thinking. She'd not only set his body on fire

for her, she set his soul on fire for her, too. He knew
her body had been satisfied, but what about her soul?
Did she wake this morning thinking Lyon was the only
man for her?

That's sure as hell what *he* was thinking.

Lyon finished dressing and sat down to put on his
boots. He sensed that his valet had come back into the
room. The man was always quiet as a mouse and usually waited for Lyon to acknowledge him before speaking. If Lyon didn't say anything after a minute or two,
he'd slip out of the room again and wait to be called.

Sensing the man was staying longer than usual, he
said, "What is it, Dome?"

"Your aunt is here, my lord," the spry, older man
said.

A morning visit from his aunt? That was odd.

"Mr. Brewster has asked her to wait for you in your
breakfast room."

Maybe she wanted him to go with her to Lady
Wake's home again with another basket to deliver.
Lyon's lower stomach tightened at the thought of see-
ing Adeline. "Let her know I'll be down shortly."

Memories of being with the countess last night
slipped easily back into his thoughts as he pressed his
foot into his boot. He leaned against the back of the
chair and enjoyed reliving them for a few moments.
But there was another image of her that wafted across
his mind. He'd seen it briefly in her face when he'd offered her the brandy. It was pain. Not physical pain
from being sick or injured, but a much deeper hurting.
A private one. An agony that she hadn't been able to
suppress.

That troubled him.

Had she been ill? Too fond of the taste of wine and unable to control it unless she completely stayed away from the drink? It could happen. Was that inner hurt the reason she was never seen with her husband?

Lyon wasn't one to delve into another's weaknesses or past, but Lady Wake's intrigued him. Whatever it was that had kept her delicate for a time was ended. She was the strongest, most passionate lady he'd ever met, and after last night, he wanted her to be only his.

But what did she want?

A few minutes later Lyon walked into his favorite room of the house. The breakfast room had two walls of windows overlooking the back grounds and not a sheer or drapery fabric on any of them. No coverings were necessary since the room was only used in the broad light of day. On sunny mornings, the sparsely decorated area was bright, cheerful. It was where he would read the newsprint and drink coffee if he was in a hurry and passed on a soak in the tub.

Lyon walked over to the table, bent down, and kissed his aunt Cordelia's soft cheek as she kissed the air beside him. He looked at the plate in front of her and grunted. "You're only eating a scone?"

She smiled at him. "I've already broken the fast and needed only a nibble while waiting for you to come belowstairs."

He poured himself a cup of the aromatic coffee and then leaned against the buffet chest that held dishes of food topped with silver covers and emanating the mixture of smells from eggs, fried ham, and sweet fruity preserves.

"It's early for you to be out."

"I know." Her brows went up and she scooted her chair back and faced him directly. "But some things are best taken care of as soon as one awakens. The early bird getting the fattest worm sort of thing."

Lyon tilted his head, denying a sudden sense of unease, and simply said, "Now you have me curious."

"Is that all?" Her gaze stayed on his. "Really, you have no idea why I'm here?"

"There are too many possibilities for me to guess at just one."

"Hmm. I assumed you knew and you were simply being your usual mum self when it comes to your private life. Which I understand and don't mind, you know."

"Ah, I see." He sipped the coffee and casually crossed one foot over the other. "You're here to do your usual complaining about my father. Enlighten me. I have no idea what he's done this time."

"Fiddlesticks, no," she said, shaking her head for emphasis and using a rare frustrated tone with him. "I wouldn't waste my morning on him. Not today anyway. But, that's not to say that I'm not looking forward to seeing Miss Ballingbrand at the Great Hall for the first soirée of the Season. Everyone is. It's been at least six years, maybe more, since her debut. No one I know has seen her since, and we're all counting the days until we meet her." Cordelia stopped and sighed, while dabbing her napkin at the corner of her mouth. "We can talk about her later. Neither she nor your father are the reason I'm here. It's much more important than those two. I had a note from Mrs. Feversham on my tea tray this morning asking that I come visit her with all haste."

"Another fall?" he asked, placing his cup on the table in front of his chair. "Is she all right?"

"Yes, she's well. For all her complaints, she's almost as robust as you. Except for her hip, of course. She is fine, but I fear you are not."

The way his aunt said the last sentence worried Lyon, but calmly, he asked, "What do you mean?"

"To put it bluntly, my dear, she saw Lady Wake march into your house yesterday afternoon as if she owned the place and had every right to do so while your gaming club was there. How many men is it each week? A dozen? In any case, Mrs. Feversham was outraged the widow would do such an unacceptable thing even if it was raining buckets on top of her head."

Doing the unacceptable was one of the things that drew him to Adeline. A primal feeling to protect her rose up inside him.

"Mrs. Feversham is watching my house again?" he asked, outraged at the thought.

"Again?" Cordelia asked incredulously. "She's never stopped. And what's more, now she never will because she's purchased a sailor's spyglass for herself so she can see up closer."

"Blast it!" Lyon said, muttering an oath under his breath. He pulled out his chair but didn't bother to sit down. "A telescope? Has the lady no sense of decency or shame for such behavior?"

If she were a younger, able-bodied lady, he'd go over and rip the damn thing from her hands and stomp it to pieces right in front of her. He didn't like the idea of anyone snooping on him, knowing who came and went from his house. Once he'd thought about trying to have the school moved out of the neighborhood. Now he was wondering what he could do to get Mrs. Feversham out.

"It's all she can do."

"No, she could knit and keep her eyes on the yarn instead of her neighbors. I can't believe this is the way she repays me for taking her enormous basketful of pastries to Lady Wake," he said angrily. "She shouldn't be spying on a gentleman's door. She's gone too far."

"Are you saying it would be all right for her to watch a lady's door with her spyglass?" his aunt asked rather guardedly as her brows went up again. "Perhaps Lady Wake's door?"

"No one's door," he insisted. Suddenly Lyon's gut tightened. He looked closely at his aunt. "She didn't."

"Of course she did," Cordelia said, pushing her chair back from the table and refolding the napkin in her lap with no small amount of consternation. "She saw you enter Lady Wake's house last night after the lights on the servants' floor went out."

Lyon refrained from speaking aloud the oaths that would have felt so good spewing from him. No one should have known he went to the countess's house last night. He made sure there wasn't a carriage or a soul in view and most every light within his sight was out.

"Homebound or not, friend or foe, Mrs. Feversham will have to be dealt with," he said through clenched teeth.

"Indeed, but how?"

"Wait a minute, Aunt," he said, his voice unusually

heavy with aggravation toward her. "I'm not admitting to anything she has told you about the countess."

"Dash it all, I wouldn't expect or want you to. You know I'm not here for an admission, details, or to pass judgment on anyone." Cordelia rose, laid her folded napkin by her plate and, to his amazement after his firm tone, smiled up at him as confidently as always. "I'm only here to advise you of what your neighbor saw and to suggest you use the back gate when you visit the widow."

Lyon's instinct to protect Adeline soared again as he stared at his aunt. "I won't allow Mrs. Feversham to ruin Lady Wake's reputation."

"You don't have to worry about Mrs. Feversham talking to anyone else about this," his aunt said in a practical tone. "I took care of that so you wouldn't have to."

"How?" he asked, not convinced anything other than matrimony could salvage Adeline's reputation.

"I said that I'd asked you to pick up the straw basket that I'd left at Lady Wake's the day we delivered the tarts and biscuits to her. And that you had been so busy entertaining your gentleman friends all afternoon you must have forgotten about it until the evening. I had no idea why she couldn't see my basket in your hand when you left, and she might need to have someone with knowledge of the instrument look at her spyglass and adjust it. That seemed to satisfy her."

It didn't satisfy Lyon. "What about Lady Wake coming inside my house? How did you leave that?"

"Oh, she knew the reason for that. She could see clearly that the area in front of Lady Wake's home was blocked with your friends' coaches. Mrs. Feversham knew it wasn't the first time it's happened. It's been going on for years. I told her I was very sympathetic with the countess on that account and that she had every right to knock on your door and express her displeasure. In the end Mrs. Feversham agreed with me."

"Are you sure?" he asked skeptically.

"Yes—I made certain all was well with her before I left." Cordelia paused, seeming to consider her next words. "She admitted you weren't in Lady Wake's house long enough to have even taken off your clothing and gotten into bed with her."

"Aunt," Lyon said, returning to his cautionary tone, "this is not a discussion I want to have with you. Now or ever."

"Understandable. Brewster said he would personally walk over and retrieve the basket from Lady Wake's housekeeper—the back way, of course—and have it waiting for me at the front door. I'll take my time leaving and make sure Mrs. Feversham sees it in my hands as I walk out. Now, I must be running along. I do try to never overstay my welcome. I'll be over for a drink soon, my dear. I enjoy having a glass of claret or brandy with you."

"You never even taste it," he grumbled.

"Oh, that's not true," she denied hastily. "I have. Once or twice. Enjoy your breakfast. I'll see you at the Grand Ball—if not before."

With that, his aunt swept from the room.

Lyon picked up his cup and took it back to the silver coffee pot to refill. Instead he put it down with a clamor and hit his fist upon the buffet chest. What could he do about his snooping neighbor? An old widow who was crippled.

After a few moments to calm himself, Lyon poured more coffee into his cup and gazed out one of the windows. The gray skies promised more rain for the already sodden earth. His gardeners were busy on his grounds. In the distance over the yew hedge and near barren trees he could see a good portion of the school, but from this room he could see only the roof of Adeline's house.

Adeline.

After last night, how could he be so formal to think of her or even talk to her in such formal terms as Lady Wake? She had him guessing like no other lady and had him feeling things he'd never felt before. Like she was his.

Damnation!

He couldn't shake the straightforwardness with which she said she didn't know whether or not she wanted him or just someone—anyone. He had to admit he'd been with countless women, especially when he was younger, where all he needed was just to fulfill his driving need for release. Is that the way she felt? Any man would do?

Lyon didn't like the way that made his gut wrench.

To be fair to himself, perhaps there was a little of that in him last night, too. It had been a long time since he'd been with a woman. There was a desperation in him, as well. He hadn't taken the time to trace the curve of Adeline's waist, stroke the plane of her hip, or let his hands stray leisurely between her thighs. Their urgency had been too intense and too heated to unfurl their passion slowly. There had been no time for long glances or tender caresses. Not even soft, sweet kisses or seductive words about how intoxicatingly fresh she smelled, how delicious she tasted, or how smooth her skin felt beneath his touch. He didn't even tell her she was the most beautiful woman he'd ever seen or held in his arms.

But he had known whom he held and *she* was the *he'd* wanted.

There was one thing for damn certain. He was going to make sure she would know it was him, that *he* was the one she wanted, the next time they came together.

And there would be a next time.

"What the devil are you looking at that has you so enthralled?" Marksworth asked, walking up beside Lyon. "I called your name twice and you didn't answer."

"The grounds," Lyon said, feeling no guilt about the lie to his father. "We had a storm yesterday afternoon."

"I was aware of it." Marksworth picked up a cup from the buffet and poured himself coffee. "I fear there's an even bigger storm going on in London today."

Unlike his aunt's news, Lyon was sure that he knew what his father was going to tell him. How could any hot-blooded man stay quiet about seeing and hearing Adeline yesterday afternoon? Still he said, "What are you talking about?"

"You and Lady Wake."

Exactly what Lyon thought.

"I had three notes delivered to my house before I'd even awakened. The Duke of Middlecastle and a room full of others were already waiting at White's by the time I got there. Apparently the arrival of Lady Wake in your drawing room yesterday afternoon has spread faster than the whirlwind storm that brought her to your door. By the time I'd heard all that was said about how resplendent she looked dripping from head to toe and how valiant she spoke, I was wishing I hadn't missed the afternoon and had been there to witness the spectacle myself."

The knot of anger that had formed in Lyon's chest with his aunt's tale of his neighbor's spying started growing.

"Some of the nodcocks were arguing over who would pursue her since you hadn't laid claim to her after she left," Marksworth added when Lyon remained silent.

But Lyon *had* in the most intimate way possible.

"That wasn't even the worst of it," his father continued after taking a drink from his cup.

"What else?" Lyon asked, holding his anger at bay and his feelings in check. His relationship with Adeline wasn't anyone's business, and he didn't intend to discuss what happened between them with anyone.

"Pritchard started asking if anyone had seen you at White's or any of the other clubs last night and no one had. You can imagine how that kindling added to the flame of intrigue about widowed Lady Wake without me even telling you."

Another oath whispered under Lyon's breath.

He looked his father straight in the eyes. "That doesn't mean I was with her."

"Of course it does," he argued effectively, lifting the

lids off the serving dishes and looking inside. "Because everyone wants to believe you were with her so they can gossip about it."

Lyon plunked his coffee onto the buffet, causing the cup to rattle in the saucer. This was madness. "I will vehemently deny being with her last night. I won't have her reputation ruined over a half-dozen carriages piled up at the front of her door."

"Very gentlemanly of you," Marksworth said, putting the cover back on the last bowl. "But no one would believe you. I took care of it for you and now you don't have to say anything about it to anyone and Lady Wake will remain unblemished."

Lyon's eyes narrowed. "What did you do?"

"I told them you came over to my house to find out why I missed the card game and stayed to have a late supper with me." Marksworth stopped, took a sip of his coffee, and then smiled. "The whole lot of them believed it."

"Because they aren't fools," Lyon finished for his father.

"Exactly. They don't want her reputation ruined. They want it pure as the first blossom of spring so they can pursue her themselves."

Lyon huffed a short laugh. His father and his aunt had managed to cover for him and Lady Wake before he'd even had a chance to defend Adeline himself.

"Why did you miss the card game?"

"Do you really want me to tell you?"

"No," he said. "I can guess."

"Good. You'd be right that I was spending the afternoon with someone else. However, I was rather remarkable in delivery of the made-up dinner between us," his father said. "Though I really didn't have to put too much outrage into my denial of your whereabouts. They had already made up their minds to court the lovely widow who captured everyone's attention, scandal or not. Knowing they didn't have to compete against you was all they really wanted to know. So what I said settles any mark against her reputation for now, but I fear they may talk about how improper, suggestive, and stimulating she looked in her wet clothing for years to come."

Lyon wasn't likely to forget the image anytime soon, either.

"At least now you know where you stand."

Yes. Lyon knew where he stood with the men. The problem was he didn't know where Adeline stood.

"Have you had a bite yet?" Marksworth asked.

"No."

He looked at the place where Cordelia had been sitting, but didn't ask any questions about who might have left the half-eaten scone. Instead, he grabbed a plate in one hand and lifted the cover off a bowl of steaming scrambled eggs with the other. "Good," he said. "Me either. I'll eat with you. All this talk of gossip has me starving." But before he picked up the spoon and dipped into the fluffy yellow mound, he turned back to Lyon. "There's one thing I forgot to tell you."

Lyon didn't know what that possibly could be. Between his gaming club, Mrs. Feversham, and Aunt Cordelia, nothing seemed to have been missed.

Still, he asked, "What?"

"The wager at White's as to which of us will be the

first to have a son. The bets are more than one hundred to one in my favor."

That didn't surprise Lyon or please him.

"You might want to keep that in mind the next time you want to visit Lady Wake. At your age, if you're going to finally have a son, he should be a legitimate one."

"Marksworth, you go too far," Lyon said in a warning tone.

"It's not the first time and I daresay it won't be the last. I'm your father and have the right to say what I damn well please to you. You don't have to like it or agree with it. She's young, a countess, and from what I heard today, she's a raving beauty and certainly looks shapely enough to bear you a healthy son. If she caught your fancy, as I have reason to believe by the murderous expression you're giving me, you're going to have a lot of competition for her hand. You best ask for her before someone else steps in front of you."

Lyon's jaw tightened as he struggled not to respond. The last thing he wanted was what happened between him and Adeline playing out in the gossip halls and gaming clubs, or in his father's mind. A shudder went through Lyon. He'd already considered that marriage would put a quick stop to any gossip about her. His chest constricted.

Lady Wake, his bride?

His admiration for her, his desire for her, that continuous leap in his chest at just the thought of her was immense. Were his feelings for her what he'd always been looking for in the lady he wanted to be his wife?

Love.

Marksworth strode over to the window nearest him and looked out. "What's that noise I keep hearing?"

"It's the girls from the school Lady Wake and her friends opened behind her house," he answered, much calmer than when his father first arrived. "They sing for about an hour around this time every morning."

Since they stopped playing outside because of him. No wonder they thought him a monster.

"Sing for an hour? Every day? Hmm." His father walked back over to the buffet, picked up a spoon, and dug into the eggs.

Lyon was sure of one thing. He wanted Adeline Wake for his own. Not just for a night or as an occasional lover as the members of his card group had bantered about. That thought made his stomach twist.

Did that mean he'd finally fallen in love?

If he had, it was looking as if he might have to go through half the men in London and a girls' school to prove that to her, but he would. Thankfully his father had just given him an idea as to how to start knocking down all the obstacles between him and the countess, one at a time.

He hoped his father ate quickly. Lyon had a lot to think about.

Chapter 14

It was ridiculous, but Adeline had been smiling all day. And it wasn't because Mrs. Le Roe had delivered the first four of Adeline's new gowns for the Season bright and early that morning or simply because it was a beautiful spring day. No, she'd awakened with no doubts, no concerns, and no regrets about the few passionate minutes she and Lyon had shared last night. She had finally felt wanted for who she was. Desired. Not used for a purpose. Their time together was indescribable and she wasn't going to try to understand why or how it all came about. The only thing she wanted was to enjoy how she was feeling today.

Wonderful. Joyous. Free.

And, in some ways it might be selfish, but she felt

deserving of everything she'd experienced with the earl.

She hadn't been sure what exactly she'd expected or wanted when she'd left her gloves behind at his house. But Lyon had left her no doubt that he'd known exactly what to do and how to accomplish it. She laughed lightly. As far as she was concerned, their coming together couldn't have been any more perfect for her.

Many times throughout the day her happy mind had betrayed her and turned to thinking about the possibility of a next time with Lyon. She would immediately shut down the thoughts. Those were for another day. She didn't want to think about the answers. For now, she only wanted to enjoy reliving the memories of every embrace, kiss, and stroke of his hand. Tomorrow would be soon enough to worry about the future and what it would hold for her.

Adeline stood beside her bed, one arm folded across her chest and tapping a finger on her chin as she looked down at the gowns draped across the bedcoverings. Amber, midnight blue, a faded mulberry, and a deep forest green. The dark colors were sedate enough to satisfy the harshest critiques for what was acceptable for her status in Society now. The sheer overdresses had enough trim, beading, and satin bows and ribbons to be formal enough for a candlelight ball.

Married ladies could be flamboyant, extravagant, and push the boundaries of fashion beyond the pale as far as color, fashion, and showing off their bosoms. Young unmarried misses and widows were not given the same freedoms.

They had rules to follow.

Adeline had topped each gown with three pairs of gloves, several decorated combs, and more than a few pieces of jewelry to match each one. Now all she had to do was make the decision as to which gown to wear first and what adornments she would settle on for each ball. She should send notes to Julia and Brina to find out if either of them had decided on a color. But what would it matter if they were all in the same color? In fact, it might be entertaining if they all arrived in the same shade of widow weeds. The talk that would start made Adeline smile, too. It had always been their plan to be companions for one another and attend the first ball together. They'd decided that more than a year ago when they were meeting once a week and making plans for the school.

Adeline sighed softly and looked at the gowns. After last night, she really didn't care which she wore. In truth, all the dresses looked alike. Demure because her station in life required it. But what she had on couldn't change what she felt inside. Lyon had shown her what she'd always thought. She was filled with un-inhibited fire and passion, and she knew how to share it and accept the same from him.

It had always been a battle of wills between them until they came together, each wanting the same thing. Each receiving. They came together as equals with the same goal in mind. He had fulfilled her long desire and brought lovemaking to life for her. He'd left her no doubts she'd satisfied him as well. There was a time early in her married life when she'd longed for Wake to look at her, touch her as Lyon had last night. That desire perished when time after time he treated his union with her as no more than doing a business deal.

Lyon showed her the difference and gave her hope it might happen again. That gave her much to smile about.

Adeline kept all her clothing simple. The fewer things one had to worry about, the fewer servants one needed. The still-fashionable high-waist shift was easy to slip on without help. Simple was good for Adeline. When her required period of mourning was over, she'd left her brother-in-law's house and moved into a small, leased house in Mayfair where she'd lived until buying Mr. Bottles' property. Adeline had hired Mrs. Lawton and quickly discovered the house-keeper was so efficient she needed no other fulltime staff. Two women came early in the mornings to help Mrs. Lawton with laundry, building the fires, and other such duties that required more help, but they were usually gone before midday.

Within a few tries and failures, Adeline had learned how to skillfully pull up her own hair, shape it into an acceptable chignon at her nape or sometimes the top of her head, and secure it with combs and pins. She found she needed no help deciding what dress to don for the day or someone to lay it out for her. Managing the clasps on necklaces and earrings was really quite easy, too. Most of her stays and bodices were made to fasten in the front or to crisscross and tie in an easy string bow at the center of her back. And Mrs. Lawton was always available for clothing that took more effort.

A light knock on the doorframe sounded. Adeline

turned and said, "Ah, Mrs. Lawton. How did you know I was just about to call for you? I'm thinking I should wear the amber-colored gown for the first ball. What do you think?"

The woman walked over and glanced down. "That will go very nicely with your hair, but—"

Adeline frowned. "But what?"

"You know buttercream is my favorite color, my lady. Whether it's a man's shirt and neckcloth, an apron, or a lady's fancy gown."

Smiling, Adeline said, "Yes, I do remember. And I love the crisp clean look of it, too. But it's not suitable for me. What do you think about the blue? It's really dark, isn't it?"

"It looks black to me, my lady, but I suspect I best leave the decision to you, and tell you that Mrs. Tallon sent Miss Peat over with a message for you. Asking if it might be possible for you to come over to the school for a minute or two."

"Now?"

Mrs. Lawton nodded. "She mentioned that the girls wanted to give you a proper thank-you."

"I don't mind going to the school, but heavens, they should know a personal thank-you isn't necessary. Besides, they've already been here almost a month. If anything, I should thank *them* and their families again for having made the sacrifice to come here."

Doing this for the girls was really the only thing she'd ever done in life that was of any consequence and she was grateful they'd given her the chance to do something so worthy. It made her feel useful. Happy. She needed no thanks.

"They're learning to sew, aren't they?" Mrs. Lawton asked. "Maybe they made a handkerchief for you. Or now that they are learning to write, they could have written something for you. Best you go there rather than all of them come over here."

The worried look on Mrs. Lawton's face made Adeline chuckle. "You're right, I'll go."

She looked back at the gowns. The amber it would be. She removed the white-and-beige gloves, the long strand of pearls, and the large teardrop amethyst that hung on a gold chain. She would go with the dark brown gloves, the choker of amber beads and matching dangling earrings, and combs for her hair.

"Prepare these for the first ball. I'll choose the things for the other dresses when I return, but at least I'm set for one evening. Thank you for helping me make up my mind, Mrs. Lawton."

The sky was blue and the day not so cold so Adeline didn't bother with bonnet, cape, or gloves. Once she was down her back steps, it was hardly more than fifty or sixty steps to the front door of the school. A spirited walk would do her good. Her gray woolen dress should be sufficient enough for a quick, though completely unnecessary, thank-you from the girls. However, it would be lovely to see them close up again, and to look at their shining eyes and rosy cheeks.

The short brisk walk added to the invigorating disposition Adeline had felt all day. It was simply amazing what a few minutes of passion could do for one's temperament. Nothing seemed as bleak and dour as it once had. And she owed it all to Lyon. The usually ornery earl had turned into a blessing in disguise. Now she was looking forward to the first ball of the Season when before she'd dreaded it.

Within a minute or two, Adeline opened the door of the school and walked inside. An eruption of noise exploded, startling her. In the far corner Miss Hinson was seated at a grand-looking rosewood pianoforte, playing a lively tune. The girls were gathered nearby smiling from ear to ear and clapping and squealing. Mrs. Tallon and Miss Peat stood behind Miss Hinson with even bigger smiles. The usually serious teachers were clapping, too!

Everyone curtsied and yelled out, "Thank you, Lady Wake!" The students then started jumping and cheering loudly as only kids could do.

All Adeline could think was *who in the world had something as large as the pianoforte delivered to the wrong address?* She hadn't bought that glorious-sounding, beautifully carved instrument for them and neither had Julia or Brina. Whoever had was going to come looking for it and take it back! What was she going to do? The girls were so excited and happy.

"I can play it, too," Mrs. Tallon was saying when the girls quieted down and Miss Hinson switched to a softer, more subdued score. "Though not as well as Miss Hinson."

"I've never heard one before," Fanny said, stepping closer to the pianoforte and running her hand along the side of the wood. "How does it make that beautiful sound?"

"You never mind about that," Mrs. Tallon said, reaching over and gently taking hold of the little girl's wrist with her thumb and forefinger and removing her hand. "And don't you be touching it, either. Not any of you," she added looking at the other girls.

Adeline could understand Fanny's natural curiosity about the pianoforte. When played correctly it could be as soothing as warm water washing over your shoulders and back. It was sobering and heartbreaking to realize that most of the girls had probably never heard music other than the voices of their mothers or fathers humming or singing.

But her heart ached. What was she going to do? She wouldn't let the pianoforte be taken away now that the girls had been exposed to it.

"Not that either of us will try to teach any of the girls how to play, of course," Mrs. Tallon continued with her conversation. "They are here to learn more beneficial things, but it will be such a wonderful luxury for all of us when we have our singing lessons in the mornings and in the evenings while everyone is getting settled for bed. We are grateful for such a generous gift to the school, Lady Wake."

Adeline swallowed hard. She would have gladly already purchased one if it had once crossed her mind the girls might enjoy hearing melodic music. She had been so focused on what they needed to learn, the skills they needed to find work that she hadn't given enough thought to what they needed to enjoy in the present. Mrs. Tallon was right. Playing an instrument wouldn't earn them a wage like sewing a fine stitch, cutting a straight pattern, or making fancy bows from silk and satin, but she could see it was going to add great enjoyment to their lives at the boarding school.

But Adeline had work to do.

There couldn't be many businesses in London that sold pianofortes. She'd have to find out which ones did and discover who had made this mistake. It was doubtful, but she would be hopeful the school could keep this one and the company have another just like it delivered to the rightful owner. If not, she'd have to come up with a good reason why the pianoforte was switched out for a different one. But she couldn't stand the thought of the girls watching that pianoforte being carried from the school.

"I'm glad everyone is so pleased," Adeline said and then smiled. "It's important to have something lovely to look forward to each day. But now, I must bid you good day."

Adeline started to make a hasty retreat but noticed several of the girls still staring at the rosewood with awe. It was indeed a rare refinement for a charitable school. She turned to Mrs. Tallon and added, "Why don't you let the girls line up and take turns coming by one at a time to touch the pianoforte? Let them press the keys if they want to. Their small hands won't harm it."

The headmistress gave her usual frown when she didn't like what Adeline said. "I'm not sure that's a good idea, my lady. It might encourage them to touch it at other times."

"Maybe. I think it's more likely that it would satisfy their curiosity about it and keep them from wanting to look it over when you aren't nearby. Better they do it now when you can control them." Refusing to take no for an answer, she added, "Don't be stingy with their time. Give each of them plenty to give it a once-over."

"Of course, if that is what you want."

"It is," she said, feeling delighted the girls had this opportunity.

Adeline said goodbye to everyone and walked out. There was no time to waste in getting to Town and finding out where the beautiful piece came from. At any moment it could be snatched away from the girls, leaving them heartbroken and wondering what was going on, and that would make Adeline feel absolutely wretched. Hurrying under the trellis, her gaze strayed to the back grounds of the earl's house. She saw he was standing near the low garden wall between their properties, looking at the school. She stopped and then he noticed her, too. He quickly backed out of sight as if he hoped she hadn't seen him.

Why?

Did he not want to see her after last night? No, that didn't feel right. He wouldn't hide from her because of what had happened between them. From her husband she knew that men handled dalliances very well. Had he heard the pianoforte playing and thought to stop it as he had the girls playing outside? Now that wouldn't surprise her but somehow that didn't feel right either. The noise might have caused him to come outside but it wasn't the reason he hurriedly tried to blend into the afternoon shadows to avoid her.

Another possibility leapt into her mind, causing her heartbeat to quicken, and her chest swelled at the thought. That explanation felt right. It would be just like him to do something so roguish.

Without taking time to really consider the likelihood or viability of what had entered her mind or what she would say to him about it, Adeline changed direction and marched alongside the tall yew border that separated her grounds from the school. She hurried across the small patch of garden and over to the vine-covered wall between her house and the dashing earl's. As she rounded the corner, she saw he was about to disappear into his house.

"Don't you dare go through that door until you have spoken to me," she called to him. When it came to Lyon, she was always compelled by emotions, not sensible reasoning. If last night proved anything, it was that.

Lyon turned toward her. "If you insist." He smiled innocently and headed back down the steps, saying, "And good afternoon to you, too, Adeline."

Adeline?

Of course, he would now feel familiar enough with her to call her by her first name. And she familiar enough with him that the informality of it didn't bother her. Without considering the violation of invading his privacy, she followed the wall down to the wooden gate that had been mounted at the end of the stone wall, opened it, and went through to his back garden and met him at the bottom of his portico.

"It doesn't appear as if you are surprised to see me," she said, trying to subdue the tingling awareness of desire that always assailed her whenever she was near him.

"Why should I be?" His gaze swept up and down her face, making her feel as if he were looking at the most beautiful thing he'd ever seen. "We are neighbors."

She met his gaze without flinching and said, "I believe you know why I'm here."

"That's not entirely true."

His answer caught her unaware and for a moment she didn't know how to respond. A crisp wind blew a strand of hair across her cheek and she brushed it behind her ear. "What do you mean?"

Apparently sensing her caution, he said, "There is more than one reason you could be here. I have no way of knowing on which to bestow the honor."

Unable to deny the truth of his words, she said, "One of them we decided not to talk about."

"Did we?" he asked in a husky voice and with an attractive quirk of his head. "Or did *you*?"

"Both of us," she answered firmly. "I asked that we not discuss what happened between us, and because you are a gentleman you agreed and it was settled. So that can't be the reason I'm here."

"All right," he said, moving over a few steps and leaning his rump against the back of a marble bench in an attractively easy manner. "Another reason you could be here is because you are returning the umbrella you borrowed yesterday, but it's not in your hand."

"No," she admitted guiltily. Because of how it came to be in her possession, she hadn't even remembered she'd used it. "I'll see it's returned later."

"Then you must have come over because you wanted to see me again." He gave her a gentle smile. "That would be a sound motive for us to meet again."

Adeline's heart pounded. So he did want to be with her again. She hadn't wanted to think about that today and she couldn't think about it now. She could play this cat–and-mouse game with him the rest of the evening, but if her instincts weren't right, she was wasting valuable time. Trusting her intuition, she said, "You sent a pianoforte to the school."

He took in a long breath but remained silent.

So it was true. She walked closer to him. "I want to know why."

"Perhaps I grew tired of hearing the girls sing off-key each morning and thought some softly played music might be a welcoming respite."

She swallowed a shivery gasp of chilling air before saying, "You are every bit the beast I thought you were."

He smiled. "Do the girls like it?"

"They love it," she said, and flew into his arms so quickly she almost knocked him over the top of the bench.

Lyon caught himself and her to keep them from falling backward. He laughed. Adeline laughed.

He spread his knees, and in an unthinking response she stepped in intimately close to him as he settled against the bench again with his feet firmly planted on the ground. He gathered her up against his chest, closed his thighs around hers and pressed her tightly against him. The warmth of his body, the tightness of his embrace, the humor in his face, instantly soothed her ruffled spirit and delighted her. She rested against his body, letting him hold her up.

Adeline slid her arms under his coat and around his waist. Reaching up, she placed her lips against his and gave him a long, soft, and gentle kiss. It was relaxing, heavenly. Natural and right. Savoring. His response was all she could want it to be. When she thought to break the kiss and pull away, his hand slid up her neck to hold the back of her head.

"Not yet."

She willingly accepted the pressure of his grasp, not caring that he wasn't ready for their embrace to end. She didn't mind that he took control. It kindled and enhanced all she was feeling for him.

"I needed to thank you."

With his lips hovering just above hers, he whispered, "Then go ahead and thank me again before I let go of you."

Their kisses weren't frantic, searching and demanding as they'd been last night. They were languorous, cherishing but with no less feeling of wanting and needing to be closer. She felt as if she would be happy to never stop kissing him. It was magical how her lips pressed to Lyon's, her breasts flattened against his chest, could stir up and awaken the most wonderful spirals of sensations in her body, making her feel totally agreeable to being possessed by him.

When his lips finally moved to the corner of her mouth and then across her cheek to nuzzle around the warmth of her ear, he whispered, "We shouldn't be doing this out here but I can't seem to stop."

Adeline leaned away from him and asked, "Lyon, I need to know, did you purchase the pianoforte because of what happened between us last night?"

He questioned her with his eyes, "What exactly are you asking?"

"Why did you give the school the pianoforte?"

His arms tightened around her. His body stiffened. Slowly, he lifted his head and looked at her. Anger crinkled around his eyes and mouth. "Do you think it was a thank-you for giving me something I've wanted since I first saw you? Do you think the pianoforte was an apology for that or a recompense for guilt? Is that what you think?"

"I don't know," she answered, wanting him to see the concern in her expression and hear it in her voice. "I don't want it to be for any of those reasons."

"Then why would you ask?"

"Because it crossed my mind. It was an expensive gift."

He slid his hands under her arms, picked her up, and gently set her away from him and straightened to his full height. His gaze lingered on hers only a moment before saying, "The truth? Yes, it was guilt that made me do it, but it had nothing to do with you. It was the girls. It was guilt because I yelled at them and I shouldn't have."

Relieved and pleased that his gift had nothing to do with her or what happened between them, she swallowed a deep breath. She jerked her hands to her hips, but instead of giving him a disapproving scowl, she gave him a bit of a grin. "So, days later, you finally admit you raised your voice to them?"

"Yes," he said disgustedly as he turned away from her but just as quickly turned back and pulled her into his arms once again. His silvery gaze burned right into hers. "Don't make light of it. They deserved better from me than they got. So did you. I yelled at you that day, too."

"I remember."

"I also will admit I have never held anyone in my arms that I wanted more than I wanted you last night. I've never been with anyone who had more passion and eagerness for my touch than you had and I want to be with you again. Right now is not soon enough for me, Adeline. No guilt, no apologies, and no regrets for that. Can you say the same?"

Adeline sucked in a deep yearning breath. She'd needed to hear that from him, too. "Yes. You have me feeling things I shouldn't feel, saying things I shouldn't say, doing things I shouldn't do. I don't know what makes me want to kiss you every time I see you but I do. I have no guilt, no apologies and no regrets either."

"So we understand each other?" he asked, his expression still serious.

"We do."

His arms squeezed her tightly and claimed her lips in a long passionate kiss. All he had to do was touch her and she wanted to be with him again.

"We are taking too many chances out here even if we are in the back garden." He let go of her and stepped away. "There's always a chance someone may see us."

"Yes, of course. You're right. We must be more careful. I seem to lose all reasoning when I'm with you. Thank you for your gift to the girls," she said hastily and turned to go.

"Wait, Adeline."

"Yes."

"I should let you know there may be gossip about

your visit to my house yesterday. Someone will talk and it will get discussed."

"I've expected as much and I'm prepared. Should the staunch pillars of Society show up at my door and forbid me to attend any of the parties or simply shun me when I attend one, I think I am strong enough to survive it."

"I believe that, too. I don't think anyone would dare say anything to you, but they will be looking at you. You and your friends have already created great interest with the school and now this is bound to cause more gossip."

Adeline hugged her arms to her chest, suddenly feeling the cold of the afternoon after Lyon's warm embrace. Once her husband had told her she was the subject of tittle-tattle because she hadn't given him a son. "I have endured much worse, Lyon."

He walked closer to her. With the backs of his fingers he brushed a strand of hair away from her face. "What?"

She looked into his dreamy eyes. The concerned look on his face and in his eyes had her suddenly wishing she could tell him, and share her burden. It wasn't just idle curiosity that made him ask. He cared and wanted to help. That made her throat thicken and her gratitude run deep. Adeline knew she was feeling way too much for the earl. Against her wishes, against her best efforts, her heart was involved in what she felt for him. It was difficult for her to say no to him.

Her hesitation prompted him to say, "Tell me. I want to understand."

His voice washed over her as silkily as an embroidery thread pulled through a delicate fabric. For reasons she couldn't understand she was tempted to tell him what she went through, but where would she start and where would she end?

"No." She stepped away from his touch. "Nothing in particular."

"All right." He slowly lowered his hand and accepted her words. "There's something else I should tell you. Our neighbor across the street, Mrs. Feversham, saw me enter your house last night."

That concerned Adeline more than her verbally accosting the gentlemen. That was done in daylight and she had good reason for entering his house.

"She saw you come inside? How could she see in the dark? Mrs. Lawton had already extinguished the outside lamps. Only one small light burned inside the house. Did Mrs. Feversham tell you this?"

"I've never met her. My aunt let me know this morning when she came over. Cordelia said she took care of the lady's concerns and there will be no more talk about it."

"Are you sure?" she asked more breathlessly than she would have liked. "I'm not fearful for myself but for the school. I wouldn't want anything to happen that might cause someone to think the school needed to be closed because I behaved inappropriately."

"I don't believe there is any chance of that. If Cordelia Carbonall says she has it under control, she does."

"You trust her that much?"

"I do. She can be fierce when she needs to be. Mrs. Feversham would listen to Cordelia because she's the only one who has consistently visited with her since she fell. She wouldn't want to lose such a good friend. It's troublesome that Mrs. Feversham doesn't have much to do other than watch her neighbors."

"Like you," Adeline said with a sudden smile.

"Me?" Lyon grimaced.

She lifted her chin and tossed out, "You admitted to watching me from the window of your bedchamber, my lord."

"That was different." He smiled, too. "I did, but I didn't have a spyglass."

"Oh my," she said, her lighter attitude fading as quickly as it had arrived. "Truly?"

He nodded.

"That is troublesome. Do you suppose it can see around the side of your house to where we are now?"

Lyon laughed. "No, I'm sure of that, but there are still risks to being out in my back garden together. You should go."

She knew he wasn't trying to get rid of her. He was sincerely worried about her reputation, but she couldn't say it was worrying her overly much—except where the girls were concerned. Gossip about her might in some way endanger the well-being of the school. And while it hadn't happened so far, she could be taken to task about it at any time. For the school she needed to be as proper as possible—when she wasn't in the privacy of her own home.

"Yes, I agree. I probably shouldn't have come over. I wanted you to know the girls are very happy."

"I'm glad. And, Adeline?"

"Yes," she said hopefully.

"I don't want the girls to know the pianoforte came from me."

"Why? They should know that—"

"That's the way I want it, Adeline."

Chapter 15

The water was just the way Lyon liked it. Cold. The day was starting as he preferred when he had no early meetings to attend, no plans to meet anyone for a ride in the park, or fencing competitions to watch or participate in. Sitting in a tub reading the morning's newsprint while downing his morning coffee.

Lyon sensed that his valet had come back into the room but he hadn't heard him leave. That was odd. Dome didn't usually intrude once the water was delivered but if he did, it was only long enough to see if Lyon needed anything and then he'd quietly slip away. Lyon turned his attention back to the article about the Prince's extravagant expenditures on three pieces of art the writer considered less than worthless and more unnecessary spending by the Regent's unrestrained appetite for anything he wanted. No doubt his father would have a few choice words to say about the author of the piece. Not that either the ridicule or the spending was likely to change.

Another rustle of movement in the room disturbed Lyon. He was about to ask his valet what the devil he wanted when he heard a slight whisper. Was Dome talking to himself? Before Lyon could ask there were more whispers and the scurry of soft-soled shoes padding on the wood floor.

Small shoes.

He tensed, and the fine hairs on the back of his wet neck rose. What he heard was not coming from his quiet-as-a-mouse valet. Someone else was in the room. He slowly lowered the newsprint until he could peek over the top. Without moving his head, he gazed first at the open door that led from his dressing chamber into his bedchamber. No one was there. He slowly shifted his gaze around the room. He saw nothing out of place and no movement, but knew someone was with him.

Who? And where?

Remaining still but watchful, something caught his eye. The face of a little girl peeked from behind the large upholstered wing-back chair that stood near the entrance. His gut tightened. His fingers started slowly closing tightly around the newsprint, crumpling it in his palms. She was the little redhead he'd seen playing outside the morning he'd been at the school.

Suddenly the head of another girl appeared. She had light brown hair and big popping blue eyes that stared straight at him. *Damnation!* How many were there? And how did they get into his bedchamber?

What could he do? He couldn't stand up but he had to get the girls out of the room. In frustration, Lyon splashed the paper into the water and yelled, "Dome!"

The girls squealed and raced out the door. He heard them collide with his valet in his bedchamber. More screams rang out.

Lyon yanked a towel off the table and wrapped it around his waist as he rose and hopped out of the tub calling for Brewster to help Dome. He should have never felt sorry for the little imps. He should have moved them out to the countryside when he'd thought about it. By the time the towel was secure and he'd made it to the top of the stairs, the girls had already reached the bottom step where Brewster was standing, blocking their exit, and Dome preventing their retreat.

The little chicks were cornered. It would serve them right if he had them both thrown in a workhouse.

"Hold them until I can dress and get down."

Once again, Lyon found himself in too big of a hurry to confront the girls than to clothe himself properly. He threw a shirt over his head and stepped dripping wet into his trousers and then into his boots. That wasn't the normal order or manner of dressing but ever since Adeline moved next door his whole life seemed out of harmony with what he expected. The folly and energy of the moment caused him to rapidly descend the stairs and stand towering over a tall, brown-haired, lanky girl who leaned against the wall trembling with fear and a stout freckle-cheeked younger lass who seemed perfectly calm with the disorder going on around her.

"How did you two get in here?" he asked, unbelievably calm for what had just happened.

Neither girl answered.

"The doors are locked, my lord," Brewster insisted. "As always to protect your privacy and avoid anyone without an appointment disturbing you."

"Are you going to cut us up and have us for your dinner?" the taller girl asked in a shaky voice.

"What?" Stunned, Lyon looked at Brewster who seemed just as shocked by her comment. What the devil was he going to do? Just a few days ago he'd tried to make amends for scaring the life out of the girls by sending a pianoforte over for them to enjoy, and they had. He'd heard them many times. Now he had to contend with this madness.

"No, of course not," Lyon declared. "Where did you hear such nonsense?"

"It happened to a boy in a story Miss Hinson read to us," she answered timidly.

"But the boy came back to life and was haunting the man," the girl with the freckles covering her face added. Lyon couldn't help but notice she didn't appear the least perturbed by him or the fact that she'd been caught snooping in his bedchamber.

"A ghost story," Lyon grunted. "Miss Hinson needs to be taken to task for what she reads to you."

"It's not scary to me, but most of the girls didn't like it," the redhead said.

"I can see why," he grumbled. "Now tell me what you're doing in my house."

Both girls remained silent, staring up at him with

their innocent-looking eyes. Lyon supposed it wasn't up to him to question the girls anyway. Only to return them.

"All right," he said. "Come with me."

"Where are you taking us?" the taller girl asked.

"You can't take us back to the school," the shorter lass said with a tinge of defiance in her tone. She folded her arms across her chest and stared at him with her lips in a pout. "We'll get in trouble for leaving."

"You should. I think you are in more danger from slipping into my house than you are for slipping out of the school. Besides, I'm not taking you there. I'm taking you to Lady Wake. It will be her decision as to what's to be done about you. Now, one of you on each side of me. Let's go."

Brewster quickly opened the front door. "No, we're going out the back. There will be fewer eyes to watch us leaving if we use the garden entrance."

Lyon stomped across the lawn at a fast pace, flanked by the errant girls who struggled to keep up with his much-longer stride. He hurried the girls alongside the tall yew and under the budding trellis, hoping they could get through fast enough that Mrs. Feversham wouldn't see them.

He knocked loudly on Adeline's back door and completely understood the shock in the housekeeper's expression when she saw him standing there with the girls. "We need to see Lady Wake. Now."

"She's in the drawing room reading her mail."

"Lead the way," he said and stepped aside, nodding for the girls to follow her.

Adeline slowly rose from the secretary where she

was sitting when they walked into the room. His first thought was she was the most beautiful lady he'd ever seen. The second was that she belonged to him and he would challenge any man who tried to take her away. Only thirdly did he notice the frown of surprise and confusion etching her lovely features.

The shortest girl had somehow slipped behind him and now stood beside the other girl. They were holding hands. To her credit, the taller child still looked frightened. On the other hand, the redhead still seemed quite calm. She was looking around the countess's drawing room, taking in its blue velvet draperies, damask settees, and carved dark wood tables as if she'd been invited to do so.

Lyon knew this wasn't the way to Adeline's heart. He had no doubt he would once again be seen as the ogre to Adeline in this scenario. He was on her property with wet hair, half-dressed and scaring the girls.

So be it.

"Here they are, my lady," Lyon said, the only way he knew how—in a matter-of-fact tone. "Your wandering students."

With her gaze intent upon his face she said, "I'm not sure what you mean by that or why you are with them."

Feeling quite sure she wasn't going to like his answer, he said, "I'm returning them to you. They were in my home."

She stared at the girls in disbelief. "Fanny? Mathilda? Is this true? You were in the earl's home?"

Fanny nodded.

Lyon was certain Adeline's legs went weak, but she straightened her shoulders and looked back at him in an accusing way. "How did they get inside your house and why were they there?"

"I have no idea," Lyon admitted. "They were uninvited guests I assure you."

"That can't be." In disbelief, Adeline walked closer to the youngsters. "Did you just walk inside his house?"

They remained silent again.

Adeline swung toward Lyon again, her soft gray skirts swishing attractively about her legs, her eyes sparkling with more questions than he had answers. "You should have had your doors locked so they couldn't get in."

"They were locked," he said, trying not to be irritated with Adeline. He knew this would upset her, and it had.

She clasped her hands together at her waist and turned to Fanny. "How did you get into his house?"

"I climbed on Mathilda's shoulders, opened a window, and crawled inside. I helped her climb in after me."

"I can't believe that!" she said breathlessly. "That was dangerous. You could have fallen and been injured."

"And against the law," Lyon muttered to himself, realizing whether or not Adeline knew it, the girls needed to be taught a lesson they wouldn't soon forget—only it wasn't up to him to do that. He'd have to leave chastisement up to her.

"Why would you do something like this?" Adeline asked them, clearly distraught and desperately trying to hide that fact.

"We heard a dog whimpering," Fanny said, so innocently Lyon might have believed her himself. If he didn't know better. "Like he was in pain and needed help." She elbowed Mathilda.

"And starving for some food and water," Mathilda said, her big blue eyes opening wider. "It was a puppy." Her voice softened and her lashes fluttered as if she were remembering a happier moment, the earlier fear completely gone from her face. "He was a playful little puppy. With soft, warm fur. He was white with big black spots all over him. He wiggled a lot and he—"

"But he couldn't play because he sounded like he was hurt bad and needed us to help him," Fanny said, interrupting her friend's reminiscing.

Adeline glanced back at the earl, her eyes filled with hope and searching for him to give her a reason she could accept the paltry explanation. "A puppy. See? There was a good reason for them to have done this—they wanted to do an act of kindness."

"I don't have a dog, Lady Wake," he said brusquely, his annoyance with what the girls had done beginning to show in his tone and no doubt his expression, too.

She moistened her lips. Lyon knew she was desperately attempting to make sense of what she was hearing, "Maybe it was some other kind of animal. Or maybe they heard a servant crying in distress over breaking something of great value and mistook the sound for that of a dog in pain." She paused for a second and then added, "Maybe you should get a dog. It might help your gruff attitude."

"My attitude was just fine until I looked up and saw these two snooping in my dressing chamber."

"Your dressing chamber?" she repeated, obviously horrified.

Adeline's words had hardly been above a whisper. Still Lyon couldn't resist the urge to add, "While I was in the bath."

Both girls snickered.

At that admission from him, Adeline gasped. "They didn't."

He nodded. "Don't worry, they didn't see anything other than newsprint in front of my face." *Hopefully.* "My butler and valet quickly apprehended them and held them until I could get dressed."

He watched Adeline inhale deeply and collect herself. "I understand. Thank you for bringing them back. I'll have a chat with them. Later, of course." Adeline walked past him to the doorway and called, "Mrs. Lawton, please come here."

"We didn't touch anything in his house," Fanny said, swinging her friend's hand ever so lightly.

"No, we didn't," Mathilda said, the earlier fear gone and a more penitent expression on her face. "It was a big house. We couldn't find our way out after we went upstairs."

"But you went into his house on purpose," Adeline said earnestly. "Into his private chambers. That was wrong and very disheartening."

"We didn't know he'd be washing," Fanny said. "We just wanted to see what the inside of the earl's house looked like. We didn't want to take anything."

"I should hope not!" Adeline exclaimed, obviously furious this had happened and devastated she didn't seem to know what to do about it.

"What can I do for you, my lady?" the housekeeper asked, walking up to join them.

"Take these two back to Mrs. Tallon. Tell her to put them in separate corners, their faces to the wall. She's to watch one and you the other. I don't want either of you to take your eyes off them until I get there. I'll be over later to discuss what needs to be done."

"You won't send me back home, will you?" Fanny asked, looking up at Adeline. For the first time since she'd been caught, she had a worried expression. "My mum would be mad with me if I had to come home before I learned how to read."

"Mine too," Mathilda agreed. "She wants me to make her a pretty blue dress one day. It was my dad's favorite color."

Lyon's stomach squeezed uncomfortably. *Damnation!* Why did the girls have to suddenly seem so innocent? Why did he suddenly feel such compassion for them and like he was the guilty one?

Adeline looked over to Lyon, and his heart felt as if it melted. In that moment he knew he'd do anything for her. His anger over the girls' infringement had dissipated and in truth he didn't want them to be sent home. They wanted to learn how to read! He didn't want to be the cause they couldn't have the opportunity. He gave Adeline a gentle shrug and a nod.

What could he say? Rules were broken. Children get in trouble.

"I can't make promises about anything right now," Adeline said, turning back to the girls. "This is serious misbehavior. I'll have to talk to Mrs. Tallon. Off you both go with Mrs. Lawton."

The moment the girls turned to leave Adeline folded her arms across her chest and walked back over to stand in front of the fireplace. "I can't believe this. I thought they were all afraid of you. Well, maybe not Fanny. She doesn't seem to be frightened of anything except going home. I don't know why they would enter your house. Leave the school again."

"Again?" he said, walking over to join her by the fire. "So this isn't the first time they've slipped out of the school and into someone's house?"

"No. Yes. I mean, Fanny has left the school building before but not broken into anyone's home. Not that I know of. I don't know what I'm going to do with her. She has been told not to do it, reprimanded, and punished."

"Those two must have struck a good friendship between them when they met," Lyon offered. "Or perhaps there's a kinship. What they did took a fair amount of trusting on both their parts."

"Perhaps even some planning, too." She swallowed hard before shaking her head and saying, "For them to go all the way up to your chambers is just so shocking. I'm mean you were—you're hair's still wet."

Lyon knew Adeline was imagining him in the bath because he was imaging her in the water with him. His body stirred. He reached up and smoothed a strand of honey-colored hair away from her beautiful, worried face. She didn't back away but watched him do it with a soft expression that let him know she welcomed the comforting gesture. The undercurrent of sexual awareness that always flowed between them was coming startlingly alive.

"I'm not one that can give advice on children, Adeline, but I do know boarding school by its nature is difficult to adjust to for anyone. It's constrictive especially for children who have been free to roam about alone and explore whatever's before them be it the streets or the countryside. Suddenly being forced to live by someone else's rules is not easy no matter your age or station in life."

"Yes, I can understand that," she conceded softly; but then in a stronger voice she added, "But when there are rules, we must obey them or suffer the consequences."

He touched her hair again, thinking he could look at her all day and not grow tired, but that thought brought others with it. The more he looked at her, the longer he wanted to stay, take her in his arms, comfort her, and make her forget everything but the thrill of being in his arms again.

"I'm sorry I had to bring them over here. I thought you'd want me to. That you'd want to know."

"Yes, of course, I needed to know." She rubbed her arms as if she were cold. "I'll talk with Mrs. Tallon. We must do something."

"Nothing as harsh as sending them home, I hope," he said, knowing how easy it was for children to get into trouble. "They both seemed concerned about disappointing their families."

"I know, and it's kind of you to be so forgiving after what they did, but stop trying to make me see reason right now, Lyon, and kiss me."

He placed his hands on each side of her face and claimed her lips with a chaste, closed-mouth, but lingering kiss. His lips moved slowly across hers, pressing softly, leisurely, leaving her no doubt about how much he wanted her, but sensing Adeline only needed him to calm and reassure her that she could handle this problem with the girls.

Taking his time, he slid his hands down her cheeks. His thumbs caressed her skin, while his fingertips lightly touched the soft, sensitive areas below and behind her ears. He knew she would let him know when or if she wanted ravenous kisses and touches or just wanted to be gently kissed, touched, and held as he was doing now. It was her decision to make how far they'd go right now. He'd continue as he was doing and give her all the time she needed to decide.

Difficult as it would be, he could wait.

He wasn't sure if either of them had had a choice in how it happened the last time they came together. It was primitive, wild, and had been destined since they'd met. Surrendering to his lovemaking today had to be her decision.

With the same slow movements, he tenderly massaged the tight muscles at her nape.

She sighed against his lips.

"I feel tension inside you," he whispered. "Does that feel good?"

"Immensely," she answered and rolled her shoulders.

He skimmed his hands across the top of her delicately rounded shoulders, and down her firm upper arms, occasionally squeezing just enough so she could feel his strength. He wanted her to know that even though she invited the kiss, and he was taking direction from her, he was in control.

When he sensed she was completely relaxed beneath his touch and his lingering kisses, he lifted his head, looked into her eyes, and asked, "Are we alone in the house?"

She nodded. "I don't have a maid."

That was most unusual. He gave her a questioning smile while his hands continued to caress her. "How does a lady get by without one?"

He felt her tremble and saw she had the same troubling, faraway look in her golden brown eyes that she'd had when he'd offered her the brandy. Why would talk of a maid bring back disquieting remembrances for her? He wanted to know, but this wasn't the time to ask. She would only turn silent on him as she had before.

Wanting only to reassure her, he bent his head and placed his nose on the soft warm skin at the slope of her neck and breathed in deeply, filling himself with her fresh, womanly scent. He wondered if she knew he felt desperate to possess her every time he touched her. Every time he looked at her.

"I prefer not to have a lot of servants around," she said. "I have my clothing made in a simple fashion. Most of it is easy for me to get into and out of on my own. When necessary, Mrs. Lawton helps me."

"I think we've found something that we have in common. I don't want a host of servants around either."

He claimed her lips in another slow, easy kiss that suddenly seemed more erotic than eager, breathless kisses. His hand slid down her chest to capture her breast and cover it with his palm, gently squeeze it with his fingers. A spiraling heat consumed him.

Adeline lifted her arms to circle his neck and melted willingly, easily into his arms. At her invitation, he took the time to run his hands down to her waist, hips, and buttocks, and then up to flatten his palm against her breasts. Her body was firm and trim, and yielded to his touch.

"You are pleasingly made, Adeline," he whispered against her lips.

He felt her smile. She opened her mouth and gave him her tongue, feeding his hunger. Lyon moaned his approval and lifted her buttocks up to meet him where there could be no mistake he was hungry for her. Ready to give and to take pleasure at her command.

With deliberate quickness, her warm hands slid under his untucked shirt and raced up his cool, bare back to caress his shoulders.

"Yes," he whispered. That was a welcomed sign. He deepened, lengthened, and sweetened their kisses with every breath he took. He plundered inside her mouth and her shape with growing anticipation as they pressed together.

It was so easy to completely lose himself in her and take what she offered without worry, but that wasn't wise. Before they went too far he said, "Adeline, I must protect your reputation. Can Mrs. Lawton be trusted if we are caught?"

"She is faithful, but there is no worry today. She won't leave the girls until I go to the school and dismiss her."

"I will take your word for that." He looked over at the settee. Larger than most, but still small for a man. "This will not be easy," he said and then swooped one arm under her knees and the other across her shoulder. He lifted and carried her over to the settee and laid her down.

With one hand, Lyon jerked his shirt over his head and dropped it to the floor while at the same time unbuttoning his trousers with the other. He then swung one booted foot and leg over her and with some effort nestled it between her and the back of the cushion, keeping the other foot firmly planted on the floor to steady himself while resting his lower body on top of her.

While he positioned himself, Adeline untied the knot in her long-sleeved bodice and he helped slip it off her shoulders. Two pulls on the laces of her stays released her beautiful, small breasts. Gently he swept his fingertips over the swell of one and then the other.

It felt so damn good to be with her like this again, loving her, touching her. He looked into her eyes for a long moment before his gaze drifted down her face, lingered over her breasts, and swept back up to her eyes again. He whispered, "You are so beautiful I don't want to stop looking at you."

She smiled so sweetly at him. Lyon wanted to take her immediately, satisfy them both and forego the sweet building of pleasure that they both needed and deserved.

Instead he tamped down his rigid desire and buried his lips in the hollow of her throat, trying to ease the rage of his passion for her. When he was in more control of himself, he fondled her breasts. First one and then the other, taking his time to feel their soft, firm shape and loving the arousing tautness of her nipples beneath his fingers. His body kept urging him to be as aggressive as they'd been last time they were together.

But no, not this time.

He held himself in check. Slowly, letting his lips trace down to tease, circle and cover the rosy tip of her breast into his mouth to heighten both their desires. He felt her body quicken beneath him.

Lyon savored the taste of her, taking his time to properly adore her body. He glided his hand down the plane of her hip, and when he brought his hand back up he caught the skirts of her dress and brought them with him. He caressed the warm bare skin of her shapely outer thigh and slowly let his hand slip between her legs.

"You wouldn't believe how much I have wanted to touch you like this again," he whispered in a heated voice against the cool, silky skin of her chest.

"Do you mean that?"

Lyon lifted his head, his expression questioning her. "Adeline, I will never lie to you about anything."

She smiled shyly at him. "Thank you."

"For what?" he whispered. "For wanting you? I've never desired anyone the way I have ached for you."

"I have dreamed and longed to be with you again, too," she answered softly.

Lyon saw and felt her words were as true. She wanted *him*. Not just anyone to satisfy her.

"After the last time we were together like this you

said you didn't know if it was me you wanted or just someone to satisfy your desires." A smile narrowed his eyes just enough to let her know he wasn't being too serious when he asked, "Are you sure it's me you want to be with or would just anyone make you feel this way?"

Her expression was almost shy. "I might have been unsure at the moment I said it, but no longer," she answered. "I want only you."

Adeline grabbed hold of the band of his trousers and slid them down his hips. She arched her hips toward him and surrounded his back with his arms, urging him to continue without hesitation. Her response was just what he wanted. Now he would to take over. Moments later Lyon claimed her once again for his own.

He made love to her with all the gentleness his eager body would allow. His movements were leisurely, sensual, and reverent. He kissed her, caressed her, and moved gently on top of her until he sensed that indescribable pleasure rising up inside her.

Lyon had never experienced such raw craving for a woman he'd already lain with once. With Adeline it was just as exciting and fervent as the first time. Her impatience for him was elating, the power she'd just given him exalting. His decision to go slow and follow her lead in the beginning was the right one. He reached down and swathed the tip of her breast, pulling it gently into his mouth, tugging lightly on it.

More tremors flowed from her and she whispered, "Lyon."

He smiled against her breasts, knowing her desire

was for him, her pleasure coming from his touch. Her hands moved over his body, making him ache with deep longing.

They both inhaled with deeply satisfying gasps. Their movements were no less eager or frantic than when they last came together. Their passion was too strong to go slow or be tame. He swallowed every soft sound made, gloried in every touch she gave him. When he felt her body tremble and heard her soft moan of peaking pleasure he allowed his own fulfillment to follow. Their chests heaved, and both sucked in ragged breaths of ebbing, all-consuming sensations.

Lyon slipped one hand under her shoulder to hug her up close and relaxed against her body. With his nose, he nestled her neck and he kissed her over and over again.

Finally, his breathing started to slow, his heartbeat calmed, and he tried to move. His body was stiff from the awkward position he'd been in. He grunted and then chuckled low in his throat as he tried to move his leg and lift it over her.

"It was much easier to get down on this damn thing than it is to get up from it."

Adeline whispered a laugh, too. "Then stay here with me a little longer."

He kissed her deeply again and felt the urge to accept her invitation. But there were hazards in doing that. He didn't want the housekeeper or the headmistress to come looking for her.

"Your drawing room is not the place for such intimacy between us," he said, and then lifted himself off the settee with no small amount of struggle and effort.

"There has to be an easier way to do this," she said, lowering her skirt and then reaching for her bodice that had been slung to the other end of the settee.

"I agree," Lyon said and started adjusting his clothing as he smiled at her.

His attraction to her was even stronger than it had been the first night they'd met. She was different from any other lady. It wasn't just the explosive desire he had for her that made him want her for his own. It was more than that. He welcomed her independence, her free-speaking, her strength, her generosity and kindness to the girls. He even enjoyed arguing with her. It was refreshing to know someone who took him to task when he was wrong and even when she knew he was right, as Adeline had a few minutes ago when she'd first heard the girls had entered his house.

Watching her lace her clothing, Lyon felt a new protectiveness stir deeply in his chest. He'd known earlier he wanted no other man to touch her, and he didn't want her to desire anyone but him. What he was feeling now went further and was stronger than just a man being jealous of a lady's attention. It surprised him to realize it, but what he was feeling had to be love. There could be no other explanation.

His heart pounded. She was the one he wanted for his bride. Without reservation, he said, "There is a better way. Marry me."

Chapter 16

Adeline's hands stilled on the laces of her stays, but she felt a quivering in her chest and stomach. She stared at Lyon. They'd been laughing over the cramped settee, but he looked so serious she suddenly felt that way, too. There was a time she could hide all her emotions. She'd had to. It hadn't been that difficult with Wake, but with Lyon, she found it hard to do. He touched her in so many ways that her husband never had. She was sure Lyon could see in her expression that she was stunned by his statement.

Marry him.

Share this exquisite passion and pleasure with him every night? Yes, she wanted to do that, but marry him? Be his wife? No.

Lyon walked over and bent down on one knee in

front of her. "I don't want anyone but you. I don't want us to hide that we want to be together. What's between us and what we're feeling is too important to be treated lightly. Marry me."

The thought of marriage again sent Adeline into panic. She couldn't.

"The feelings I have for you are more than I could have ever imagined feeling. It's true I thought you a beast at first. With good reason. I now know you are kind, strong, and your touch thrills me, but I'm not interested in matrimony, Lyon."

She brushed away from him and rose from the settee, quickly shoving her arms into her bodice.

He stood up and said, "Look at me, Adeline," he said, and waited for her to do so. "Marriage is what usually follows the kind of passion we have for each other. I feel it in here." He put his hand over his heart. "This is the right thing for us to do."

"No," she said, giving her attention back to the bow she was tying in her stays. "I admit if I were to ever be tempted to do so, it would be with you, but I will never marry again."

"That is a bold statement, my lady."

"A true one," she answered earnestly, making a loose knot at the center of her back.

"Why?"

"Because I've been a wife and found I'm not suited to marriage and have no desire to entangle myself in it again."

He took hold of her upper arms, forcing her to look at him again, and said, "So your marriage wasn't a happy one?"

"It wasn't, but I don't intend to discuss it with you."

"I respect that you want to remain silent about that. I'm not demanding you tell me anything concerning your past. I am willing to listen if you ever want to. Your previous marriage is not a concern to me unless you want it to be. I want to talk about us. The future. Our future. What we will share. How we will live with each other."

She pulled out of his grip and straightened her shoulders. "I don't want to think about marriage. Past or future. I don't want to have this discussion. It doesn't mean that I don't want to be with you. I do. Often. I have since the first night we met when you—well you know. We'll have to find another solution to our dilemma of nosy neighbors and servants."

"No, Adeline," he said tersely. "I will not make you a mistress that I visit every now and then when I so desire."

"Not a mistress!" she said fiercely. "I need no man keeping me for his private pleasure. I will be an equal lover. Our coming together would be on mutual terms as it was just now."

"A lover? You mean like this?" Capturing her up in his arms again, he gave her a short, hard kiss, but it was no less passionate than any of the others they'd shared. "Is this really what you want? Grabbing a quick kiss or a longer moment or two with you on the settee or against the wall when your housekeeper is away or asleep? Is that what your heart desires?" he rasped. "Should we just go ahead and set a time and a day of the week for you to send Mrs. Lawton to the school or elsewhere so I can slip in and out of your bedchamber without her suspecting?"

"Stop it," she pleaded. "You're making it sound so tawdry. What we shared wasn't."

"No and it shouldn't be, but that's what you're asking for," he insisted angrily, turning her loose. "You are asking me to treat you less than a lady deserves. Less than I want for you and me."

"No, I'm not. Respectable widows take lovers."

"They do," he said more calmly. "Some are most content doing so. I don't want that for you. For me. I have deeper feelings for you. I can't accept you as a casual lover."

Adeline searched his eyes. She understood and believed what he was saying. But she didn't believe the good would outweigh the bad. "I want to be with you, but I won't hear more about marriage." She stepped away and pulled the tail of her bodice down over the skirt of her dress, fitting it properly.

"Then tell me why."

There was more than just one reason why she couldn't marry him. Lyon was titled and would expect to have an heir, which she could never give him. She couldn't go through another man demanding of her what she wasn't capable of giving. And she wouldn't deny Lyon what was rightfully his.

A wife to bear him a son.

Shoring up her courage with a deep breath, she said, "It would make no difference. I will not be persuaded. Now, I need to get to the school. You can see yourself out."

She started walking past him, but he caught her arm and stopped her. "What if you are with child?" he asked.

Adeline gasped. "What?" Her breath caught in her lungs and couldn't move for an instant. She felt as if she were choking. "Why would you ask that?"

"It could be true."

"No," she said adamantly. "That can't be."

"I may be a man, Adeline, but I am not naive when it comes to matters such as this. We've been together twice now and sometimes it only takes once if measures aren't taken to ensure otherwise."

"It didn't happen and it won't."

Anger clouded his features. "You can't be sure."

"I can. A woman knows these things, Lyon. I don't want to lose what we've been sharing, but I won't marry you. Being a widow gives me the right to live my life as I so choose. I have freedoms now to make my own choices that I never had before. I can go where and when I want to go. I can eat and drink what I want with no one telling me I must stay at home, or stay in bed, or—" She stopped and took a deep breath, already having said more than she intended.

"Did your husband do those things?"

She looked away from him, determined not to reveal any more of her past than she already had. It would serve no purpose. "Marriage doesn't suit me. Accept that I can't marry you and leave it at that."

"I wouldn't restrict you like that, Adeline."

"I didn't think Wake would treat me as he did, either. Now, turn me loose. I have nothing more to say about the subject."

His expression had told her he wanted to say more. He didn't want to give up, but after a moment or two, he bowed to her wishes and let go of her. He stepped back, as if realizing it was best to save his argument for another day.

"All right, I will accept your answer. And you must accept mine. I won't take you as a lover I must keep hidden."

"Then we understand each other, again," she said, feeling as if she'd stabbed herself with a knife.

"We do."

"Now, if you'll excuse me I need to re-pin my hair before I leave."

He nodded once, and said, "Usually just the threat of a ruler across the knuckles of a hand or cane on the backside is enough to make unruly children sit up and take notice that rules must be obeyed. Keep that in mind when you talk to the girls. Let them stay and give them the chance to learn. Don't send them home."

Adeline watched him walk away and her heart ached. Her arms felt cold and her stomach empty. She couldn't take back her words of rejection. Married life had been much too cruel to her. During her marriage she thought she'd learned how to endure anything that might come her way, but saying no to Lyon had been harder than drinking the foul-tasting tonics Wake had prepared for her.

Knowing Lyon wanted her, wanted to marry her would have to be enough to sustain her. She couldn't suffer through trying to be in the family way again, and she couldn't leave him childless and without an heir.

The thought of never being in his arms again was heartbreaking. Perhaps in time he would agree to keep their time together going as it was now? Surely being together sometimes was better than not being together at all.

For now, she had to put thoughts and feelings for Lyon aside. She had to decide what to do about the girls. Their violation of the rules of the school and decency could not go without a strong punishment.

After a visit up to her room, Adeline walked over to the school and into the large open front room. Mrs. Tallon and Mrs. Lawton rose from the teaching table where they were sitting and walked over to the door to stand with her. Fanny and Mathilda rose from the opposite corners at the back of the room where they'd been seated on the floor facing the wall.

Adeline looked away from the girls. She didn't like the way it made her feel to see them punished. "I'm sorry to have kept you, but the earl is a difficult man to get away from." That was no prevarication.

"Is he going to do anything terrible to the girls?" Mrs. Lawton asked worriedly. "Will he send them to the workhouse for their mischief?"

"No, no," Adeline answered softly. "I don't know what would make you think he'd ever do anything like that. He's not really a harsh man. It wouldn't even enter his mind to do something so reprehensible. He wanted to have his say, of course, and I listened. In the end, he has left all punishment to me and Mrs. Tallon. Thank you for helping her, Mrs. Lawton. You may go back home."

"Yes, my lady," she said and left the room.

"Where are the rest of the girls?" Adeline asked Mrs. Tallon.

"I had Miss Peat and Miss Hinson take them to the workroom."

"Good. Let's stand over here by the window where Fanny and Mathilda can't hear us talk." The woman followed her to the other side of the large room and Adeline asked, "Have you been thinking about what might be a fitting punishment for these two?"

"Oh, we must send them home," she said without hesitation. "They're a hindrance to all the girls."

Adeline was sure that would be her answer but she still didn't want to do it. "Do they disrupt the class in any way?"

"No. They participate in everything. Quite good at all they do, but as soon as my back is turned they're off to look at something. And it's not like they haven't been warned not to do it again. Mrs. Lawton said they were found on the earl's property. That's unpardonable as far as I'm concerned."

Was it? Adeline pursed her lips and studied over that. It had been her first reaction for their disobedience, too. If she did that, they would have few recourse for their futures. Helping the girls had been her only goal when she started the school. Not doing so would mean she'd failed and they had taken control away from her. That thought stiffened Adeline's back. She wasn't going to let the ten-year-olds win this battle.

Mrs. Tallon had been right when she said Fanny would start engaging the others with her mischief. Mathilda was her first quarry. Adeline intended to make sure she was also the last.

"If I don't agree to dismiss them, what other punishment would you suggest?"

The woman looked at Adeline as if she'd lost her mind. "What else is there, my lady? We've already tried extra work. Fanny didn't seem to mind that at all. You told me not to use my cane. Not to even bring it to the school with me. I don't know what else we can do."

Lyon had mentioned just the threat of the cane might bring about change in their behavior, and she knew it was a common practice in boys' schools. Adeline didn't even want to consider it but she must. Desperate measures were needed if she was going to keep the girls at the school.

Adeline rubbed the back of her neck, and memories of Lyon massaging her nape invaded her thoughts. She closed her eyes for a moment and allowed the memory of his gentle strength, the warmth of his touch, and the taste of his kisses wash over her. For a few minutes he'd made her forget she had to make a difficult judgment on the problem before her.

Her eyes popped open. Suddenly she was clear on what she needed to say. "Fanny and Mathilda will not be allowed to play with the other children for a full month. When you take them to the park, those two are to take writing and number lessons with them and work the entire time the others are there enjoying themselves. That is their punishment."

Mrs. Tallon's back bowed but she remained silent. The headmistress didn't know Adeline wasn't finished.

"That is their punishment for leaving the school. For their recompense to the earl for trespassing on his property, while the other girls are enjoying their time of singing, have Miss Peat keep Fanny and Mathilda in the workroom. They are to learn how to make a neckcloth—more than one design would probably be good. Once their quality of stitch has been perfected, and it has been inspected and accepted by you as flawless, they will then make the earl a dozen neck-cloths. Each one to be perfectly stitched, washed, pressed, and ready for wearing. That should keep them too busy to wander off."

A victory smile eased across the older woman's face. "That sounds adequate to me, my lady. Though, it may take a while. I've not even started teaching them how to cut a linen cloth or to make a fine stitch."

"I don't think you need to be in a hurry. Take all the time you need. When all is finished, we'll set a day for you to bring the neckcloths and the girls to me, and I'll see to it they deliver them to the earl bearing their written and verbal apologies, too."

"I'll see it's all done to your satisfaction."

"Thank you." Adeline then strode over to stand be-tween Fanny and Mathilda. She glanced from one to the other, hoping guilt and sorrow over what they'd done would show in their expressions. All she saw was girlish innocence in their faces. Sick to her stomach and denying her innate reluctance to be harsh, she squared her shoulders and said, "I don't know the reasons for your misbehavior today, but your of-fense justifies being dismissed from school and sent home."

Fanny's mouth opened in shock before she quickly said, "Don't send Mathilda home. She didn't want to

go into his house. I made her go with me because I
didn't want to go alone."

Adeline wasn't expecting either of them to say anything, but she turned to Mathilda and said, "You are
more than a head taller than Fanny. Did she force you
to do anything you didn't want to do?"

Mathilda rolled her big eyes toward Fanny and
slowly shook her head. "I wanted to see inside the
house, too."

"I thought as much. Fanny, do you want to go home
and be able to read to your mother?"

The little girl looked down at her feet for a moment
and then back to Adeline and said, "Yes, my lady."

"That's what I want, too, and because of that I won't
send either of you home today. You will remain here.
Your families sent you to this school to become a
seamstress, to be able to write, add numbers and to
read. I will not fail them because of your selfish behavior or because of a rebellious spirit or even girlish
inquisitiveness. But as of right now *you* will start obey-
ing the rules—all of them or I will have Mrs. Tallon
bring her cane to the school and give her permission
to use it on your backsides if you disobey her." Adeline looked directly at Fanny. "Do I make myself
clear?"

Fanny nodded and so did Mathilda.

"Mrs. Tallon. Please place your cane in one of the
corners of the classroom."

"Of course, Lady Wake."

Adeline held her breath and strode across the room
and out of the school without saying anything else. She
couldn't. As soon as she shut the door behind her she

swallowed down a sob. And then another. And another. Almost choking herself to keep from making a sound until she was far enough away from the school that the girls couldn't hear her.

She couldn't stop the tears rolling down her face.

She would never allow Mrs. Tallon to do such a harsh thing to any of the girls. It had been wrenching to say it. She'd had no choice. Fanny had to be frightened and believe Adeline would do it, or she'd continue on her unruly path. Adeline hoped Lyon was right and just the fear of the cane would work wonders in making one comply.

She wiped her eyes with her fingertips, knowing that saying no to Lyon's marriage proposal was even more wrenching than threatening the girls with a harsher punishment should they step out of line again.

Chapter 17

No matter whatever else might be going on in London or the world, the elite of Society always made it to the most pretentious ball of the Season. The first one—where all the madness of the ton's wealth and prestige was on display in the lavish and colorful fashion of those attending. It was only equaled by the glimmering, golden glow of candlelight sparkling off the crystal chandeliers hanging from the painted vaulted ceilings and mounted on the pristine plaster walls. The flower-decorated ballroom hummed with the constant strum of violins and cellos flowing flawlessly in tune with the melodic tinkling of ivory-covered keys, frenetic chatter, and uninhibited laughter.

Expense for the extravagant opening of the Season

was never spared. Many members of Society vied for the opportunity to be one of the chosen few who gave generously for the honor of being a host for the spectacular evening of debuting the new bevy of young ladies who were now on display and eligible for the marriage mart. Amidst the glamour of the evening there was also a tremendous amount of rubbing elbows for business and political purposes, kissing of ladies' hands, and dancing for everyone as the London Season began. Smaller parties would be held at the Great Hall all through the spring, but none would compare to this one.

That's the way the ton wanted it.

Lyon and his father stood facing the entrance to the ballroom with three other gentlemen, drinking champagne and discussing with, or rather listening to, Marksworth defend the Prince's continuous pageantry week after week and the outrageous expenditures that were allowed at Carlton House, the Prince's London residence. Marksworth was on the watch for his intended, Miss Helen Ballingbrand. That was remarkable. The marquis actually seemed eager for her to arrive so he could introduce her.

The room teemed with elegantly gowned ladies and splendidly dressed gentlemen. Some stood in small groups chatting and laughing while others twirled and swept across the dance floor that was a mere stone's throw away.

Tonight was the first time Lyon had ever been early to a champagne-toasting event and the infectious merriment of the crowd wasn't the reason. Adeline was. He'd been telling his father that he wanted love before marriage almost since the day he entered Society. Now he had that. But it had to be real love both for him and for the lady he chose.

He should have told Adeline that afternoon in her drawing room that he loved her before he asked her to marry him, but he wasn't sure that would have made a difference. And he wasn't sure he'd realized it himself until after he left. Love was the reason he wouldn't agree to the kind of relationship she was asking for. That wasn't the way to treat the lady he loved. Her feelings for him wasn't the problem.

It was marriage she was rejecting. Not him.

Lyon had no doubts that Adeline was the lady he wanted to spend the rest of his life with. Within moments of seeing her the fateful night they met, he'd known he was attracted to her, to her courage to stand up to him, her boldness in striking him. His attraction to her was fast and hot from the beginning. She'd tempted him, challenged him, and angered him that night. And she continued to do so. She was brave, caring, generous, and so passionate he ached to be with her again. She satisfied him. Completed him. And he believed she felt all those things about him, too.

But she wasn't willing to marry him.

She had deep hurts that haunted her. He'd seen glimpses of them. But she was so damn good at hiding her emotions most of the time that they weren't easy to detect. Her husband had obviously limited her freedoms. What else had happened in her marriage that kept her out of Society? An ailment? A fondness for drink that she hadn't been able to control for a time?

Whatever it was, did it now keep her from committing to him?

He couldn't press her to tell him until he knew she was ready to face her past herself.

It had been almost a week since he'd seen her. That made for a difficult week. It would have been so easy to send over a note and tell her he'd be over after her housekeeper's light went out. She'd made it clear that was what she wanted. An occasional lover. Lyon had scoffed at the idea. Just the thought of it had made him angry. Yet, he'd lost count of the times he'd written the note, thinking to accept her offer, her affection the way she wanted him to. As a lover. But no. All of the notes had been thrown into the fire and never sent.

He wouldn't give in to a life he didn't want for her or himself. He might be an impatient brute but he was a man of honor and he couldn't bend to her will in a matter as important as this.

There was another reason he'd wanted to be at the ball when Adeline arrived. He had assured her no one would dare say anything to her about her impromptu visit to his home. Regardless of his aunt's believable fib to Mrs. Feversham, the problem was, Lyon hadn't completely convinced himself. Society was fickle as a whole, though they prided themselves on being stable and consistent. Because the gentlemen of the ton had reasons of their own for not wanting to besmirch Lady Wake's reputation, he hoped the ladies of the ton would follow their lead.

However, it was best he be available when she arrived in case a toffee-nosed matron decided to take her to task over one of her assumed transgressions. It wasn't that Lyon didn't think Adeline could handle herself if rebuked by one of the formidable ladies of the ton. He had first-hand knowledge of just how strong and capable she was. And he'd have to let her do it alone, just as he'd remained quiet and let her have her say to his gaming club that afternoon in his home. But then, she'd need someone to talk to.

That would be him.

He would have to fight Lady Kitson Fairbright and Mrs. Brina Feld to do it. They had shown him they would take up arms for Adeline the afternoon he took the tarts over to her house. As soon as they saw him, they each rose to stand slightly in front of her so he'd know she wasn't alone. He didn't mind. They were true friends, but Lyon was now her protector. They would have to step out of that role.

Adeline was his to defend now.

He wanted to see her. Wanted her to see him watching for her. Letting her be herself at the ball without hindrance from him but all the while reminding her he was there and the only man for her. Pursuing a lady in earnest was a new way of life for him and he was still getting used to it. He'd always assumed that whenever he fell in love, the lady would consequentially fall in love with him. That she didn't want to marry surprised him, and had angered him for a time. Now he was resolute in making her change her mind. One thing he was certain of, she wasn't ready for him to go charging over to her door with flowers and another proposal of marriage.

Not yet.

But she would.

That he'd been the first man to touch her since her husband's death was further evidence they were meant to be together. Two years had been ample time for her to find comfort in the arms of a man. Something had held her back. He felt certain it wasn't lack of offers, and he had no doubts there would be others who would vie for her favors until he could publicly claim her heart and her hand.

Something had happened in her marriage. Something that disturbed her so greatly she didn't want to consider marriage again. Maybe it was just her lack of freedom to do the things she wanted. She didn't know him well enough to know he wouldn't take that away from her? He wanted her just the way she was. Every self-confident, passionate inch of her.

Lyon scoffed a short laugh to himself. Ah, but it appeared Adeline was demanding of him the one thing that was hardest for him to do. Be patient. So he would wait until she realized she wanted him for a husband—not just as a lover. It was damn difficult for a man who didn't usually have to work for what he wanted.

For her, he was willing.

There was no reason for Lyon and his father to move from their ideal position near the entrance and mill through the crushing crowd. Other gentlemen were quite willing to make the trek over to them in order to have a moment or two of the marquis' time.

Lyon and his father had their differences, but Lyon loved him. He was one of the most respected and approachable members of the peerage. Patience and intelligence concerning matters people brought to his attention encouraged his popularity. He was genuinely fond of most everyone and was always willing to listen to their questions, arguments, stories, or rants no matter how unimportant they seemed to him or others.

Not so for his son. Lyon had never found it within himself to be as forbearing as Marksworth with people who wanted a favor, an introduction, or to just be seen with a man who wore a title along with his name.

"Good evening, Marksworth, Lyon."

Lyon shifted restlessly. Annoyance shuddered through him at the voice but he and his father turned and acknowledged Viscount Thurston with polite greetings and exchanged pleasantries about the celebratory ball. Because the viscount was a member of Lyon's gaming club, he knew Thurston to be a fair gentleman in all his business dealings and treatment of others. He was good with a bow and a pistol, and a blade. He could handle a horse better than most. The two got along amicably, and the man had visited at Lyonwood a time or two. Lyon hadn't disliked the viscount until he'd shown an interest in Adeline. He couldn't blame the man for that, but Lyon now saw him as an adversary.

"I wanted to ask a favor of you, Lyon," Thurston said.

"What's that?" he answered, though he knew exactly what the viscount wanted.

"I was hoping you'd introduce me to Lady Wake tonight. I understand she's going to be here."

"Unless you find someone else who can do it," Lyon answered, seemingly uninterested, when truthfully the thought of her smiling at Thurston had Lyon tight as a violin string. It would be a cold day in Hades before he'd introduce the viscount or any other man to Adeline. He had no intention of helping another man pursue her.

"I'm not sure how many people remember her or have been formally introduced to her. I dare say not many are as *familiar* with her as you seem to be"—he smiled—"with her being such a close neighbor."

Lyon's hand tightened on his champagne glass as his eyes narrowed. If Thurston was trying to rile him, he was successful. "You dare say?" he repeated the viscount's words, feeling the string about to snap.

"I'll do it for you, Thurston," Marksworth said in an easy tone that took the matter at hand away from both men. "Be happy to as soon as she arrives. I'll find you and do the honors."

"Thank you," Thurston said with a nod, noting that the marquis was dismissing him as well as humoring him. "Very kind of you. I'll look forward to it." He gave another nod to Lyon and walked away.

Certain his expression hadn't changed, Lyon looked at his father. "I thought we agreed you stopped speaking for me when you sent me off to Oxford."

His father clapped him once on the back gingerly. "I'd never do such a foolish thing. A father never ceases to come to his son's aid. You were about to give away every card you had in your hand. Next time you might want to look at them before you start laying them down. I don't think you are holding a fist full of aces when it comes to the countess."

Lyon shrugged off the truth of his father's comment. "I don't care if Thurston knows. I'd rather chew nails into powder than introduce him to Adeline."

"The man has the right to ask for an introduction. From what I understand, you still haven't claimed her."

He had. He just couldn't announce it. Until Adeline was ready. Her reservations about marriage and what she wanted had to be respected. Whether or not he agreed with her wishes.

"Stay of out this," he muttered to his father and stopped another server to exchange his empty glass for a filled one.

"Wouldn't dream of getting involved in your life," Marksworth said with an easy smile. He turned back to the gentlemen standing with them and continued his conversation about the Prince.

From the corner of his eye Lyon saw Prichard. The man nodded to him and then tilted his head toward Thurston. Lyon grunted under his breath. Was every man who saw Adeline at his house going to ask for an introduction? He'd known tonight wouldn't be easy. Gentlemen were already lining up to win Adeline's favor. His gut twisted. He didn't know a one of them who would reject an offer to just be a lover. Hell, that's what most of them would want anyway.

Ignoring the man, Lyon went back to watching the door, and a few moments later Adeline stopped at the entranceway with Lady Kitson Fairbright and Mrs. Brina Feld. Each looked stunning, but he had eyes only for Adeline. She wore an amber-colored gown banded with thin strips of yellow ribbon. Her beautiful, slender neck was perfect for the choker of amber stones nestled around it and woven into her hair.

Lyon quickly glanced around the room. A few ladies had stopped their conversations to watch the three widows. Others joined them. The noise level softened around the room as more people looked their way. There were nods, glances and whispers. He wanted to be the first to greet her, gently squeeze her fingertips and kiss the back of her gloved hand as a proper gentleman would do. Instinct told him that wasn't the way to woo her. She knew she already had his attention and she needed no show of outward affection from him. He'd let her settle into the room, talk with people, maybe even have a dance or two before he approached her. It'd be a struggle, but he would manage. This was her first evening back in Society. He had to let her handle it as she wished. He would talk, laugh, and sip his champagne. Maybe he'd have a dance or two himself. Anything to hurry the night along.

The Duke of Sprogsfield, Lady Kitson Fairbright's father-in-law, walked up to the three ladies. Not surprisingly, the young and strapping Mr. Harvey Brightstone was with him and the first eligible gentleman to sidle up to the three ladies as they descended the steps into the ballroom. Brightstone had been looking for a bride with a plump purse for two years. Mr. Edward Wallace was another and he was the second to approach the threesome.

The crowd around the widows quickly became so thick Lyon could no longer see Adeline.

As he suspected, there would be no small amount of gentlemen standing in line for Lady Wake and her two friends this evening. Nor it appeared would there be shunning by any of the matrons of the ton. They watched for a few seconds longer and slowly went back to their conversations as if completely uninterested in the widows' arrival. Perhaps his father and his aunt had nipped the gossip in its tracks after all.

Marksworth turned away from the other men standing with them and in a quiet voice said, "Lady Wake is here."

"So you remember her," Lyon said.

"No. I don't remember ever seeing her before, but I remember the two widows with her so I'll pretend I do when I speak to her later this evening. It's easier to do that than go through an introduction. Lady Kitson Fairbright and Mrs. Brina Feld didn't quit Society after they married as did the countess. But recognizing the other two ladies isn't the reason I knew the countess had entered the room. I felt the change in you."

"That's not good." Lyon stopped a server and again exchanged his empty glass for a full one.

"Don't worry. No one else knows you as I do."

"Somewhat reassuring," he answered and sipped his drink.

"Do you think this time you might have found love?"

Yes.

Lyon remained silent. His feelings for Adeline weren't something he could discuss with his father. Marksworth knew it but never stopped trying.

"I didn't expect an answer," his father grumbled. "But then you know that silence can be an answer. I take it that for some reason you decided someone else should be the first gentleman to greet her tonight."

"There's no hurry."

"Oh, good lord, I know that," his father said in a frustrated tone. "I've lost track of how long I've been trying to get you in a hurry to settle on a bride and marry."

"Eight years," Lyon said.

"Ah. You're right. No reason to rush anything tonight. You're wise to let the flurry of flapping coattails slow down before you approach her. That might give you an edge."

Lyon grunted a laugh.

"I saw Lady Wake's eyes. She was searching for you."

"What?" Lyon's breath kicked up.

"Ah, so you are interested in her. It's not as if you couldn't dominate her time as I feel free to do with Miss Ballingbrand since we are betrothed and will be married shortly after the Season ends."

"This is not the night to start that conversation again, Marksworth. That is not a route I intend to travel."

"I didn't think so, but it is the night for you to meet all the young ladies who've just entered Society. I still hold hope one of them will please you. If not the countess, perhaps another. Turn around, I'm about to introduce you to the lovely young lady I met a few weeks ago. I mentioned her to you. Mr. William Palmont's daughter. She'd be perfect for you."

Lyon turned and saw the stout, bearded man and his daughter. "I've already been introduced to her," Lyon said.

"Really?" Marksworth raised his eyebrows.

"I can't believe something happened in London that you don't know about." Lyon lifted one corner of his mouth in a grin. "I was invited to his house for a dinner party last week and accidently met her. Much as you did a few weeks ago I suspect. I think Palmont wanted to make sure every eligible peer saw her before tonight in case any of them wanted to make an offer for a match before the Season began."

"Hmm. He must not have had any takers," Marksworth murmured just before the two stopped in front of them.

Lyon greeted the cheerful, green-eyed Miss Palmont and her father. There didn't seem to be anything about the young miss to dislike. As a gentleman, he did all that was proper and expected of him concerning her, including asking her to save him a dance later in the evening. After a few minutes, he found an easy way to excuse himself from the trio when he looked up and saw Cordelia walking into the ballroom.

"You are looking beautiful enough to be the diamond of the Season, Aunt," he offered and kissed her hand.

She laughed. "You are such a dear. You make me wish I had more nephews to flatter me."

"I would never do that. I only tell you the truth and you know it. You are looking exceptionally beautiful tonight."

"Well, it's a wonder. I do get weary of telling Mrs. Feversham that it doesn't matter if she has a spyglass, it wasn't you she saw with Lady Wake in your back garden. Nor was it you she saw a few days ago traipsing past the hedgerow half-dressed with a girl from the school on each side of you."

"So she saw that?"

"By the saints, Lyon! Was it true? I've convinced the poor lady she's drinking too many elixirs for the pain in her hip and she must stop. Heavens! What is going on at your house?"

"Nothing you want to know about."

"I do want to know if I'm going to keep defending you. Please get me a glass of champagne, Lyon. You know I love the taste of it and I'm suddenly feeling in need of a sip."

Giving his aunt an indulgent smile, Lyon answered. "I know you like holding the glass." His gaze swept over the room. He saw Adeline talking with Thurston. He couldn't say the man hadn't warned him.

"For the love of heaven, Lyon, you and Lady Wake need to be more careful."

"Aunt," he cautioned, "I can't speak to that."

"Don't tell me this isn't a discussion you want to have with me because I think it's high time we had it. I've been a widow for twenty years now. I've had my share of lovers, but I was careful to keep my affairs of the heart a secret and so should you."

Lyon blinked at the surprising admission. "You've had lovers? I didn't know."

"Of course you didn't," she said. "That's the way it's supposed to be. These things are kept private."

"Why didn't you marry?" he asked, wondering why she wouldn't want the more acceptable way of life. "I know you had offers."

"Yes, but none I ever wanted enough to give up my freedom for."

"Because you didn't love them?" he asked, thinking of Adeline's wishes and wanting to understand his aunt's reluctance to marry.

"Heavens no. Unlike you and my dear sister, love was never something that interested me. Thanks to your father I didn't need money or prestige. And I didn't need love or marriage for what I wanted from my lovers."

Lyon studied over her words. He could accept that there were some women who didn't want or need a husband, but he had to believe Adeline wasn't one of them. For some reason a lover was all she wanted from him.

"I don't know what to think of young widows today," his aunt said with a wisp of exasperation in her voice. "It's as if they have no care for the proprieties Society expects of them. Lady Wake shouldn't be seen in your back garden again under any circumstances, and you shouldn't be using the girls as a reason to go to her house."

"Is that what you think I was doing?"

"I can only assume as Mrs. Feversham does. Please do me a favor and take better care with your dalliances."

"That woman doesn't miss a thing. What kind of spyglass does the woman have?"

"A good one," Cordelia stated. "The problem is that you and Lady Wake keep giving her things to see with it."

Chapter 18

Adeline realized she didn't remember the steps of the slow quadrille as well as she'd expected she would. It had been four years since she'd danced, and the steps were quite intricate. And, she'd hadn't had much practice dancing with a man before she'd married. Viscount Thurston didn't seem to mind that she lifted her hand at the wrong time, hopped on the wrong foot, or started turning in the wrong direction.

He was handsome to look at, tall and slender. His hair and eyes were a classic dark shade of brown and his features had a boyish charm. After only a few minutes with him, his light chuckle told her he didn't take life too seriously. Very much unlike the Earl of Lyonwood, who was too serious about most things.

Including her reputation and respectability.

Adeline, Julia, and Brina had entered the ballroom at the same time. They'd planned it that way more than a year ago so they could be one another's companions for the evening. Brina looked beautiful in a dark gray dress that was softened only by sheer sleeves and cuffs. A row of dainty silk roses edged the neckline and outlined the waistband of her gown.

Julia had always had her own idea when it came to what was and wasn't desirable attire for widows. Of the three of them, her gown was the most fashionable. Some in Society would consider the purple she wore much too bright with one too many flounces on the skirt. A few of the older ladies might even say it was scandalous and inappropriate that each one was scalloped and banded in a wide gold-colored ribbon.

Their entrance had quieted the ballroom for a few seconds. Thankfully the hush hadn't lasted long before everyone went back to their conversations. Adeline was fairly certain it was because the Duke of Sprogsfield was the first to greet them. Not many would be willing to slight anyone the crusty old duke greeted. Adeline had caught a few haughty looks and more than one sniff of a nose high in the air but she didn't let it bother her. Many formal introductions had been dispensed. Most everyone reminded her they'd met the year of her debut. For most of the hour she'd been at the ball it had been enjoyable listening to the chatter and the music, and trying to remember the dance steps.

The music ended, and she and Lord Thurston clapped as they left the dance floor.

"I must apologize for not being as polished on my

feet as I once was, my lord," she said with a smile as they walked toward the side of the room. "I felt as if I was missing every other step."

"I don't know what you're talking about, my lady. I didn't notice anything other than how graceful you are," he replied.

"You are too kind, and I appreciate it."

"I'm not being kind, Lady Wake. Truthful. Would you like for me to get you something to drink?"

"No, thank you. I don't want to hold you up if you have someone else to dance with."

"I have no one else on my mind tonight." He stopped and looked directly into her eyes. "I'm interested only in you. I thought about it while we were dancing and decided I want to make my intentions known before I get lost in the trail of gentlemen I know are headed for your door and your heart."

Intentions?

That was about as blunt as one could be. She knew offers would be forthcoming. A wealthy widow was a prize in Society, as her brother-in-law had told her on more than one occasion when he'd offered to arrange another marriage for her. He'd gently told her that most men would be respectful but not shy in seeking her attentions. A marriage would help her avoid the indelicacy of such. She'd politely made it clear to him she planned to remain a widow and needed no help.

"I'm flattered that you think that."

"Good. I believed you were the type of lady who would appreciate candor. I was at Lyonwood's house during the storm when you—shall we say, came to borrow an umbrella."

"Yes, that is a kind way to say what happened that afternoon."

"I saw your courage and fervency that day, and it was quite stunning."

"I remember that afternoon, too." Which had led to that night when she'd been held and kissed with all the desire she'd dreamed about. Adeline swallowed down the sweet memories. "And I do appreciate your straight-forwardness about what transpired," she said, realizing she wasn't offended at all by his direct approach.

"You are the kind of lady many men dream about but few will have the opportunity to get to know personally. Perhaps intimately."

There was no reason for Lord Thurston to treat her as an innocent young lady who knew nothing about the intimacy that happened between a man and woman, but she would have expected a more subtle approach from him. He was as fit and handsome as Lyon, but she felt no desire to be with him in an intimate way when she looked at him.

"I can't speak to that, but I do think one should always know where they stand with the other person."

He smiled. "I would welcome the invitation to call—"

"Oh, I apologize for interrupting you, Lord Thurston," she said suddenly. "I see Mrs. Feld motioning to me and she looks distressed. I fear the modiste might have left a pin in her gown or she's lost the heel of a shoe. Please excuse me, my lord. I must go see what she needs."

Not taking her word for it, the viscount turned and looked at Brina who was motioning for Adeline to come to her. "Yes, it does appear your friend is trying to get your attention." He bowed. "Of course, go to her. We'll talk again later."

"Yes, at parties and dinners. I would be happy to dance and converse with you, but as you were direct with me, before I go, let me be so with you. I am not accepting any gentleman's attention, so there will be no invitations from me forthcoming."

Adeline made a hasty retreat and went over to Brina. "What's wrong? You look frantic."

"I am." Brina huffed. "Mr. Brightstone was almost making our wedding plans before I could get off the dance floor with him. What an oaf! Doesn't he know I'm still in mourning?"

"No," Adeline said softly. "He doesn't. Brina, you must accept that as far as Society is concerned you have passed your time of mourning."

"I don't feel as if I have," she answered softly and lowered her lashes over her eyes. "Not yet, anyway. And, I don't think I want to be."

"There's nothing wrong with continuing to feel that way." Adeline's heart felt heavy for her friend. "I know you still miss your husband very much. Give yourself more time to grieve him. Everyone will understand. Well, most everyone anyway."

"Yes," she said, giving her attention back to Adeline. "I was worried about you when I saw Lord Thurston looking at you as if he were ready to have you as a tasty dessert at the end of the night. I assumed he was sending you the same message Mr. Brightstone sent me. I was trying to save you the embarrassment of being propositioned your first night back in Society."

Adeline laughed. "I think I can handle the viscount's forward behavior. I wasn't the least put off by it. And you don't need to be upset by any gentleman wanting attention or favor from you. You are eligible. But you are also free to accept their attention or brush them off."

"Then perhaps I'm not ready to come back into Society."

"You can't hide away from life any longer. You can't hide from men. None of us can. We are moving forward as we've discussed many times."

"I think all men consider we are easy prey."

From the corner of her eye, Adeline saw Lyon talking to his aunt. "Not all of them," she said. "Some are honorable."

"Most of them think that just because we are widows we want a man slipping into our bedchamber."

"Well—"

"Well, what?" Julia said, coming from behind Adeline to join them.

"Yes," Brina said, looking a bit horrified. "Well what? What happened between you and the viscount? Did he offer to pay you a visit?"

"Yes," Adeline declared. "I declined. I have no interest in the man."

"But you do have interest in Lyon," Julia said.

Adeline thought about that and said, "Yes." She was surprised at how easy it was. "I've admitted as much to both of you before."

"How much of an interest?" Brina asked. "You haven't—I mean you haven't—"

"She has," Julia answered quietly.

"Adeline, you told Julia and not me!" Brina exclaimed.

"She didn't have to tell me," Julia answered. "I see it in her face every time his name is mentioned. He tapped into her soul."

"My feelings for the earl really haven't changed since the first night I met him. They were vivid and passionate then and they still are. I knew then he was different from any man I'd ever met."

"But now there is a different kind of passion between you two," Julia offered as more of a statement than a question.

"Yes, or maybe it's more like an addition. He— he—" Adeline glanced toward Lyon as she searched for the right words to describe what she was feeling, and suddenly realized it was more than the wanton desire they shared. That was how it started but now it was love. Beautiful, sweet love.

"You don't have to explain," Julia whispered.

"Of course she does," Brina exclaimed, wide-eyed with questions and not wanting to give up on wanting to understand. "He what?"

Adeline felt as if a weight had lifted from her shoulders now that she'd admitted to herself that she loved the earl. She looked at Brina and said, "He makes me feel wanted. He makes me happy and angry. He makes me feel peaceful and so many other things. I can't explain all he makes me feel other than to say *everything*. Brina, I don't know why so many emotions rise up in me and take notice whenever I look at him."

"Do you think you've fallen in love with him?" she asked.

Hesitating to be so open with her feelings while she was still sorting them out for herself, Adeline said, "My feelings on marriage haven't changed. I want no part of being bound to a man as his wife and all that he would expect of me. I know I'm not strong enough to put myself through that burden again."

"How does he feel?" Julia asked.

"I believe his emotions are as conflicted as mine, but for different reasons." Adeline glanced to where Lyon had been standing. He was gone. Her gaze searched the room. He was walking away from his aunt and heading toward the entrance to the ballroom. Was he leaving? Before they had a chance to speak to each other? How could he be so callous toward her?

For a moment she thought to turn away and think good riddance. But then she knew she couldn't— wouldn't—let him get by with treating her so shabbily just because she refused to marry him.

"What are you going to do?" Brina asked, gently touching Adeline's shoulder.

"Right now," she said, feeling more than a little slighted and angry, "it looks as if Lyon is already leaving the ball. I'm going to talk before he does. Excuse me."

Adeline tried not to rush and cause attention to herself, but the fear of Lyon leaving before they spoke gripped her. She knew he was upset with her because she rejected him. That was nothing new. He was always upset with her. Perhaps that was part of his allure. She smiled or nodded at everyone she passed, but didn't allow anyone to slow her progress as she made her way through the crowd, up the three steps to where he was speaking to the attendant in charge of everyone's wrap.

So he really was leaving and without saying hello or goodbye to her. That tore her heart.

"Lord Lyonwood," she called, hoping her voice didn't sound as shaky as she felt.

He turned around. Their gazes met. She was winded and her chest heaved. She realized she wasn't angry. Just hurt.

She swallowed and tried to catch her breath. "Were you going to quit the ball without speaking to me at least once?"

His eyes questioned her. "Would it matter to you if I was?"

"Yes. Of course. I wanted to say hello to you."

"You look angry."

"Do I? Perhaps I am. I didn't think you would leave without so much as a nod in my direction."

"Is that what you thought?" he asked.

"Isn't it true?"

He walked to stand before her. "You're beautiful."

Adeline's stomach felt as if it turned over.

Other gentlemen had said she looked beautiful, but they had added the word *tonight*. Lyon hadn't. She could tell by the way his gaze swept her face that to him she was always beautiful. Not just because she was fancied up for a ball tonight.

"I do have to say, Lady Wake, that crimson is your color."

Her hurt that he was leaving didn't vanish, but she

smiled and then laughed softly, briefly. She knew he would eventually get around to mentioning the red stays she had on the first night they met. She didn't mind. Thankfully she'd gotten over the embarrassment of being caught in the moment of fantasy.

"Every lady should wear a forbidden color at least once, don't you think?"

"Indeed I do. And, I like seeing you laugh."

"I laugh and smile, too, my lord," she said.

"Then I'd like to see you do both more often."

"Our conversations don't seem to lean to the more frivolous topics that merit such humor. They are usually so, so—"

"Heated."

"Yes. I suppose that sums them up well."

"I must take the blame for that."

"Good," she answered and smiled again.

"I will take the fault for many things, Adeline, but I won't take the responsibility for us not being together. My feelings haven't changed. Marry me."

Adeline lost her breath for a few seconds. "That is one of those serious discussions that doesn't bring about many smiles, my lord. My feelings haven't changed either."

He nodded.

Adeline squared her shoulders and said, "I hope the girls aren't singing too loudly in the mornings now that Miss Hinson plays the pianoforte for them each day."

"Not at all. However, I now find myself wishing they were running outside laughing, squealing, and shouting at the top of their lungs to one another rather than singing inside."

"What?" She gave him an incredulous look. "I believe you would grumble about anything, my lord. Not even wanting the girls to sing after you gave them the pianoforte? Next, you'll be upset if you hear one of them breathing."

Lyon chuckled. "I hope I never get that bad, Countess."

"You *are* that bad, my lord."

"Perhaps I have good reason this time. I do find it maddening when I can't get the tune of *'Here we go 'round the bramble bush on a cold and frosty morn'* out of my mind no matter how hard I try. I find myself humming the tune while I'm walking down the stairs, looking over the account books, or in the middle of a card game."

Adeline laughed, too. "You cannot be pleased."

His gaze swept up and down her face. Their gazes wouldn't separate. "No, I *can* be. *You* please me."

Yes. And he pleased her. A bond of respect and desire had developed between them the first night they met, and it hadn't been broken. But neither of them was willing to accept the other on their terms.

"I admit the same thing has happened to me about the song. I'll have to ask Mrs. Tallon to let that one rest for a while."

He nodded. "What did you decide to do about Miss Fanny and Miss Mathilda?"

"After talking with Mrs. Tallon, I came up with what I considered an appropriate punishment for them, and I haven't heard of either of them doing anything wrong since."

"So you didn't send them home?"

"No. I couldn't. That went against every reason I wanted to open the school. Besides, your advice was true. I decided if I wasn't going to let an earl get the best of me, I couldn't let two little girls do it either."

He chuckled softly. "That's what I expected. I hear you and Lady Kitson Fairbright and Mrs. Brina Feld are being heralded for your courage in opening the school for such unfortunate children."

Adeline saw in his expression and heard in his voice admiration. Still, she said, "Heralded? That word seems much overstated."

"I'm not making it up. I'm sure you've heard some of the comments tonight. I must have heard *those wonderful widows* at least three or four times already."

Adeline gave him a bit of a grin and then sighed. "I've received some questions about it. Mostly what I've heard is curiosity. I'm sure there are times you think we're more like wicked widows for putting a boarding school next door to you."

"Wicked? I would never think of the word *wicked* in the same thought with you, my lady. Well . . ." He grinned. "Maybe wickedly wonderful."

"Perhaps that is why I find that some of the older ladies are not receiving me as well as they are Brina and Julia."

"I neither see nor hear any jealousy in your voice about that."

"There is none. Ladies have a right to be upset with me for barging in on a men's card game if they wish—though I truly didn't know what was going on when I entered. It was scandalous just the same and could have been more so. I have a feeling you had something to do with minimizing and quelling the severity of it. I am only concerned if it reflects badly on the school."

"A scandal would only bother me if it hurt you in any way."

The attendant Lyon had been talking to walked up and said, "Excuse me, my lord. Here is the cape you asked for."

"Thank you," he said, taking a lady's black velvet wrap from her and placing it over his forearm.

"Aunt Delia was feeling chilled and asked that I get it for her. I was going to hand this off to her and go find you."

Adeline's breath sped up. "So you weren't leaving?"

He gave her a roguish grin. "Without speaking to you? Without dancing with you? No, but I like that it made you angry to think I was going to."

"You are a scoundrel," she said.

He reached out and took two glasses from a tray as a server presented it. "I'd never leave without sharing a glass of champagne with you." He gave a glass to her. "For tonight, a truce. There will be no more heated conversations. No talk of a subject that doesn't bring a smile to your face."

"For tonight only?"

"I can't promise more than that. I want you to tell me about your childhood, Adeline."

She gave him a curious look. "What kind of statement is that?"

"One that should make you smile. Most childhoods are happy ones, aren't they? See you are already smiling."

"That's because I can see the boredom settling into your eyes before I even get started."

"No. You don't see that, Adeline. You could never be boring to me."

"You're serious. You want to hear about my childhood."

"I do. I want to know everything about you. Where and how you grew up seems a good place to start."

Adeline felt a tightening in the center of her shoulders. No. She couldn't tell him everything. She didn't want him to know everything.

"Excuse me for interrupting Lyon, Lady Wake." The Marquis of Marksworth bowed. "I'd like to introduce my intended, Miss Helen Ballingbrand."

Adeline looked into one of the sweetest faces she'd ever seen as formal introductions were carried out. Miss Ballingbrand wasn't exceptionally lovely but her complexion was flawless. She had light brown hair and eyes and a fragile smile that seemed more fixed than natural. The marquis was an older Lyon. Tall, regal, and about as handsome and confident as a man could be.

"Lady Wake," Miss Ballingbrand said, "Lord Marksworth told me about the school you started. I think that's one of the most wonderful and compassionate things I've heard of anyone doing."

Adeline quickly glanced at Lyon, who gave her an *I told you so* look. "That's kind of you to say. There aren't nearly enough boarding schools for girls and certainly not for the more unfortunate ones."

"I'm afraid I didn't know there were any, but then I was tutored at home and my knowledge of such things is limited to what my teachers wanted me to know. Your school must be one of the first?"

"Perhaps. In any case, we have much hope for its success in helping these young girls."

"Do you think it might be possible for me to call on you one day for a visit so I can hear more about it?"

"Yes, of course. I enjoy talking about the school and welcome your interest."

"Ah, Lyon. There you are with my wrap," Mrs. Carbonall said, stepping up beside him. "I wondered what happened to you. Lady Wake, you are looking lovely as are you, Miss Ballingbrand."

"Thank you, Mrs. Carbonall," Adeline answered, feeling a note of sadness that her time alone with Lyon had come to an end.

"And, Marksworth," Cordelia added, "I hear congratulations are in order—for the fourth time."

"Yes, thank you," the marquis said. "And I see you are in your favorite color tonight—green."

"So you did learn something from Shakespeare's plays when you were at Oxford. I wondered. I think it's the first time you've let your knowledge of any of his writings be known."

"Oh, I've done it many times, Mrs. Carbonall. Perhaps you weren't fast enough to catch on to them."

Adeline moved closer to Lyon and whispered, "Are your aunt and father always so contentious?"

He smiled. "No. Usually they don't even speak to each other. That's the way that makes both of them happiest. I just heard the call for a waltz. Since you won't marry me, dance with me."

Chapter 19

A canopy of blue sky and warm sun covered Lyon and his father like a blanket as their horses slowly picked their way across the acreage of Hyde Park. There was enough chill in the air to make his wool coat comfortable without needing a cloak or scarf to keep his neck warm. The wide expanse of sloping, tree-dotted land was sprinkled with carriages, carts, and people out enjoying the late spring weather or making their trek to attend their daily chores. Some on horseback, others walking, and a few seated on the ground enjoying refreshments from a straw basket. The park was loud with sounds of wheels rumbling over less-than-favorable terrain, shouts from drivers managing stubborn mules, and horses galloping in the distance.

His father didn't often ask Lyon to go for a ride with him anymore. They used to ride together several times a week when they were both in London and the weather as fair as it was today. The past couple of years Marksworth had found he'd rather use the more convenient and comfortable velvet-cushioned carriage to carry him around than a leather saddle strapped to the back of a horse. Lyon never minded. He would be happy with a stroll. His father irritated the devil out of him at times but Marksworth was still his favorite companion.

Both their mounts knew the paths well, and they allowed the mares to pick the pace. Lyon and Marksworth's conversation had been the usual topics they'd discuss on a mid-afternoon outing—the usual issues facing parliament, the King's declining health, the Prince's lavish spending, and the gossip of who had or hadn't caught up his wagers at White's.

A lull in their discussions gave Lyon time to think about Adeline. He'd seen her thrice in the last month at parties they'd attended. That wasn't nearly enough. They exchanged plenty of long glances at each other but their conversations had been limited. The most important issue between them was never mentioned. There were too many dinners, balls, operas, and such events each evening for him to guess which she'd be attending. He'd tried. Short of asking her, he couldn't know where she'd be or the time. At the Duke of Middlecastle's house he'd actually been seated across from her. They each talked more with the guests on their right and left than to each other. It wasn't what he wanted. By the way she looked and smiled at him, he was convinced it wasn't what she wanted either. She hadn't found it within herself to trust him with her heart or that he would be a different kind of husband than her first one.

It was as if each was waiting for the other to make the move to give in to the others' wishes. He still watched for her as he shaved each morning, but that hadn't proved rewarding either. She hadn't been back to that part of her garden.

"I suppose you've heard the latest gossip," his father offered after a time of quiet.

There had to be a reason his father said that. Lyon didn't want to react, but found himself asking, "Probably not. It seems to change daily. What is it?"

"Not one of the three widows has allowed anyone to call on them. Have you heard?"

"That none of them has? No," Lyon answered as his horse shuddered beneath him and pulled restlessly on the bridle. He had heard some of the men in his card club grousing that they'd been snubbed by Lady Wake and Mrs. Feld. Lyon couldn't say that bothered him.

"Don't you find that surprising?"

Hearing that his aunt had had lovers during the past twenty years was surprising. It was downright heartening to hear that Adeline hadn't accepted anyone's overtures. He'd thought as much, but couldn't be sure. On the occasions they were at the same gatherings, she'd had no shortage of gentlemen by her side, but Lyon hadn't noticed that she'd given any one of them more attention than another.

"Some of the gents think the three of them have made a pact not to accept callers this Season. It seems a reasonable conclusion since they all three decided to sit out the first year they could have returned to Society after their mourning had passed. They attend every party together and seem to stick together like poesies in a bouquet wrapped tight with a ribbon."

"Could be," Lyon offered carelessly. "The ladies are quite fond of each other. They visit Lady Wake, but I haven't seen any gentlemen's carriages at her house."

"So you're watching."

"Only when I'm home." Lyon looked at his father and grinned. Marksworth laughed. Lyon probably looked more closely than Mrs. Feversham with her spyglass.

"I'm sure you have your reasons for not declaring for her."

"I do."

"I'd ask you what they were but I know you won't tell me. I'll leave you to them. However, it's certainly not because she's not interested in you or you in her. I've watched her. She can't take her eyes off you."

Lyon grimaced. "Are you watching her?"

Marksworth shifted in the saddle and rolled his shoulders. "I couldn't do anything else the other night at Middlecastle's dinner party. She was right in my line of vision and you were in hers. But since you won't tell me what's going on between the two of you, I'll tell you why I asked you to join me for a ride today. I'm getting married on Friday. You'll come?"

"Of course. I like Miss Ballingbrand. She seems to suit you. I'm just surprised you're not waiting until the Season is over and parliament has ended."

"I had expected to." Marksworth chuckled under his

breath. "But there's hardly two weeks left of the parties so I can forgo them. She's ready to marry me, leave London, and begin our travels. I had hoped she'd learn to enjoy the parties, teas, and shopping, but that hasn't happened. She's quite miserable here and loves the quiet of the country so we'll go ahead, say our vows, and then visit my estates while the weather is comfortable."

"I'm surprised and glad you're acquiescing to her wishes."

"Why do you say that? I've done my best to make all my wives happy." He grunted. "Besides, she's eager to start a family."

"Marksworth, we are not on that path today," Lyon said, suddenly annoyed.

"I don't suppose you ever have been," his father mumbled. "I'm glad she wants children. There's no reason for us to wait for a few more parties and a few more votes. Especially since it looks as if another Season will end with you unwed."

The devil take it! If Lyon could change Adeline's mind, he would be happy to do so. But she'd made it quite clear her first marriage was enough for her. He was doing his best. He had to trust his instincts. Pressing her every other day to marry him wouldn't help him to earn her trust. It was difficult enough to accept the way things were without his father's constant harping about him marrying and having a son.

Marksworth continued to talk, but something else had caught Lyon's attention. In the distance he heard high-pitched girlish squeals, yells, and peals of childish laughter. He pulled on the reins, stopping his horse and scanning the area around him. To his right he saw a group of children playing.

His body tightened. They had to be girls from the school. He recognized their sounds. Maybe Adeline was with them in the park. A perfect coincidental meeting.

"I'm going this way, Marksworth," he said, and without waiting for his father to agree, he guided his horse to change directions.

His father had no choice but to follow and catch up to say, "Where are you going all of a sudden? This isn't the way to run away from a conversation you don't like."

"I'm not," he answered. "There's something I have to do. I'll see you at your wedding on Friday."

Lyon nudged the horse, and the mare started trotting. He didn't slow the animal until he was close enough to recognize the girls' coats and bonnets. Making a wide circle around the merrymakers, he looked at the three women standing guard.

Adeline wasn't with them.

Disappointment and aggravation gathered in his chest. There was no reason for her to be with them but for a brief moment he'd had hope. As he watched them, something odd struck him. Two girls were apart from the rest. They weren't up running around wildly, holding hands and swinging around, or laughing and chasing with the others. They were sitting on the ground, a good distance away from the playing and from each other. Looking closer he realized the two girls sitting as the ones who'd entered his house that morning. The headmistress was standing an equal distance between them. Fanny and Mathilda each had a slate and chalk in their hands and seemed to be writing something.

Writing? While in the park? Instead of playing?

He watched the red-haired girl hand her board up to the mistress. She looked at it, picked up the tail of her apron, wiped it clean, and then handed it back to the girl who started writing on it again.

Lyon's hackles rose. Was this the punishment Adeline had told him about or had the two done something else? It had been a month since the wayward lasses had entered his house, so this shouldn't be over that incident. But he didn't know and wanted to find out.

Lyon turned his horse again and kicked his heels into the mare's flanks. She took off at a gallop. Not wanting to take the time to return the animal to the stables, he raced around curricles, pedestrians, and vegetable carts to get out of the park. Carriage and wagon traffic was heavy on the streets, but he didn't let that stop his pace either. Without slowing down, he nudged the horse around the slow-moving coach he was behind. Then, one at a time he passed all the conveyances in front of him until he made it to his house in St. James. He quickly dismounted and tethered the mare.

Two carriages were in front of Adeline's house. Probably Mrs. Feld and Lady Kitson. He didn't care that he'd be interrupting them. They'd seen him at her house before. So had Mrs. Feversham. If he hadn't been so intent on getting to the bottom of the girls in the park, he might have turned around and waved to his neighbor.

He strode up to the front door and knocked.

"Mrs. Lawton," he said, removing his hat when she opened the door. "I'd like to see Lady Wake."

"She has guests, my lord."

"I know, but tell her I'll only take a moment of her time. You can show me to another room to wait until she's free, but I'll see her today."

Mrs. Lawton smiled at him. "Her ladyship told me that you're the one who gave the girls the pianoforte."

What could he say? He'd asked Adeline not to tell the girls. He never told her not to tell her housekeeper. He nodded slightly.

She smiled. "I like hearing it in the evenings when all else is quiet. Puts me right to sleep." She inclined her head toward the corridor. "Go on in and see her. She's not standing on ceremony today. She has the little one here."

"Little one?" he asked.

"Lady Kitson Fairbright's son. He's a fine boy. Running about here and there and all over the house. No rest for anyone when that one's around. He can't be still or stay in one room for long."

Lyon handed his hat and gloves to the woman, walked to the drawing room doorway, then stopped. His heart slammed against his chest. Adeline was sitting in a chair holding a little dark-haired boy. She had a small wooden horse in her hand and was hopping it across the child's knees as she said, "Clip-clop, clip-clop."

They were all laughing.

"My lord," Lady Kitson said and rose.

From the corner of his eye, he saw Mrs. Feld stand

up, too, but he couldn't take his gaze off Adeline. She lifted the child into her arms, sweeping her gaze up and down Lyon's face as she did so.

"Lyon, what are you doing here?"

"My apologies." He bowed ever so slightly. "It seems I've interrupted you three ladies again."

"No, not at all," Lady Kitson said, taking the child from Adeline. He went willingly into his mother's arms. "We were just getting ready to say our goodbyes. Weren't we, Brina?"

"Yes," she said brightly. "We were." She turned to Adeline. "It was a lovely visit but, we must go."

Adeline looked from one friend to the other and back to Lyon. "If you'll excuse me, my lord, I'll see them out."

"No," Lady Kitson said as the little boy chattered and struggled to get down. "No need for that. We must hurry before Chatwyn gets more restless."

"Don't forget this," Adeline said, handing the horse to the child. He grabbed it eagerly in his hand and then cupped it to his chest.

"You must not spoil him and have a toy for him every time I bring him," Lady Kitson said.

"I can't promise I won't. I've heard it said a man can't have too many horses. Chatwyn needs a collection."

The ladies said goodbye the way ladies do. Earnest hugs, kisses on the cheek, and promises to see one another soon. During the flurry of their parting, all Lyon could think was that Adeline would be a caring mother. In just the few moments he saw her with the little boy, he could see that she had patient, loving hands and a tender touch and voice.

"Will you always just barge into my house, Lyon?" she asked him after her friends cleared the doorway.

It always got her attention when he did. Lyon walked farther into the room. "I don't know. Perhaps I should be punished for doing so."

"Punished?" she asked curiously. "What are you talking about?"

He stopped just inches from her. "Why did I just see the two girls who entered my house sitting in the park writing on their boards, while the other girls played?"

Adeline's shoulders lifted. "Because that is their punishment for leaving the school and trespassing on your property."

"It's been at least a month since then."

"Obviously not," she challenged.

"How long do you intend for this to go on?"

"The reprimand was only for a month. I don't remember the exact day it started. Perhaps this is the last week. Or the last day."

"Four weeks is a lifetime for a child. Have you no heart?"

"I have plenty of heart," she insisted. "I didn't know you knew so much about children, my lord." She folded her hands across her chest. "I don't need you to tell me about punishment for the girls."

Lyon relaxed his stance. She was never more beautiful to him than when she was angry at him. "A week should have been long enough," he stated. "Two at the most."

"It wasn't your decision to make. You agreed I couldn't send them home and it was your suggestion that I threaten them with a cane."

"Did you?" he asked, advancing on her again.

"Yes," she answered without equivocating. "You knew I had to be severe or they would have continued to disobey. As it is, there have been no further instances and they are both still doing quite well."

He smiled. "Good."

Adeline's expression softened. "You aren't worried about the girls. You just wanted an excuse to come over."

"No, I was worried about the girls, too."

"My lady."

They both turned to see Mrs. Lawton standing in the doorway. "Everything is fine, Mrs. Lawton. I need no help."

"I'm glad of that, my lady. I told Miss Peat I couldn't disturb you, but she insisted I tell you it was very important you read this note at once. She said it was pinned to the coat of a little girl who was left on the steps of the school."

"What!" She gasped. "Someone left a child at the school?"

"Mrs. Tallon is going to give her something to eat while she waits for you to come over and let her know what to do."

She looked at Lyon, and he nodded. "Go ahead and read it now."

"All right. Thank you, Mrs. Lawton. Tell her I'll be over shortly."

Adeline unfolded the note and started reading. Her

hand started trembling. Her eyes closed and she whispered an almost silent "No."

Her gasp was violent and rending, sending a shudder of alarm through Lyon.

"I can't believe this." Adeline grabbed her stomach and bent over double as if in pain.

Lyon caught her in his arms and helped her to sit on the settee as the note fluttered to the floor. He knelt protectively in front of her and placed his hands on her knees, chilled by how hard she was taking the news. "Adeline, tell me what's happened? Who's it from?"

She lifted her head and looked at him. Her golden-brown eyes glistened with shock. "My husband's mistress. She left Wake's daughter at the school. She wants me to take care of her and let her attend the school."

Chapter 20

Adeline tried to slow her breathing, but it was impossible to do. Nor could she stop her limbs from trembling or her body from shaking.

He looked back at her and asked, "Did you know he had a child?"

The roaring in her ears was intense but she managed a nod.

"That's damn brazen of her to bring the girl to you." Without asking, Lyon picked up the note and started reading.

"I can't believe she'd ask this of me," Adeline whispered. Heartache and bitterness that she'd long since buried boiled from her heart and mind, consuming her. "I won't do it. I can't. It's vile of her to even ask it of me." She looked up at Lyon. "The girl must be given back to her mother. I don't want to see either of them. Would you please go tell Mrs. Tallon for me?"

Lyon looked up at her. Concern edged his features, and it threatened to deplete what little control she had on her emotions. She didn't know if she could withstand his sympathy without collapsing into tears.

"Did you read the note to the end?" he asked.

"No," she said curtly.

"Adeline."

"No," she answered in a harsher tone. "I don't want to read it. Why should I want to see her, hear from her, or read anything she has to say to me or anyone else?"

Lyon seemed to think about his words, before answering. "All right, but you must know what she said, so you'll hear it from me. Your brother-in-law, the Earl of Wake, has not honored your husband's allowance to her in over a year. She no longer has the means to care for her child and is giving you guardianship."

The anguish and destroying despair that Adeline had seen on Fanny's mother's face that afternoon near the docks flashed across her mind, wounding her further. Because of that, Adeline understood a mother wanting, deserving the right to adequately take care of her children. But this wasn't fair. She viciously blinked the image from her mind. She had to. This was different from Fanny and her mother and all the other children she saw that day. This tore at her soul.

"I'm sorry. I can't help her. Not either of them." Adeline shook her head, the shock wearing off and anger at this woman building inside her. It was wrong to be forced into a situation that was impossible to bear.

"I owe her nothing. She must take care of her child as best she can."

"The note says she left London yesterday and paid someone to deliver the girl to your school today."

"It doesn't matter. I will have someone find the woman," she said, wiping at the wetness she felt gathering in the corners her eyes. "I won't have her daughter at the school. Why would she even ask me to do this? She must know how I feel about her."

Lyon took hold of her trembling hands and held them tightly in her lap. His touch was warm and comforting. The understanding she saw in his face was depleting the little control she had on her emotions, making her want to melt into his arms and cry from the pain this caused her. "Everyone in London must know by now that you helped start a school for unfortunate girls."

"For girls whose fathers and brothers were lost at sea on the *Salty Dove*! No one else and certainly not for the benefit of titled men's illegitimate children. I don't know why she's doing this. No, maybe I *do* know. She wants to remind me one more time that she gave Wake a child and I didn't."

"Adeline, no," Lyon said, gently touching one side of her face. "I don't think she was thinking about you at all. She was thinking of what's best for her child. When the earl stopped her income, she probably had to turn to a life that wouldn't be suitable for a little girl to be around. She must be desperate."

"I don't care," she insisted fiercely. "I can't help her."

"Adeline, take time to think about this reasonably. It's unlike you to be so unkind."

"Me? Unkind? Did you actually say that to me?" Adeline shoved Lyon away and rose, raking his arms away when he tried to take hold of her. She turned to him, striking her fist to her chest, and said, "You have the nerve to call me the unkind one?"

"You must think of the welfare of the child."

He reached for her again, but she spun away. "No! I am not the unkind one. You don't know what I went through."

"I don't, but I know you can't put your husband's daughter in an orphanage or out on the street."

"His brother did and so can I."

"You aren't like that."

"I am like that!" she yelled, inhaling a bitter sob. "You don't know how many times Wake threw in my face *'My mistress can give me a child but my wife can't.'* You don't know how many potions he mixed and forced me to drink with brandy because the taste was so vile I couldn't otherwise get them down. How many examinations I had to endure from men and women. The horrors of being probed and poked by a physician, a midwife, an apothecary, or some other person Wake had found who promised he could make a miracle happen. They all promised they could help me conceive. And none of it ever made a difference. Not once." Another sob heaved from her chest. "So no, I won't take her child into my school and care for her! I never said one unkind thing about her to Wake. That's what I did for her, and all I can do for her now is stay quiet about what I think of her."

Lyon stood quietly watching her. Letting her say what was buried deeply in her heart. What she should never have let be spoken. She didn't want him to see her like this. Didn't want him to know how she'd suffered. Without thinking, she rushed over to the doorway and pointed to the corridor. "Get out."

Her throat and chest hurt. She watched Lyon stride over to where she stood, but instead of going out he closed the double doors.

"I asked you to leave," she said in a softer tone, not wanting to believe he wasn't leaving her alone to drown in her anger, hurt, and bitterness.

"No," he replied quietly, with a hint of a smile twitching his lips. He turned the key in the lock. "You told me to get out, but I'm not going to." He reached for one of her hands.

She pulled back from him and held her arms stiffly at her side. "I want you to leave."

Lyon reached for her hand again and caught her wrist. "I know, but I'm not going to." He let his fingers slide down and grasp her palm.

"Give me the other hand," he said softly.

He had her attention, but she still answered, "No. What are you doing? I don't want to hold your hand. I want you to go away and leave me be."

"I will, but not right now. Come on, take my other hand."

He walked toward and she walked backward as he continued to advance on her.

"Your other hand, Adeline. Let me hold it."

Finally, she lifted her arm and he grasped her fingertips. He stopped moving forward and started sidestepping. His upper arm bumped hers, and she was forced to sidestep, too. Taking faster steps, he knocked into her again.

"You're going too slow."

Adeline took wider, hastier steps.

"Don't let me step on your ankle," he said. "Keep going."

"No—I—what are you doing?"

"What I've seen the girls at your school do from my window. Hold hands and spin."

"I don't want to do this, Lyon," she whispered softly. "Please."

"Go faster. Pick it up or I'll run over you."

Suddenly they were holding hands tightly and making circle after circle, spinning around as fast as their feet would move. Her skirts swished and twirled about her legs, her hair fell from its bun and danced across her back.

"Don't stop."

And she didn't. Swinging round after round, step after step, spinning until she was so dizzy she fell against his chest, out of breath and laughing. Lyon caught her in his strong embrace and kissed her hair just above her ear several times. She snuggled deeper. It felt so good to press her cheek into the soft padding of his quilted waistcoat, to rest her head and her heart, and to allow her inner balance to return to normal. She soaked up the comfort of his hands running soothingly up and down her back.

Her breathing was labored but she was calmer. Lifting her head and her arms, she clasped her hands together at his nape. He bent and kissed her tenderly, sweetly on the lips. His touch was delicate, enticing, and brief.

"You're breathing heavy," he said.

She smiled and murmured, "So are you."

For a long time, he simply held her close. She lifted her head and placed her lips on his and kissed him the same way he'd kissed her. Slow and soft. Sensuous and enticing.

The longer they kissed, the more she wanted it to go on forever. She wanted to forget everything but her love for him. She opened her mouth, and his tongue explored inside with eager yet soothing strokes. His hands moved down her chest to palm and mold her breasts, lightly caressing. Her nipple stiffened beneath his gentle touch. Adeline moaned and leaned into his hand, enjoying the intense feeling. She ran her hands down the front of his trousers and moaned.

Yes, this is what she wanted. "I've missed being with you like this."

"Adeline," he whispered.

"Yes?" she answered, enjoying the ripples of sensation tightening in her stomach, sending waves of pleasure flowing down her body to settle into her most womanly part.

"We are back to where we were a month ago."

She turned around and looked at the settee. "I know. It's all I can offer."

His eyes narrowed and his lips tightened. "I want more. I love you, Adeline. Marry me."

She swallowed hard as she gazed into his eyes. "You know I wanted a child, too. I suppose that's really the reason I drank every brew and endured every examination. I wanted a child to love. I married Wake because I thought he loved me. But I soon found out all he wanted was an heir. Not me to love. Not a child to love, but an heir to carry on his title. You'll need an heir one day, too, Lyon. You will inherit your father's title one day and you will give your son yours. The burden of not being able to do that is too heavy and I can't go through that again."

"Have you so little faith in me?" Lyon asked in an exasperated voice. "Don't you know by now that I would never do to you or ask of you what Wake did?"

"Yes." She tried to tell him with her eyes she meant that. "I do believe that. But I know you deserve a son. I won't go through the pain of not being able to give you that."

"I'm not asking you to. I'm only asking for your love and for you to marry me. No matter who I'd marry I might never have a child. Or I could have five daughters and no son."

"But at least you would have a chance. With me there is no chance."

"Having a child has never been a reason for me to marry, Adeline." He stopped and ran his hand through his hair and inhaled deeply. "My father has been after me to marry and produce an heir since I was twenty. I have always told him love comes first. Then marriage. Having or not having a child with you would not change my love for you. I've waited to find the love of one woman sharing my bed, my mornings and my nights beside me in all things till death do we part. You are the lady I want. The only one I've ever wanted. I love you and want to marry you. I've never forced my attentions on any woman and I'll not force my love for you on you. You must come to me as my wife willingly or not at all."

"I love you, too. You must know that."

"I do. That's why it's so hard to understand you not wanting to marry me. It's time for you to trust that I won't be like your first husband. I won't demand anything from you but love."

"You have my love," she exclaimed. "You have my devotion. Why can't that be enough? You are being stubborn for not understanding why I can't marry you."

"I am being fair to you and to me. A lover is not what I want and a lover is not what you deserve." His voice softened. "I have had lovers, Adeline. They are very good at satisfying the body but they don't satisfy the heart or the soul. Marriage is a shelter, security. It is love that will hold us together and keep us content. I want a wife who loves me for me, for who I am, not whether or not she can give me a child. Love is the only thing I am asking from you, and if you can't trust me with your love then I agree, we can't marry."

Adeline backed away from him. "It's settled then."

He nodded. "Except for Nora. That's her name. She's only five years old. What happened is not her fault. Keep the child Wake's mistress sent to you. You are a kind, tenderhearted lady. You are capable and you must take care of your husband's child. In a way, by doing what his brother and mistress are failing to do, you are finally giving him the child he wanted."

A sob rose in Adeline's throat again. "You ask too much of me. She doesn't belong here. She needs to be with her mother."

"No, you're making excuses. You don't want to see her each day and be reminded of the past."

"Why is that wrong?"

"Because you must put what he did to you behind you so you can forgive and start new. And trust me that your love will be enough for me after we marry."

She straightened and blinked away more tears, hating the reality that she was still afraid to trust him. "I don't think I can do that. I will let her stay at the school while I will search for her mother."

"Good. Maybe that will be a start to healing, Adeline."

Lyon turned the lock in the door, opened it, and walked out.

Chapter 21

Adeline stood in front of the earl's door, resolute in what she had to do. It had taken her no small amount of time, courage and soul-searching to get to this point. At first she hadn't known what to think much less what to say or do. She'd struggled for days with her own tense emotions for the right answer to what she should do, and found there was only one solution.

On one side of her was Fanny and on the other side, Mathilda. Mrs. Tallon stood watch behind them. Each girl had her arms out and palms up carefully holding six neckcloths. It had taken the girls almost two months to get the dozen lengths of cloth finished to the head-mistress's satisfaction. They had met Adeline's approval, too, after she had looked them over. On top of the stacks were short hand-written notes from each girl apologizing to the earl for entering his house.

Really more important than the recompense to the earl was the fact that neither girl had broken a rule since they'd been given the punishment of no play time for a month. Their good behavior could very well be because Mrs. Tallon kept them so busy cutting, sewing, washing, and pressing the fabric over and over again that there was no time for mischief. Or maybe it was that they had finally settled into boarding-school life and were content. Adeline didn't want to think it had anything to do with the cane that stood in the corner of the classroom, but she couldn't be sure it didn't. The actual cause for the change in their naughtiness didn't matter. That it had happened was all that mattered. The school was functioning the way she'd always envisioned—except for Nora.

That wasn't likely to change anytime soon.

Adeline hadn't found it within herself to speak to the little girl yet, but Mrs. Tallon said she was adjusting.

Squaring her shoulders up tight, Adeline drew in a deep breath of late-afternoon air and knocked on the door. Moments later, the butler opened it and looked from her to the girls to Mrs. Tallon. "The earl received your note and is expecting you, Lady Wake."

"Thank you, Brewster. Would you please ask his lordship to come to the door, the girls won't be coming inside."

He nodded. "As you wish, my lady."

Brewster left the door open, and Adeline heard Lyon coming down the corridor. Her stomach tightened.

She'd only seen him at a distance lately and was eager to see him up close again.

"Lady Wake," he said, "I didn't realize the girls would be with you. "What is this?"

He looked splendid. Maybe even more handsome than ever. Trepidation filled her but she touched each girl's shoulder, ushering them forward. Fanny lifted up her offering to him and in a loud voice said, "I'm sorry for entering your house without permission. I wish to give you these."

"I'm sorry, too," Mathilda echoed, though not quite as forceful, as she stepped up closer to the earl and offered him the load in her arms, too. "I brought you this gift and hope you'll accept it."

"Me too," Fanny said and smiled so brightly Adeline wanted to hug her. "We had to work extra hard until we made every one of them perfect. Mrs. Tallon said so."

Lyon continued to look at the girls but didn't offer to take the neckcloths from them. "That's quite a few you have there."

"Twelve," Fanny said. "We counted each one. More than once, so we know we're right."

"That many?" he said and glanced at Adeline.

"Mrs. Tallon said sometimes a gentleman has to wrinkle three or four neckcloths a morning before he gets one tied the way he wants it," Fanny informed him.

"Did she?" he asked, still making no attempt to receive the gift.

Adeline cleared her throat. "The girls would like to know if you'd accept these along with their apologies."

"Yes. Of course." He looked over his shoulder and

called, "Brewster." He bent down to Fanny's level and took hers first. "They're—handsome."

"Don't wrinkle them," she said, handing them over to him. "They're not easy to press." Lyon glanced over at Adeline and smiled. He then took the neckcloths from Mathilda and thanked her, too. He gave them to Brewster. "Have Dome put these away."

The girls beamed.

"If you'll pardon me, my lady," Mrs. Tallon said, stepping forward. "The girls have a gift for you, too."

Adeline looked at Fanny and Mathilda. "For me?"

Each girl pulled a folded handkerchief from their pockets and handed it to Adeline.

"We knitted the lace and then we had to sew it on," Mathilda said.

"That wasn't easy either," Fanny said and rolled her eyes. "I'd rather cut and sew than knit."

"I'm sure it wasn't, but they're lovely." Adeline's heart constricted. "It wasn't necessary to do this for me, but I do like surprises. Thank you, girls. It must have taken quite some time to learn how to do all this. They're very delicate and look perfect."

"My fingers were sore, but I'm glad you like it."

"Mine, too," Mathilda agreed.

Adeline laughed lightly. "I do, but now it is back to school for you two."

She handed the handkerchiefs to Mrs. Tallon. "Would you please stop and give these to Mrs. Lawton for me? I need to speak to the earl."

Adeline watched them walk down the stone steps and out the gate before turning back to Lyon. "May I come in?"

His brow rose. "I think you must have forgotten about Mrs. Feversham and her spyglass."

"I haven't forgotten. Is she still watching our doors?"

"According to my aunt she hasn't missed much that has happened around our houses."

"Didn't you tell me you've never met her?"

"Yes. She has no qualms about sending me a note if she wants me to deliver a basket full of tarts to a girls' school, but we've never met."

"I haven't been over to see her either. Maybe she's just lonely. Perhaps if we did—if I did—she'd see me more as a friend and not just a neighbor, and not feel right about spying on a friend."

Lyon smiled at her. "You try it first and let me know if it works."

"I think I will, but not today. I'll take my chances with her snooping, if you don't mind." Adeline's heartbeat was racing but she found the courage to say, "I do have something to tell you that I'd rather not say standing out here. If you don't mind, I'd like to come inside."

"You are always welcome in my home, Adeline." He stepped aside. "Though as you know, doing so has its risks."

"In more than one way," she answered softly, letting her gaze flutter down his face.

"Aunt Delia saved us once before. Perhaps she can work her magic and do it again if Mrs. Feversham isn't taking her afternoon nap."

He waved Brewster away and helped Adeline with her short black cape. "Would you like for me to have some tea brought in?"

"No," she said with a bit of a smile. "I believe I'd like to have a snip of brandy."

She was sure it was alarm she saw on Lyon's face, and that made a soft laugh flow past her lips.

He slowly laid her wrap on a chair. His eyes searched hers intently. "Are you sure about that?"

"Quite."

He didn't question her further, but motioned down the corridor. "Join me in the drawing room."

Adeline walked past him on shaky legs. His footsteps echoed behind her. She gathered strength and was heartened with each step she heard. She didn't stop until she stood before the low-burning fire.

They remained quiet as he covered the bottom of a small delicate-looking stemmed glass with the amber liquid.

"I heard your father married," she said.

He handed her the glass. "Yes. They quit the Season early to travel to his estates so he could introduce his new bride. Helen wanted it and surprisingly, he agreed. I haven't heard from them, but assume all is going well with their ventures."

"I thought she was very nice. She came to visit me before they left, and we had an enjoyable time."

"Good," he said, and then dismissing that subject, he asked, "Have you come to tell me you've found your husband's mistress and reunited her with her child? I know you have someone searching for her."

"No. The runners haven't found a trace of her. Julia and Brina agree that we should continue to look for her, but so far no one will admit to knowing her whereabouts. I wrote to the Earl of Wake and asked for his help. He responded that he had nothing to say on the subject."

"I think he'd already made that clear."

"Yes, and while we search for her mother, Nora is safe, cared for, and adjusting to her new life."

"Have you seen her?"

"Yes. From a distance."

"You are doing the right thing for her."

"I could do no other. As you pointed out. When we started the school, it was never our intention to get involved in the lives of any of the girls. Only to provide a place for them to learn. Fanny made that an exception by her escapades. She's settled down now and isn't wandering away from the others in the class."

"That must make it easier for everyone."

"Yes. I am letting Mrs. Tallon handle everything. That seems to be working well for both of us."

"Good," Lyon said and blew out a deep breath. "Is that what you came to tell me, Adeline?"

"No. I want things settled between us. First, I want you to know that I love you."

"And you need a shot of brandy to tell me that?" he asked, suddenly sounding angry.

"No." She looked down at her glass.

"Just telling me you love me settles nothing between us. I haven't doubted your love for me."

"You didn't pour one for yourself," she said. "Must a lady drink alone?"

His gaze swept over hers again. "Of course not."

He walked back to the table and splashed a dram in his glass and joined her again. Not waiting for her, he downed the nip in one swallow. Her hand trembled, but refusing to think about the past, she inhaled deeply and put the glass to her lips. She sipped a small amount and swallowed. There was no foul taste, no bitter remembrances, just a sweet sting and then the flash of warmth that always flamed her cheeks and neck for a second or two.

"Thank you," she whispered. "That was one of the fears I needed to put to rest. The easier one."

Lyon put his glass down and then took hers, placing it beside his. "You are troubling me, Adeline. Something's wrong. What is it that you want to tell me?"

"I am carrying your child."

He looked astounded. "A babe?"

She stepped back, suddenly feeling frightened and alone, despite all her earlier thoughts of courage and determination about her admission of the situation she found herself in. "I swear to you I haven't been with another man."

Lyon took hold of her upper arms. "Damnation, Adeline, I know that. It's just that you were so sure you couldn't be in the family way."

"I know," she whispered earnestly. "I have disbelieved all the signs myself."

"How can you be sure then? What's changed?"

"You." She stopped and inhaled deeply. "It was you making love to me. It's the only possible answer. You made the difference."

His eyes glistened. "Me?"

Her heart was full of love, of happiness for the child she carried, and of dread in not knowing how Lyon would respond to this news. "I know of no other reason. I have been to see a physician and two different midwives. One of whom I saw when I was drinking the tonics that were made for me every day. She was the only one I trusted during that time, so I went back to her as well." Adeline touched her stomach lightly. "They all agree with me that it's true I'm carrying a child. I don't know how this could have happened. I went through hell trying to have a child for Wake and now I am more than three months carrying yours."

His fingers tightened around her arms. His gaze fluttered up and down her face. "So it happened our first time together."

Adeline's throat tightened more and she shivered. "It appears so."

"Can you feel it move?"

"Not yet. It will take a little longer for that to happen."

He let go of her arms and placed his hand against her lower stomach as if he were in awe of a precious stone he was touching.

"Yes," he said, looking up at her with joy beaming on his face. "I feel it. The small swell of life is there."

"I knew all the signs to watch for indicating I was with child. They were drilled into me. I've waited extra time to be sure."

His eyes narrowed. "You waited to tell me I'm going to be a father?"

"I had to be sure. Lyon, I love you with all my heart, but I couldn't get past the ugliness of my first marriage. The torture, the feelings of failure. I can't explain it."

He placed a finger on her lips. "Shh, my love. You don't have to think about that ever again."

"All I can do is say again that I love you and I'll marry you if you still love me and want me."

"Love you? Want you?" He caught her up in his strong embrace. "I wake every morning wondering what I can do or say to make you change your mind about marriage. Adeline, it was always only you that I wanted. I understood your reasons for wanting to remain a widow. I had to respect your wishes."

"Thank you. I love you for that, Lyon, but now will you marry me?"

"I was beginning to think this day would never come and I never could have dreamed it would be a babe that brought you back to me."

He kissed her long, hard. "I didn't know how it would happen or when, but I had faith that if I gave you enough time you would realize love conquers everything and you would want to be my wife." Lyon squeezed her tightly and whispered, "I love you so much."

"And I love you."

Suddenly he leaned away from her and asked, "Do you know if you will have a son?"

Adeline breathed a soft laugh. "Of course not. Many try, but no one can predict son or daughter."

"Good. I want to be surprised by you one more time."

Lyon captured her lips with his again.

Adeline thrilled to his touch.

Epilogue

$\mathcal{L}$yon stood before the fire. They were all trying not to stare at him, but at various times during the night they all had. It was as if they expected something from him other than the calm he was presenting. Adeline had assured him she would have no problems delivering the babe and that after it arrived, Lyon would be sent for. He had no choice but to take her at her word and let her handle this very important matter of giving birth without his assistance or pressure. It wasn't that he didn't have concerns.

He was filled with them.

Everyone was gathered in the drawing room with him at his London home. He and Adeline decided to winter there rather than Lyonwood. She would be near the midwife she wanted to attend her. There would be time for them to enjoy the last of winter at Lyonwood, after she delivered.

Marksworth and his bride had returned to London and were on one settee. Mrs. Brina Feld and Cordelia were on the other. Lady Kitson Fairbright was also present, but she was the only one who had the honor of being above stairs and in the room with Adeline—because she'd had a child and might in some way be of service to her during delivery.

Lyon would have rather this be a private time, but Marksworth had made Lyon promise, as had the others, to let him know when the time was close for the baby to be born. They all wanted to be at Lyon's house for the joyous occasion.

The midwife had been sent for early in the afternoon, and she confirmed the time was near. But that was several hours ago. Lyon was told to vacate their room and find a way to keep himself busy. He'd written the notes that brought the others rushing to his house and then tried to concentrate on some of his account books before they arrived. That proved impossible to do. Every little sound had him looking up at the door and losing his place.

"It's been long enough," Marksworth said, rising from the settee. "I think it's time someone went up there to check on what's taking so long."

"Why don't you go?" Cordelia said dryly.

"Me?" He exclaimed, giving Aunt Delia a hard look. "I have no business going up there. It's no place for a man."

"Neither is it for the rest of us," she answered. "She has a midwife and Lady Kitson. She doesn't need anyone else interfering."

"What do you know about birthing a babe?" he asked. "You've never had one."

Cordelia gave him a mocking smile. "Neither has anyone else in this room. Which is my point. We don't need to be barging in when we don't know how to help. Lady Kitson said she would come for us after the babe was born, and she will."

"Marksworth, come sit back down," Helen said in her sweet, calming voice, patting the cushion beside her. "Your bluster is worrying everyone."

"Well, it should," he said, pacing in front of Lyon. "I've been through this before. It's been too long. We should have heard a wee little cry by now or at least Adeline yelling out in pain." He walked over to Lyon. "Aren't you worried?"

Very.

He'd wanted to be with her, but her insistence there were reasons husbands were kept out of the room had to be honored. He would only get in the way, she'd said. She was probably right about that. Besides, the last thing he wanted was to see her in pain, even if the pain was from bringing his child into the world. This was delicate enough without him adding to her worry by insisting he be with her. When they'd married, he'd promised to always be sensitive to her wishes, and he would.

Even at stressful times as this.

So he waited. Just as he'd waited for her to come to him in love, and ready for marriage. He smiled. The natural order of things. Love, marriage, and then a baby. He needed nothing more to please him.

"Adeline has said not every woman screams during birth," he said to his father. "I'm not concerned." Over much. "This is the way she wanted it and we'll—"

A door shut above. Lyon's gaze flew around the room. Everyone was riveted. For a heartbeat. Lyon rose and took off running out of the drawing room. He heard the shuffling of feet right behind him.

By the time he made it to the vestibule, Julia had gotten to the bottom of the stairs.

"Is she all right?" he asked.

Julia smiled. "Yes, yes. She and the babe are fine."

"Is it a boy?" Marksworth asked excitedly.

"That's not my news to tell." Julia looked at Lyon. "She wants to see you."

Lyon took the stairs two at a time. He opened the door and rushed into the room. Adeline was sitting up in bed looking glorious with her honey gold hair framing her shoulders and holding a small bundle of blankets against her breasts. He smiled, laughed, and sat down easily on the bed beside her. He brushed a strand of damp hair away from her face. "Are you all right?"

"Of course," she smiled. "I am fine."

He pressed a quick kiss to her lips. "It took so long. I was worried."

"Not that long, really. Aren't you going to ask about your child?"

"Yes, but I don't have to. I can see all is well in your face. I didn't know how you would look after your— your labor, but you are beautiful."

"Is it a boy?" Marksworth asked, bursting through

the doorway. Cordelia, Helen, and Brina entered right behind him.

"Come see for yourself."

Everyone crowded around the bed. Adeline folded back the layers of blankets one at a time and then turned the pink, wrinkled, kicking, and naked little babe so that all could see him.

"I knew it!" Marksworth shouted. "And a fine boy he is."

The baby jumped and started crying. Happy wishes echoed around the room.

"Now look what you've done," Lyon said. "You've scared him."

"What can you do to quiet him?" Brina asked, distress marking her features. "I don't want him to cry."

"It won't hurt him, Brina," Adeline said with a smile. "It's good and will help strengthen his lungs."

"I do hope you will consider naming him Paston after your dear mother's surname," Cordelia said as she peered down at the little one.

"What kind of name is that for a son?" Marksworth argued.

"A good one," Cordelia answered.

"That's enough," Lyon said firmly when the babe continued to cry. "Out. All of you for now. Mother and child need their rest."

"Don't worry, I'm going," Marksworth said, pulling on the tail of his coat. "I must get down to White's and let them know you've had a son and settle my wager."

Lyon grimaced at his father. "Did you put money on the wager as to which of us would have a son first?"

"Of course." He smiled. "And I put my money on you." Marksworth smiled and walked out the door.

Helen, Cordelia, and Brina followed him and Lyon closed the door.

Lyon eased back down onto the bed beside Adeline. She had the baby wrapped tight again snuggled to her chest. She was rocking him in her arms whispering, "Shh, little one."

"He's really unbelievably small," Lyon whispered.

"No, he's a healthy, handsome size. Does his crying bother you?" she asked.

"If I can handle the screaming girls next door, I think I can manage a soft baby's cry."

Adeline laughed. "You will never forgive me for moving the school next door, will you?"

"I have many times over." He smiled and kissed her forehead. "I was just thinking today that I should have a swing hung from that big tree on the other side of the school. Do you think the girls would like that?"

"They would love it, Lyon, but it would give them another reason to play outside and make more noise." She looked down at the infant in her arms. "I fear you will never have order in your life again."

Lyon stared at the tiny scrunched face. The babe stopped crying but continued to make sweet sounds. He'd never seen anything so peaceful-looking. His eyes were big, dark blue, and looking straight at Lyon. He felt as if his heart turned over in his chest. The intensity of his feelings was matched only by what he felt for Adeline.

He looked into her beautiful gleaming eyes. "I'll be

all right with that. I'm learning that not everything has to have order."

"Do you want to hold him?" she asked.

"No, I expect he should be walking on his own two legs and feet before I try to hold him."

"Don't be afraid."

"I am." He gave her a humorous grin. "He's so little. I don't want to hold him too tight and hurt him."

Adeline laughed and placed his son in his arms. "You won't. He wants to be held tight. Take him."

He took the little fellow gingerly but with steady hands. Lyon felt the warmth of his son's body through the blankets. The babe wiggled and squirmed just as Lyon thought would happen. His arms tightened at first, but then he slowly relaxed as the baby's eyes closed. Lyon didn't know why, but he reached down and kissed his son's forehead. It was soft.

"I like seeing you hold him," Adeline said.

He glanced at Adeline. "I think I like this, too." He reached over and kissed her gently on the lips. "You close your eyes and sleep, too, my love. I have him. I'll take care of him while you rest."

"I know, and I think I will rest for a bit. I love you, Lyon." She snuggled down onto the pillow and closed her eyes.

"And I love you, Adeline."

Author's Note

Dear Readers,

I hope you have enjoyed the first book of my First Comes Love series. I had tremendous fun dreaming up and writing Lyon and Adeline's story. It's always a challenge to mix a hero's and heroine's inner conflicts with the external trappings of their lives and make it all develop into a sexy, satisfying romance. In this book, the story gave me a couple of mischievous little girls to help.

The sinking of the *Salty Dove* and The Seafarer's School for Girls have no particular historical reference. Both are completely from my imagination and, therefore, I felt free to write about them as I did for the sake of this story. The downing of a ship at sea seemed the perfect way to have three young and beautiful widows in Society all at the same time. Though a boarding school for girls wasn't common during the Regency, it was a touching way to show how a charitable act of kindness can transform someone's life.

In our modern times it's often difficult to understand the strict rules of behavior Regency Society placed on ladies while having relatively few for gentlemen. Many of the rules are restricting for an author who writes historical romance, but as always, I try to conform to most of the dictates of Society at the time, while filling my stories with all the passion a romance deserves. And I love sharing my stories with you.

I hope you will be watching for book two in my First Comes Love series, *Gone with the Rogue*, and the third, *How to Train Your Earl*.

I enjoy hearing from readers. You can e-mail me at ameliagrey@comcast.net, follow me on Facebook at Facebook.com/AmeliaGreyBooks, or visit my website at ameliagrey.com.